SERVE AND
PROTECT

BOOKS BY SHELDON SIEGEL

Mike Daley/Rosie Fernandez Novels
Special Circumstances
Incriminating Evidence
Criminal Intent
Final Verdict
The Confession
Judgment Day
Perfect Alibi
Felony Murder Rule
Serve and Protect

David Gold/A.C. Battle Novel
The Terrorist Next Door

SERVE AND PROTECT

A Mike Daley/Rosie Fernandez Thriller

SHELDON SIEGEL

For Ben, Michelle, Margie, and Andy Siegel

"Oro en paz, fiero en guerra."

"Gold in peace, iron in war."

— SAN FRANCISCO POLICE DEPARTMENT MOTTO.

1

"I HOPE IT ISN'T SOMEBODY WE KNOW"

The Honorable Elizabeth McDaniel tapped her microphone, and her overflowing courtroom went silent. She looked my way and flashed a wry grin. "Haven't seen you in a few months, Mr. Daley."

I stepped to the lectern and returned her smile. "I'm not spending much time in court, Your Honor."

"Neither am I."

Now in her mid-sixties, Betsy McDaniel was a fair-minded jurist and a gracious soul who had gone on senior status to spend more time with her grandchildren. While she adored them, the former prosecutor had grown bored playing with Legos and going to Pilates classes, so she came back to pinch-hit for her former colleagues from time to time.

She arched an eyebrow. "I didn't expect to see the head of the Felony Division of the San Francisco Public Defender's Office in Misdemeanor Court."

"One of our deputies is under the weather."

"Nothing serious, I hope."

"Just a cold."

At nine a.m. on Wednesday, February ninth, her courtroom was packed with small-time criminals and smaller-time lawyers waiting for a moment of small-time justice. A half-step above Traffic Court, Misdemeanor Court was our system's great equalizer. On good days, the windowless courtroom on the second floor of the Hall of Justice smelled a bit nicer than the men's locker room at the Embarcadero Y. On bad days, the plumbing backed up and the aroma of sewage wafted through the courts. A few years ago, the monolithic fifties-era building at Seventh and Bryant was declared unsafe from earthquakes, and it was being evacuated room-by-room at a snail's pace. If the economy stayed strong and the political winds blew in the right direction, there was a chance that the old warhorse would be replaced before I retired.

Every seat in the gallery and the jury box was taken. People were standing halfway down the center aisle and along the back wall. Many couldn't afford a Muni ticket, let alone a lawyer or a childcare provider. As a result, the courtroom and the corridor were filled with relatives, significant others, and friends. Children weren't allowed in court, so they had to entertain themselves in the hall. I felt bad for the parents who would have to write a note to their kid's teacher explaining that they were absent from school to attend Mommy or Daddy's court date. I felt worse for the kids.

Judge McDaniel put on her reading glasses and glanced at her computer. The process in Misdemeanor Court was similar to the long-closed cafeteria in the basement that was now a storage area. You took a number and waited your turn. She nodded at the baby A.D.A. standing at attention at the prosecution table. He was wearing a brand-new going-to-court suit that looked as if he'd bought it off the rack at the Men's Wearhouse earlier that morning. The judge spoke to him in a cheerful tone. "Good morning, Mr. George."

He tugged at the collar of his starched white shirt that was a little snug around the neck. "Good morning, Your Honor."

Ted George was a handsome lad and fifth-generation Californian who had graduated at the top of his class at Stanford Law School. His ancestors had planted the apricot orchards that once dotted Silicon Valley. His father had made a fortune in venture capital. He was a conscientious young man who had the potential to grow up into a competent prosecutor. It brought back memories of the day almost a quarter of a century earlier when I had made my first appearance in this very courtroom in front of a grizzled judge who took his morning coffee with a splash of bourbon. He retired a few years later and lived comfortably in the Pacific Heights mansion that he had inherited from his parents until his liver finally gave out.

"What brings you here today, Mr. George?" Judge McDaniel asked.

"The People versus Luther Robinson."

"Oh, dear." The judge pushed out a sigh and turned to me. "Is he here, Mr. Daley?"

"Yes, Your Honor."

I motioned to my client, who joined me at the lectern. Luther Robinson was a wiry man of indeterminate middle age. When he had a few bucks in his pocket, he lived in an SRO in the Tenderloin. When he didn't, he slept in an alley on Sixth Street. A gentle soul with sad eyes and gray stubble, the native of the Fillmore had returned from the war in Kuwait with a severe case of PTSD which he treated by self-medicating with malt liquor. He was wearing a navy sport jacket and a pair of khaki pants that he had selected from the donated clothes closet at the P.D.'s Office. Luther had been one of my first regulars when I was a rookie P.D. working in Misdemeanor Court, and I had a soft spot for him. He was blessed with an engaging manner and a gift for persuading strangers to part with their hard-earned cash for his low-rent scams. He'd never hurt anybody. He ripped people off when he was hungry.

Judge McDaniel's tone was more maternal than judicial. "How are you, Luther?"

"Fine, Your Honor." His voice was soft. "And you?"

"Fine, thank you." She took off her reading glasses. "I saw you here last week, didn't I?"

"Yes."

"You were selling baby wipes and telling people that they were contraceptives, weren't you?"

"Yes."

"And the week before, you were selling Tic Tacs and saying that they were Viagra tablets, weren't you?"

He lowered his eyes. "Yes, Your Honor."

"In each case, I let you go on your own recognizance after you promised not to do any more scams, right?"

"Right."

The judge rested her chin in her palm. "Did you break your promise again, Luther?"

"Sort of."

She turned to the prosecutor. "Why are we here, Mr. George?"

"Mr. Robinson was selling wooden tongue depressors on the street in the Tenderloin."

I interjected, "*Allegedly* selling."

"No, he was *really* selling. One of his customers was an undercover police officer."

I shot a glance at Luther, who nodded.

The judge looked up. "Where did he get the tongue depressors, Mr. Daley?"

"The Tenderloin Free Clinic. Luther took them during an appointment last week."

"Technically, that might be shoplifting, but it seems pretty innocuous." She looked at her computer. "It says here that Mr. Robinson is charged with misdemeanor fraud."

George answered her. "He is."

"Strikes me as a bit severe."

"Mr. Robinson was charging twenty dollars each."

"Why would anybody in their right mind pay so much for an item worth a few pennies?"

"Mr. Robinson represented to his customers that they were home STD tests."

"You're kidding."

"I'm not. He instructed them to place the wooden stick under their tongue for thirty seconds. If it didn't turn blue, they were clean."

This elicited a few snickers in the gallery.

Judge McDaniel templed her fingers in front of her mouth to hide a smile. "How many did he sell?"

"At least a dozen. Seems they're in great demand in the Tenderloin."

"Is this true, Luther?"

He nodded.

The judge's voice filled with disappointment. "Oh, Luther. Were you trying to get yourself arrested again?"

"No, Your Honor."

"Do you need dental work?"

"No."

"Were you hungry?"

"A little."

She turned to me. "Mr. Daley, would you please see that Luther gets something to eat?"

"Already did."

"Thank you. Is he prepared to enter a plea?"

"In a moment. First, I wanted to let you know that Luther is very sorry."

"That's a good start." The grandmother voice disappeared as she spoke directly to Luther. "Do you understand that sexually transmitted diseases are serious business? And if they are not diagnosed properly, someone could become very sick or die? And that they can be retransmitted to somebody else?"

Luther swallowed. "Yes, Your Honor."

"Your Honor," I said, "Luther sold only a handful of these items and nobody was injured. I would also remind you that he has never been convicted of any crime other than petty misdemeanors. He's never hurt anybody."

George did his best to muster a forceful tone. "We can't just let this go. Mr. Robinson committed a blatant fraud that could have resulted in serious medical repercussions."

Technically, that's true, but let's not get carried away. "Your Honor,

Luther made a mistake for which he is willing to take responsibility."

"What did you have in mind, Mr. Daley?"

I was hoping you would ask. "First, Luther will refund the money."

"So far, so good."

"Second, he will agree never to engage in the sale of any medical products of any type." *Especially the phony kind.*

"I like the sound of that."

"Third, he will volunteer at the Tenderloin Free Clinic one afternoon a week for the next four weeks." *And he won't pilfer any more tongue depressors.*

"Even better." The judge spoke to Luther. "Is this agreeable to you?"

"Yes, Your Honor."

"That's good enough for you, isn't it, Mr. George?"

The young A.D.A. exhaled heavily. "I guess."

"Then we're agreed." She picked up her gavel—which she rarely used for its intended purpose—and pointed it at my client. "I want to make something clear to you, Luther. I am going to suspend these charges and grant diversion, but not dismiss them. Subject to the conditions that Mr. Daley just outlined, I am going to release you on your own recognizance—*again.* If I see you back in this courtroom in the next five years, I'm going to reinstate the charges and make sure that you spend time in jail. If I'm not here, I will instruct my colleagues do the same thing. Understood?"

"Yes, Your Honor."

"Good." Her eyes shifted to me. "Nice to see you, Mr. Daley. Please give my best to our Public Defender."

"I will."

"Next case."

* * *

The Public Defender of the City and County of San Francisco

flashed the radiant smile that I still found irresistible twenty-five years after we'd met in the old P.D.'s Office and two decades after we'd gotten divorced. "How's Betsy?" she asked.

"Fine. I told her that you'd see her at the gym on Monday."

"Great." Rosita Carmela Fernandez adjusted the sleeve of her Calvin Klein blouse. Sixteen months earlier, the Mission District native had upgraded her wardrobe when she won a hotly contested election to become San Francisco's first Latina Public Defender. "Were you able to resolve Luther's case?"

"I got him off with a warning and a promise not to sell ersatz STD tests ever again."

"Making the world a little safer for victims of scammers."

"Indeed. If Luther's case appeared in a Grisham novel, nobody would have believed it."

"Out here in the real world, things are always stranger than anything you make up. Thanks for pinch hitting for Rolanda."

"My pleasure." Rolanda Fernandez was Rosie's niece and one of our best deputies. "It was fun to be in Misdemeanor Court. It brought back good memories."

"You miss it, don't you?"

"Yes."

"So do I."

"Thought so." I flashed back to the days when Rosie was a rising star who had just been promoted to the Felony Division, and I was a newbie Deputy P.D. who had gone to law school after three frustrating years as a priest. In those days, she wore jeans and denim shirts to work. Her two going-to-court suits were in plastic bags hanging from a nail pounded into her door. Her straight black hair used to flow down to her waist. Nowadays, it was shorter and styled into a softer look. She had been San Francisco's Public Defender for a little over a year, but it seemed longer. She wore the trappings of political influence naturally.

Her smile broadened. "You're a helluva lawyer, Mike."

"That's why you made me the head of the Felony Division."

"You still work for me."

"You never let me forget."

"It's important to observe chain-of-command protocols."

"You're just a higher-ranking bureaucrat."

"I prefer to call it public service."

One of the reasons that Rosie and I had remained on reasonably good terms at the office and, for that matter, in bed, was the fact that I always let her have the last word. If I had learned this lesson twenty years ago, we might still be married.

I glanced around at her immaculate office on the second floor of a bunker-like building a couple of blocks south of the Hall of Justice. The P.D.'s Office had moved here in the nineties. While our new digs were no longer under the same roof as the criminal courts and the jail, it had the advantages of adequate ventilation and, more important, functional bathrooms.

The wall next to her door was lined with law books (mostly for show). The area behind her desk was filled with citations and photos of herself with San Francisco's political and social power brokers. Rosie insisted—legitimately, I suppose—that the fancy office was required for her occasional TV appearances. While she was the most grounded human being I'd ever met, I worried that she was beginning to enjoy the accouterments of her job a little too much.

I pointed at the framed photo of our nineteen-year-old daughter, Grace, who was a sophomore at USC. "Heard anything lately?"

"She might have an internship at Pixar this summer."

"That's great. How's the new boyfriend?"

"Already an ex-boyfriend."

"That didn't take long."

"She's very particular."

Just like her mother. "Is Tommy okay?"

"Fine."

Our twelve-year-old son was a pleasant, but unplanned

surprise long after Rosie and I had split up. He was more dedicated to video games than schoolwork, but he was a good kid. "I'll be at his basketball game on Saturday."

"I'll let him know."

Rosie and I lived a couple of blocks from each other fifteen minutes across the Golden Gate Bridge in Marin County. I spent three nights a week at her house. Old habits.

I glanced at the flat-screen TV on her wall. It was tuned to the local news, the sound turned down. "What's going on?"

"There was an officer-involved shooting in the Fillmore."

"Not good. Do you know which cop?"

"They haven't released a name."

My dad was a San Francisco police officer for thirty-five years. He had died almost twenty years earlier. He always referred to SFPD as the "family business." My younger brother, Pete, had worked in the family business until he and his partner cracked some heads breaking up a gang fight in the Mission. He lost his job as part of the settlement of the inevitable lawsuit. Nowadays, he worked as a private investigator. We still knew a lot of cops.

Rosie glanced at her watch. "I need to get onto a conference call."

Her doorway filled with the imposing presence of our secretary, legal assistant, process server, bodyguard, and one-time client, Terrence "The Terminator" Love, a former small-time prizefighter who was one of my most reliable customers during my first stint at the P.D.'s Office. The light reflected off the bald head of the gentle giant who clocked in at six-six and three hundred and fifty pounds. "Pete's on the phone. He tried your cell, but you didn't answer."

I glanced at my iPhone and saw that the battery had run out. "Is he okay?"

"Yes, but he needs to talk to you right away. It sounded important."

Terrence was perceptive for a guy who had taken more punches than he had given. "I'll take it in my office."

* * *

I sat down at my metal desk and picked up the phone. "You okay, Pete?"

"Fine, Mick." His rasp was more pronounced than usual.

"Everybody okay at home?"

"Yeah. Got a minute?"

"For my kid brother, always."

"I need to see you right away. We gotta deal with a problem."

Uh-oh. "What kind?"

"You seen the news?" He didn't wait for an answer. "There was an officer-involved shooting in the Fillmore."

"I heard. I hope it isn't somebody we know."

"It is."

2
"THERE COULD BE RIOTS"

"Who's the cop?" I asked.

Pete's voice was tense. "Johnny B."

Oh, crap. "Is he okay?"

"Yeah."

"But?"

"He shot an eighteen-year-old kid during a traffic stop. The kid died."

Not good. "Stuff happens."

"This is bad, Mick."

"Yes, it is."

Giovanni "Johnny" Bacigalupi IV was a rookie cop and fourth-generation SFPD. The youngest of seven siblings, all of his brothers were police officers. His father, Giovanni "Gio" III, was an assistant chief and my high school classmate at St. Ignatius. His grandpa, Giovanni II, used to be the commander at Taraval Station. He was one of my father's best friends.

"Where's Johnny?" I asked.

"Northern Station."

"Has Gio talked to him?"

"Not yet."

"He's the assistant chief."

"Doesn't matter. You remember the chaos during 'Fajitagate.' They aren't going to let Johnny talk to anybody—especially his father—until they get his statement."

True. In 2002, three off-duty police officers had too much to drink and got into a fight outside a bar on Union Street after they demanded a bag of fajitas from two young men who were in the wrong place at the wrong time. The cops were exonerated of assault and battery charges, but two were held liable in a civil case. The situation was exacerbated by the fact that the father of one of the cops was an assistant chief. He and other members of the brass were absolved of obstruction of justice. When the smoke cleared, the three cops lost their jobs, and the big guns looked terrible. SFPD adopted a policy that the chief or an assistant must recuse himself from the investigation if his kid is accused of wrongdoing.

I kept my tone even. "He has to go through the process, Pete."

"This is going to get messy."

Yes, it is. "Who else was there?"

"Three other cops. It gets worse. The victim may have been unarmed."

In which case, this could be a full-blown disaster. "Have they ID'd the victim?"

"SFPD hasn't released a name."

"Did Gio call you?"

"No, Luca did. He couldn't reach you."

Lucantonio "Luca" Bacigalupi was Gio's older brother and Johnny's uncle. He was a "juice" lawyer downtown who used his family's connections on behalf of developers to ram building projects through the City's Byzantine permitting process. He was the only member of the immediate family who wasn't SFPD.

"Why didn't Gio call me?" I asked.

"He's at Northern Station trying to see Johnny."

"What does Luca expect me to do?"

"Line up a lawyer."

"He knows everybody in town."

"He does real estate deals. He wants a criminal defense attorney."

"The POA has people on-call."

"He wants somebody he knows."

"Johnny won't qualify for a public defender. The family has

plenty of money."

"Luca wants somebody he trusts."

So would I. "Let's not get ahead of ourselves. We don't know that Johnny did anything wrong."

"In that case, we can call off the fire drill. For now, we have four cops involved in an officer-involved shooting. Gio wants a lawyer for Johnny in case this gets out of hand."

"Is there video?"

"Probably. The world has changed since I was a cop. SFPD still doesn't have dash cams, but every cop wears a body cam. Something might have been caught on a security camera. And there's always a chance that somebody taped it on their iPhone."

"Johnny's lawyer needs to see the videos before somebody puts them up on YouTube."

"Agreed. Pop never had to deal with this."

"He would have quit."

"So would I. Local TV is all over it. CNN and Fox News will pick it up any minute. Twitter is going wild." My streetwise younger brother's tone transformed into a whisper. "There could be riots, Mick."

"Where did you leave it with Luca?"

"I told him that you and I would come over to his office as soon as we could."

"I'll meet you there."

* * *

I was walking down the corridor at the P.D.'s Office when I heard Rosie's voice from behind me. "Going somewhere?"

"I need to see Luca Bacigalupi."

"Does this have anything to do with Johnny B.?"

"Yeah. How did you find out?"

"I'm the Public Defender of the City and County of San Francisco."

"How did you really find out?"

"Twitter."

Thought so. "I'll be back this afternoon."

"Johnny won't qualify for a P.D., Mike."

"I know."

"Why are you going?"

"He's my godson."

3
"I'M JUST BEING CAUTIOUS"

The well-heeled attorney extended a meaty hand and spoke to me in a flowing baritone. "Thanks for coming in on short notice."

"Pete said it was urgent, Luca."

"It is, Mike."

Unlike many of his contemporaries who have switched to business casual, Luca Bacigalupi still wore a charcoal Brioni suit, a white oxford shirt, and a conservative tie to work. Built like an SUV, his slick gray hair, gold Rolex, and maroon pocket square meshed with the rosewood-paneled walls in the reception area of his law firm on the twenty-seventh floor of the historic Russ Building on Montgomery Street. The eldest of the seven Bacigalupi brothers had just turned sixty-seven, but he still looked like he could hold his own on the offensive line at St. Ignatius, where he had starred a few years before my older brother, Tommy. Luca went on to USF for college and law school. Tommy became an all-city quarterback and the starter at Cal before we lost him in Vietnam.

"How's your dad?" I asked as he escorted me down the hall.

"Good days and bad days."

A year earlier, his father had suffered a debilitating stroke, and Luca had become the *de facto* head of the family. "Is he still living at home?"

"For now. He has a full-time caretaker."

Pete and I had been through a similar experience with our mother, who had suffered from Alzheimer's during the last years of her life. "Tough stuff."

"Tell me about it."

"Is Pete here?"

"He's inside."

I accepted his offer of coffee as he led me into a conference room with overstuffed leather chairs and Currier and Ives lithographs. The traditional look was a welcome respite from the sterile designs of many contemporary law firms. I looked out the window. Through the heavy rain, I saw the outline of the Transamerica Pyramid and, in the distance, the Golden Gate Bridge.

Pete was standing by the credenza. My younger brother was stockier than I was, with a pockmarked face and closely-cropped gray hair. He was dressed in his ever-present bomber jacket, a cup of coffee in his hand. Luca closed the door behind him, and we took our seats around the rosewood table. There was a poster-sized drawing of a condo tower near the ballpark that Luca was trying to bulldoze through the planning commission. The conference room reminded me of the five years I had spent at a power firm at the top of the Bank of America Building after Rosie and I had split up. I took the job because I needed the money. It was a bad fit from day one. The white-shoe guys who run white-shoe firms don't like it when you represent blue-collar criminals—you know—the kind who steal stuff and kill people.

Luca's tone was somber. "This conversation is attorney-client privileged."

"Understood." Since Pete wasn't a lawyer, this wasn't true for him. Then again, he wasn't going to tell anyone about our discussion. He never said much. "Is Johnny okay?"

"Yes. He's at Northern Station."

"Is Gio there?"

"Yes, but they won't let him see Johnny."

"They have to follow procedures." I didn't need to mention Fajitagate. "They'll want to get Johnny's statement."

"Gio's an assistant chief."

"There can't be any appearance of special treatment. He's going to have to recuse himself."

"I know."

"What else did Gio tell you?"

"Johnny shot and killed a young man during a traffic stop." He waited a beat. "The kid was black. Johnny and the other cops are white."

Uh-oh. "Is there a problem?"

"Just a hunch. You know the issue. Trayvon Martin. Ferguson. LaQuan McDonald. Black Lives Matter."

"Let's not get ahead of ourselves, Luca."

"I'm just being cautious, Mike."

Got it. "Why did you want to see me?"

"Gio asked me to line up a criminal defense lawyer for Johnny."

"The POA will provide an attorney. They probably have somebody there already. If not, you know the good defense lawyers in town."

"I know you better."

"I'm a public defender."

"You're family. I trust you. So does Gio. So does Johnny. I want you to come with me to Northern Station. If they won't let Johnny talk to Gio, maybe they'll let him talk to you."

I considered my options for a moment. "Okay."

Pete finally broke his silence. "You want me to come along?"

Luca nodded. "Yes, but you can't talk to Johnny. Anything he says to you isn't covered by the privilege. I want you to work your sources at Northern Station and the Fillmore and see if you can find out what happened."

4
"THEY WON'T LET ME TALK TO MY SON"

"Where's Johnny?" I asked.

Assistant Chief Giovanni "Gio" Bacigalupi gestured with his thumb. "Upstairs."

"Is he okay?"

"As far as I know. He isn't answering his police or personal cell."

"Have you seen him?"

"No." His voice filled with frustration. "They won't let me talk to my son."

Gio's features were similar to his older brother's, but he was rail-thin, and his face bore the scars of three decades of police work. Unlike Luca's flowing hair, Gio still wore a traditional crewcut. His badge was displayed on the breast pocket of his Men's Wearhouse suit.

"We'll get this sorted out, Gio," I said. "You know the drill. They need to follow procedure."

He took a sip of room-temperature coffee. "Yeah, right."

At ten-forty-five on Wednesday morning, my high school classmate was sitting at a metal table in an interrogation room in the basement of Northern Station, a windowless bomb shelter at Fillmore and Turk. Luca and I were across from him. Given Gio's rank, I figured that he would have been given more comfortable accommodations. The desk sergeant had received iron-clad instructions to escort Gio downstairs and out of range from his son, the brass, and, most important, the press.

Gio's scowl became more pronounced. "I'm the assistant chief."

"SFPD has to be careful with an officer-involved shooting. Let's give them the benefit of the doubt and assume that they're following procedure and taking Johnny's statement."

"He should talk to a lawyer first." He turned to his older brother. "Right, Luca?"

"Yes."

Something didn't sound right. "Do you have any reason to believe that Johnny did something wrong?"

"No."

"But?"

"You know how it works, Mike. Johnny's a kid. In SFPD, crap always flows downhill. If something got screwed up, Johnny is going to take the hit."

Yup. "Who is taking his statement?"

"The chief and the commander of this station." He waited a beat. "And Roosevelt Johnson."

What? "He's retired."

"Evidently, he's agreed to help with this investigation."

I exchanged a glance with Luca. Now in his eighties, Roosevelt Johnson was the most decorated homicide inspector in SFPD history. He had handled countless high-profile cases until his retirement ten years earlier. Coincidentally, he and my father were San Francisco's first integrated patrol team when they walked the beat in the Tenderloin almost sixty years ago. His credentials were impeccable, and his integrity was unquestionable.

"Why is a homicide inspector involved?" I asked Gio.

"It's the protocol for an officer-involved shooting. The D.A.'s Office also has the authority to conduct its own parallel investigation."

"SFPD has two dozen active homicide inspectors."

He gave me a sideways look. "I guess they're busy."

"What's going on, Gio?"

"I don't know, but I don't like it."

Neither do I. Why is a highly respected and very retired homicide cop coming back to handle the investigation of an officer-involved shooting?

"Have you talked to him?"

"Not yet."

"What about the chief?"

"He ordered his people to send me down here."

It was no secret that Gio and Chief Alshon Green weren't pals. Green had been hired three months earlier when his predecessor was forced to resign after two officers shot an unarmed man in the Mission. The cops were exonerated after what some viewed as a less-than-robust investigation. The press coverage was merciless, and the former chief took the fall. When it was time to pick his successor, Gio was passed over. He never complained in public, but I knew that he was bitter.

Luca spoke up. "What else did the chief tell you?"

"Johnny was the shooter. No cops were hurt. Then he told me that I should stay out of the building and avoid the press." His tone turned sarcastic. "Optics."

Of course. "How are you and the chief getting along these days?"

"We keep it professional."

"It's better that way." I pushed back my chair, stood, and headed toward the door. "You should stay here, Gio."

"Where are you going?"

I motioned to Luca to join me. "To see our client."

* * *

"How are you, Ignacio?" I asked.

The desk sergeant looked up from the sports section of the *Chronicle.* "Fine, Mike."

"Pete says hi."

"Give him my regards."

Sergeant Ignacio Navarro was sitting at a console behind

bulletproof glass in the lobby of Northern Station. He was Pete's first partner at Mission Station thirty years earlier. Back then, he was a person of few words. Nowadays, he said even less. I've always wondered whether he and Pete ever spoke to each other.

His eyes darted from me to Luca and then back to me. "Yes?"

"We'd like to see our client."

"Who's that?"

We're going to have to do this the hard way. "Come on, Ignacio."

"Do you know how many people are in the lockup?"

I care about just one. "Johnny Bacigalupi."

"They're taking his statement."

"We're his attorneys."

"I was told that the POA was going to provide somebody."

"Change of plans."

"How come the P.D.'s Office is involved? He can afford a private attorney."

"That doesn't concern you. We want to see our client."

"No can do, Mike. I'm under orders. Nobody talks to Johnny until they take his statement."

"You know better, Ignacio. You can't prevent him from seeing his lawyer."

"As far as I know, he hasn't asked for one."

"He is now."

"Says who?"

"His lawyer."

"It's not my call, Mike."

"Could you please talk to somebody who can make the call?"

He finally put down the paper. He picked up his phone, punched in a number, and held his hand over the mouthpiece so that we couldn't hear him. He nodded a couple of times, grunted, and hung up. "Can't help you, Mike."

"Unless he's been arrested, you have no legal basis to prevent him from leaving."

"I'm sorry, Mike."

"If you refuse to let us see our client, we'll find a judge who will order you to do so."

"I'm under orders, Mike."

"We'll go to the press."

"Your client isn't here."

What? "Where is he?"

"They took him downtown to headquarters."

5
"PROTOCOL"

The police officer looked younger than my college-age daughter. "Can I help you?" he asked.

I handed him a business card. "I'm Michael Daley. This is Lucantonio Bacigalupi. And I'm sure you know the assistant chief."

"Yes, sir." He stood taller. "Of course."

Good manners. I like that. I read his name plate. "Officer Dito, are you Phil's son?"

"Nephew, Mr. Daley."

I wasn't surprised. Four of Phil Dito's brothers were cops. "Your uncle and I were classmates at S.I., David. Please tell him that I said hello."

"I will."

We were standing in the otherwise empty corridor outside the chief's office on the sixth floor of the shiny new police headquarters on Third Street, just south of AT&T Park. Officially known as the "San Francisco Public Safety Building," the glass-walled edifice also housed the Southern Police Station, a fire station, and a community center. Opened in 2015 at a cost of almost a quarter of a billion dollars, the state-of-the-art facility was an unimaginable upgrade from the old headquarters at the Hall of Justice.

A dozen uniforms had been instructed to sequester the press in the lobby. My mole at the metal detector informed me that Johnny was in the chief's office. We had made our way upstairs, where we found Phil's nephew. His only job was to keep passers-by, reporters, and lawyers out.

I invoked my priest-voice. "We were hoping that you could help us."

"I'll try, sir."

I no longer cringed when young people offered me their seats on Muni or addressed me as "sir." "You don't need to call me 'sir.' 'Mike' is fine. I presume you know Johnny B?"

"We were in the same class at the Academy."

Good. "We need to talk to him. We're his lawyers." I let my words hang. I was hoping that the young cop would feel compelled to fill the void.

My patience was rewarded. "Uh, I need to talk to my sergeant."

Yes, you do. "That's fine. We need to talk to our client." I pointed at Gio. "Assistant Chief Bacigalupi hasn't had a chance to talk to his son. Johnny's mother is worried. We need your help, David."

The kid repeated his mantra. "I need to talk to my sergeant."

"Understood."

He pointed at a nearby bench. "Would you mind taking a seat for a few minutes?"

"Of course. Given the circumstances, we would appreciate it if you would check with your sergeant right away."

"I will."

Gio finally spoke to the rookie cop. "You're doing a good job, son."

"Thank you, sir."

Gio, Luca, and I sat down and waited as David worked his way up the chain of command. Luca and I checked our e-mails and texts. Gio called his wife. Then we sat in silence.

Ten minutes later, the door opened. At forty-eight, Chief Alshon Green still had the erect bearing of a Marine. He nodded respectfully and spoke precisely. "How can I help you, gentlemen?"

"We need to see Johnny Bacigalupi," I said.

"I'm afraid that's not possible."

"I'm his lawyer."

Luca spoke up. "So am I."

The chief frowned. "Which one of you is his lawyer?"

"Both of us," I said. "We need to see our client."

Gio stood up. "And I want to see my son."

"That's *absolutely* impossible. You know our procedures, Gio. I have to follow protocol."

"He's my son."

"Protocol," he repeated.

I stepped in front of Gio, who was seething. "Chief Green, Luca and I respectfully demand to see our client immediately."

"After we've finished taking his statement."

Not good enough. "Unless he's under arrest, you have no legal authority to detain him. If you question him outside our presence, anything he tells you will be inadmissible in court. It is therefore to your advantage to let us see him right now."

"I can assure you that he's fine. We have provided him with a meal and a change of clothes. We've offered him counseling. Since he isn't married, we informed Gio—his closest relative—of his whereabouts and confirmed that he doesn't require medical attention. He's been contacted by a CIRT Team to make sure that his immediate needs are taken care of."

SFPD officers volunteer to serve on so-called "CIRT" teams, which stands for Critical Incident Response Team. They make sure that the officer gets food and clothing and that the needs of his or her immediate family are addressed.

He wasn't finished. "The POA has spoken to Officer Bacigalupi. They gave him a list of on-call attorneys."

"*We're* his attorneys. You can't deny us the opportunity to talk to our client."

The chief lowered his voice. "Can we please dial it down a little?"

No. "We need to see our client—now."

He feigned exasperation. "It would make everybody's life— including your client's—a lot easier if you'd let us take his statement."

You're stalling. "We have the legal right to talk to him."

"Fine." The chief pointed at me and then at Luca. "You two can come inside." He looked at Gio. "You're going to have to wait out here."

"But Alshon—,"

"I'm sorry, Gio. Protocol."

6

THE SEVENTH SON OF THE SEVENTH SON

"Where's my dad?" Johnny asked, his voice tense.

"Downstairs," I said.

My godson's muscular arms were folded as he sat in a windowless interview room adjacent to the chief's office. It was considerably nicer than the consultation rooms at the Hall.

The concern in Johnny's voice was palpable. "Why isn't he here?"

Luca spoke to his nephew in a paternal tone. "He isn't allowed to talk to you, Johnny."

"He's the assistant chief."

"They have to follow procedure—especially since you're his son."

Johnny was the sort of kid that I'd like Grace to marry someday. He looked as if he had been transported intact from a fifties-era *Life Magazine*. At twenty-two, he was clean-cut, clean-shaven, and, as far as I knew, clean-living. His baby face contrasted with the chiseled body of a three-sport athlete. His clear blue eyes reflected an eagerness to please. He wore his jet-black hair in a crewcut identical to his father's.

"What about my mom?" he asked.

"She's at my office," Luca said. "We'll let her know that you're okay."

"Thank you."

Johnny was holding up better than I had anticipated. Then

again, he always made things look easy. Altar boy at St. Anne's. Eagle Scout. Valedictorian and star athlete at St. Ignatius and USF. First in his class at the Academy. His nickname at S.I. was "Johnny B. Goode." And he *was* good—seemingly at everything. His father liked to say that his youngest son was special because he was the seventh son of a seventh son. In some cultures, it is believed that such individuals have healing powers. It made for a nice story, but I also knew that Johnny worked hard at school, sports, and life. He still addressed his elders as "sir" and "ma'am," and always said "please" and "thank-you." Notwithstanding his low-key demeanor, he hated to lose. When I was in high school, I wanted to be like him. Nowadays, I was immensely proud of him.

First things first. "Are you okay, Johnny?"

He nodded a little too emphatically. "Yeah."

"You should take a little time off."

A shrug. "I will."

At the very least, SFPD was going to put him on administrative leave for ten days—maybe longer. "Have you eaten?"

"A little."

"Do you need us to call anyone?"

"No."

Johnny lived by himself in the in-law unit behind his parents' house. It was a rite of passage for the Bacigalupi boys. Each of his brothers had lived in the studio apartment before they moved into their own places.

"When can I go home?" he asked.

That's always the first question. "Soon."

"How soon?"

I have no idea. "I'm not sure. They have to finish the process."

He showed his first hint of irritation. "Everybody keeps talking about 'the process.' I told them everything—twice. What else do they need?"

"To make sure that your story lines up with everybody else's."

"Of course it will. Why are you here?"

Luca answered him. "They won't let your father see you."

"You're lawyers."

"We're family. And they won't let you talk to anybody other than an attorney."

"The POA said they would provide a lawyer."

"We're family," Luca repeated.

"Does that mean you're representing me?"

"Technically, yes. So is Mike."

The confident façade showed its first crack. "Am I under arrest?"

"No," I said.

"Then why are you here?"

"Your parents wanted to be sure that you're okay. So did I."

"I'm fine."

"We'll let them know. In the meantime, they wanted to be sure that you have everything you need."

"I do."

"And they wanted you to have a lawyer in case something unexpected comes up."

"Like what?"

They arrest you. "We'll worry about it if we have to. In the meantime, we thought it would be a good idea to have somebody available who knows the ins and outs of the system."

He wasn't satisfied.

I decided to do a little gentle probing. "Who else was with you this morning?"

"My FTO."

"FTO" stood for "Field Training Officer." After trainees complete thirty-two weeks at the Academy, SFPD puts them on the street with one or more FTOs, who train and mentor rookies.

I asked, "How many weeks of field training have you completed?"

"Three."

"Is this the first time that you drew your weapon?"

"Yes. This is going to screw up my reviews, isn't it?"

"Not necessarily." *That's the least of our concerns.* "Who is your FTO?"

"Kevin Murphy."

He was in capable hands. "Murph" was a hardass from the Excelsior who was in Pete's class at the Academy. His dad was a cop. So were two of his brothers and his sister. "You're absolutely sure that his story will match up with yours?"

"Of course."

"Who took your statement?"

"The chief, my commander at Northern Station, and Roosevelt Johnson."

"Inspector Johnson was my father's first partner. He's very good."

"I've heard. I thought he retired."

"He did. Evidently, he's agreed to help with this investigation."

"Why?"

"Maybe the active inspectors are busy. Would you mind telling us what you told him?"

"Murph and I stopped for burgers at Mel's on Geary. We finished a few minutes before one. We were driving east on Geary when we saw a Honda Civic with a broken tail light."

"You were driving?"

"Yes. Murph told me to pull him over. I put on my overhead lights and he got off Geary Boulevard at Steiner. Murph ran the plate through our dash computer. The car wasn't reported as stolen. It was registered to a woman named Vanessa Jones, whose address was on Turk. Thirty-eight. No criminal record or outstanding warrants. We thought it would be fix-it ticket. The driver parked in the Safeway lot on Webster."

"Was Vanessa Jones driving?"

"It was her son, Juwon. Eighteen. Lived with his mother." He said that he and Murphy followed procedure. Johnny turned on his spotlight and aimed it at the side mirror to obstruct the driver's vision. Murphy shined his spotlight through the back window. "I grabbed my flashlight and nightstick and approached on the driver side. Murph came up on the passenger side."

"Did you try to open the trunk?" I learned this trick from Pete. The cops try to get a free look if the trunk pops open.

"It was locked. I approached the driver and turned on my body cam. I was the contact officer, so I introduced myself and asked him to make sure the ignition was off, and the car was in Park. I requested license, registration, and evidence of insurance, which he provided. I determined that the driver was, in fact, Juwon Jones. He said the car belonged to his mother. Nobody else was in the vehicle. No sign of a weapon. No alcohol or drugs in the car.

"I returned to our unit and ran Jones's information through our dash computer. His driver's license was valid. He had a conviction for grand theft auto and a 10-35."

It meant that Jones had a probation violation which allowed the police to search his car.

"On my way back to Jones's car, I told Murph about the 10-35. He said that I should follow standard procedure. I positioned myself at the driver-side door and asked Jones if he was on probation. He didn't answer. When I asked him again, he acknowledged that it was true."

"How was his demeanor?"

"He was calm at first. Then he got agitated. I politely asked if he would let us search his car, but he refused. I told him that because he had a probation violation warrant, we had the legal right to search the vehicle."

This was true. They also had the right to handcuff him. "And?"

"I asked him to get out of the car. I informed him that if the vehicle was clean, I was planning to issue him a fix-it ticket and let him go."

Seems reasonable.

Johnny's right hand clenched into a fist. "Initially, he refused to get out of the car. On the second request, he got angry. As he started to exit the vehicle, I saw a handgun in his hand. He banged the door into me and I fell down. He ran across the plaza to Fillmore. I radioed for backup, drew my weapon, and pursued him on foot. Murph followed me.

"He ran north on Fillmore, but he was cut off by a backup unit at Geary. He turned left and headed west past the old Fillmore Auditorium. Another unit closed him off in front of the post office, where he climbed over the gate into an enclosed parking lot. I followed him over the fence and cornered him behind a postal van."

"He still had the gun?"

"Yes."

"Did he point it at you?"

"No."

"Was it in his hand?"

"It was in his pocket."

"You said that it was in his hand when he got out of the car. When did he put it into his pocket?"

"I'm not sure. Maybe when he climbed over the gate. It was definitely in his pocket when I cornered him."

"How do you know?"

"Because we found it under his body."

"Let's take a step back. What happened when you cornered him?"

"I followed standard procedure and tried to de-escalate the situation. I ordered the suspect to put his hands up. On the second request, he complied."

"Did he say anything?"

"He said, 'Don't shoot.' I told him that I was placing him under arrest. I informed him that I would shoot him if he did not follow my commands. I ordered him to lie down on his stomach with his arms spread."

"Did he?"

"No. I repeated the command, which he disobeyed. The third time, he started to reach into his pocket for the gun." He swallowed. "I thought he was going to kill me, so I shot him in self-defense." He waited a beat. "I had to, Mike."

"You sure he was reaching for his gun?"

"Yes." He repeated, "I shot him in self-defense."

Okay. "You did what you had to do."

Luca spoke to his nephew. "You didn't do anything wrong, Johnny."

"I killed him, Luca."

"You had no choice, son."

I leaned forward. "You explained all of this to the chief and Inspector Johnson?"

"Yes."

"And you're sure that your FTO and the other officers will corroborate your story?"

"Yes."

I hope so. "I know this is tough, Johnny, but from a legal standpoint, your actions were completely justified."

"That's good, right?"

"Right." My mind raced. "You said that you were wearing your body cam, right?"

"I was." He confirmed that his car was not equipped with a dash cam.

"So there should be footage of everything."

"Most of it."

"What about the part where you shot Jones?"

"No. The camera came off when I jumped the fence to get into the parking lot."

"Have you seen the video?"

"No. We aren't allowed to look at it before we give our statement."

I was aware of this policy. They didn't want the cops to adjust their stories to match up with what they'd already seen on tape. "Are you sure that we'll be able to see a gun in Jones's hand when he got out of the car?"

"Yes."

"Was your partner wearing a body cam?"

"Yes, but I don't know if it was turned on."

We'll find out. "Where was he when you shot Jones?"

"Outside the fence. So were two other officers who provided backup. They must have seen what happened."

"Is it possible that one of the other officers caught this on video?"

"Possibly."

"Was anybody else around? Maybe somebody recorded something on their cell phone."

"I doubt it."

The door opened. Instead of the young cop who had let us in, we were met by the imposing presence of my father's first partner. At eighty-two, Roosevelt Johnson's baritone was hoarse, but still forceful. "I didn't expect to see you here, Mike."

"I didn't expect to see you, either, Roosevelt."

He nodded at Johnny's uncle. "Luca."

"Roosevelt."

My tone was respectful. "Could you please check with the chief and let us know when Johnny can go home?"

"I'm afraid that isn't possible."

"He's given his statement."

He looked at Johnny, then he turned back to me. "I'm here to inform you that I am placing your client under arrest for the murder of Juwon Jones."

7
"YOU CAN'T BE SERIOUS"

My stomached tightened. "You can't be serious."

"Yes, I am." Roosevelt's voice was controlled. "Please step out of the way so that we can begin processing Officer Bacigalupi."

"You're making a mistake."

"No, I'm not."

Luca spoke up. "Yes, you are."

"We'll talk about it another time, Luca."

"We'll talk about it now, Roosevelt. If you insist on filing spurious charges against my nephew, I will file a lawsuit first thing tomorrow morning against the City, SFPD, and you personally for wrongful imprisonment and false arrest."

"That's up to you."

"I can make your life difficult, Roosevelt."

Threatening Roosevelt isn't a winning strategy.

Roosevelt exhaled. "I've been doing this for a long time, Luca. Do what you have to do."

"I will."

Roosevelt turned back to me. "I need to take your client to booking at the Hall of Justice. As a courtesy to you, if he agrees to cooperate, we can dispense with handcuffs."

"Thank you." I turned to Johnny. "It will make your life easier if you cooperate."

His voice was a whisper. "Okay."

"Except for your name, address, and date of birth, I don't want you to say a word to anyone. Not to Inspector Johnson. Not to the other officers. Not to anybody from the D.A.'s Office. And, most important, not to the people in booking. Understood?"

"Yes."

"We'll take care of this, Johnny."

His voice filled with panic. "It was self-defense. I didn't do anything wrong."

"Don't say anything else."

Luca spoke up again. "Inspector, would you please give me a moment with my nephew?"

"That would violate procedure."

"Do you think we're going to try to escape from a windowless room in headquarters?"

"Two minutes." Roosevelt stepped outside, closing the door behind him.

Luca turned to me. "Would you please wait outside? I want a word with Johnny."

What's this about? "Sure."

* * *

My father's first partner stood with his back to the wall. Without looking at me, he said, "How do you like this building?"

"Not bad. Are they going to move Homicide over here?"

"Maybe someday."

The Homicide Detail was still housed in a drafty bullpen area on the fourth floor of the Hall. Efforts to find a new home were moving slowly.

"How's Rosie?" he asked.

"Fine."

"Is her mother okay?"

"Yes."

"Grace and Tommy? Pete and his family?"

"All good."

"Glad to hear it." If you listened attentively, you could still discern a hint of his native Texas in his voice. He had moved to San Francisco seventy-five years earlier when his father found work in the naval shipyard at Hunters Point. He removed the toothpick from his mouth. "Why are you here?"

"I'm Johnny's godfather. Gio and I were classmates at S.I. And I'm a defense lawyer."

"Doesn't mean you have to represent him. He isn't going to qualify for a P.D."

I'm well aware of that. "Gio asked me."

He glanced at the deputy who was standing down the hall. He turned back to me and lowered his voice. "It's bad, Mike. He shot an unarmed kid."

"It was self-defense. The kid had a gun."

"No, he didn't." He wouldn't provide any additional details.

"Why are *you* here?" I asked.

He took off his aviator-style bifocals and wiped them with a cloth. I'd seen this gesture countless times at our dinner table on Sunday nights. Roosevelt was deciding how much he wanted to tell me. "The chief, the mayor, and the D.A. asked me. As you know, we've had some less-than-satisfactory results with officer-involved shootings. They want somebody with gray hair to make sure this is handled by the book."

Good choice. "What aren't you telling me?"

"I can't talk now."

"I'll call you later."

"You know where to find me." He put his glasses back on. "High-profile cases get a life of their own, Mike. You should extricate yourself as quickly as you can."

"Thanks, Roosevelt. I will."

The door opened, and Luca appeared. "Johnny is ready."

Roosevelt nodded. "Thank you."

Johnny's face was pale as Roosevelt read him his rights. Luca and I remained silent as we watched Roosevelt escort him down the hall.

Time to get to work. I turned to Luca. "Tell Gio to meet us at the P.D.'s Office."

* * *

"What did you tell Johnny?" I asked.

Luca and I were walking out the back door of headquarters to avoid the reporters.

His eyes narrowed. "That we'll take care of this. What did Roosevelt tell you?"

"He said that Johnny shot an unarmed kid."

"Johnny told me that he shot him in self-defense. This is a publicity stunt by the chief or the mayor. I expect you to get Johnny out of here by the end of the day."

That's unlikely. "We'll talk about it later."

"We'll talk about it now."

"If they charge him with first-degree murder, it will be difficult to get bail."

"They'll never charge first-degree."

I hope you're right. "Either way, I'll help you find somebody to handle it."

"I want *you* to handle it."

"Johnny won't qualify for a public defender."

"You're his godfather."

"We have procedures."

"We'll talk about it when we get back to the office."

* * *

My iPhone vibrated as Luca and I were walking across Bryant toward the P.D.'s Office. Pete's name appeared on the display. His voice was tense. "They arrested him."

"Yeah." *Word travels fast.* "Where are you?"

"Still in the Fillmore. I'll let you know if I find anything."

* * *

Rosie stood outside her office. "I saw Roosevelt on TV. He said that they're charging Johnny with murder."

"They're saying he shot an unarmed kid."

"Did he?"

"Johnny said the kid had a gun. He shot him in self-defense."

"I just saw Luca go into the conference room."

"Gio will be here shortly."

"You can't take this case, Mike."

"I'll help Luca and Gio find somebody."

"Maria texted me. She's coming over to meet Gio."

Maria Cereghino Bacigalupi was Gio's wife. She was also a classmate of Rosie's at Mercy High. "Do you have time to join us? It'll make her feel better."

"I have to get on a call."

"Can it wait?"

"I'm afraid not."

8

"THEY'RE SAYING OUR SON IS A MURDERER"

Maria Bacigalupi sat between her husband and her brother-in-law on mismatched chairs in the conference room down the hall from my office. The retired second-grade teacher clutched Gio's hand. "Thank you for seeing us," she whispered to me. "We need your help."

"We'll take care of this, Maria."

At five-one and a hundred pounds of tightly wound energy, the daughter of a Mission District firefighter didn't suffer fools and wasn't shy about expressing her opinions. "They're saying our son is a murderer."

"Don't believe everything you hear."

Her brown eyes turned to cold steel. "Between TV, radio, the Internet, Twitter, and Facebook, you would think that Johnny has already been tried, convicted, and put in prison."

I had no good response. "It's better if you try to ignore it."

"I can't." She held up her cell phone. "Look at the headline on the *Chronicle's* website."

It read, "Rookie Cop Arrested for Murder."

Maria set the phone down. "Johnny could have been killed. The mayor and the chief are more concerned about a street punk than a police officer. They're saying he shot an unarmed man. There is going to be a march from City Hall to the Fillmore tonight. They're worried about riots."

"That's out of our control."

She let go of Gio's hand and pointed at me. "We have to do *something*, Mike."

"We will." I turned to Gio. "What have you heard?"

"Nobody's talking. The chief must have told everybody *not* to talk to me. He's playing to the media. He's using Johnny to win political points."

"You don't know that."

"Come on, Mike. The mayor brought him in to deal with situations like this one. They're worried about another Ferguson here in San Francisco." He pushed out a frustrated sigh. "And he's trying to screw my kid and me."

"You don't know that, either."

"Yes, I do. I can take care of myself. For now, we need to focus on Johnny."

"Agreed."

"I want you to go over to the Hall of Justice, find a judge, and get bail."

Bail will run well into seven figures—if I can persuade a judge to grant it. "First, I will help you find a top-notch criminal defense lawyer for Johnny."

Gio exchanged a glance with his brother. It was Luca who spoke. "We found one: you."

Maria nodded.

I held up a hand. "I can't do it."

Luca answered again. "Yes, you can."

"Johnny won't qualify for a P.D."

"We'll hire you separately."

"I'm not allowed to do that."

"Then we'll need to find a way to make it happen."

"It's written in black-and-white in my contract. I'm not permitted to moonlight."

"There must be a way around it. You can do it on your own time."

"I'd have to quit."

"No, you wouldn't."

"Yes, I would. Even if I did, you can't expect me to set up my own firm and request a bail hearing for Johnny this afternoon."

"You can work for my firm. We'll pay you a very generous hourly rate. We'll put you on our malpractice policy. If it's an issue of health insurance, we'll put you on our plan."

"This isn't about money."

"You're right. This is about Johnny."

"There are a lot of good defense lawyers in town."

"You're one of the best. And we know you."

We sat in silence for a long moment. Finally, Maria spoke to me in the voice of an anguished mother. "Please, Michael. Johnny needs you."

"I need to talk to Rosie."

9

"I HAVE A PROPOSITION FOR YOU"

Rosie's response was a succinct "No."

I figured this was coming. "Can we talk about this?"

"There's nothing to discuss. You signed an agreement with the City stating that you wouldn't work on cases outside the P.D.'s Office."

"Sometimes you need to be flexible."

"We have rules."

"They can be bent."

"Not in this case. There are some things that I just can't allow. The head of the Felony Division can't take time off to handle a case outside the office."

"We've lent out attorneys."

"Only to other public defenders in circumstances where they were shorthanded or somebody in our office had a particular expertise."

"We've let people help friends and family from time to time."

"Not on my watch."

"Rolanda helped her cousin when he got picked up on a D.U.I."

"That was different. It was one afternoon in court. It wasn't a high-profile matter. And Rolanda wasn't the head of the Felony Division."

"I'll tell Gio that I'll do this only until we find somebody else to step in."

"It's like being a little pregnant, Mike. If you're the lead attorney, no judge will let you back out at the last minute."

"Johnny wants me to represent him. Gio and I go back a long way. His dad and my dad went back even longer."

"I can't do it, Mike."

"Maria wants me to represent her son. I'll take a temporary leave of absence."

"This case could last years."

That much was true. In California, defendants have the right to demand a trial within sixty days, but that happens only on TV. The investigation and witness interviews could take months. And that didn't count pre-trial motions and other legal maneuvering. "At the very least, let me deal with this for a couple of weeks."

"It will look like I'm giving special treatment to my ex-husband and the son of an assistant chief. It will set a terrible precedent."

"What if somebody offered Rolanda a million dollars to take a case outside the office?"

The corner of her mouth turned up. "I'd tell her to take the money."

"So would I."

Her tone turned serious. "You can't do a case outside the office and get paid by somebody else."

"I'll do it *pro bono*."

"The taxpayers are still paying your salary."

"Then I'll take an unpaid leave."

"I'll get crucified by the press."

"I'll take the hit for you."

"Easy for you to say. Your name won't be on the ballot at the next election." My ex-wife, best friend, confidante, lover, and the Public Defender of the City and County of San Francisco drummed her fingers on her desk. "This isn't going to work, Mike."

"You're saying that the only way that I can handle Johnny's case is if I quit?"

"Don't put me in that position."

"I'm just trying to clarify exactly where you stand."

"The answer is yes."

I understood. Coincidentally, it was probably the right call. "I need to think about it."

There was a knock. Terrence the Terminator let himself in and closed the door behind him. "Mr. Bacigalupi wants to know if he can speak to you for a moment."

"Gio?" Rosie asked.

"Luca."

* * *

Luca's smile was sincere, and his tone was warm. "Nice to see you, Rosie."

"Nice to see you, too, Luca. Are Gio and Maria still here?"

"They went to police headquarters."

They exchanged abbreviated pleasantries. Luca was smoother than the bottle of Talisker single malt Scotch that he kept in his office. Rosie could command a packed courtroom, conference room, or political rally without raising her voice. The only people on Planet Earth who could tell when she was irritated were her mother, our kids, and me.

Luca feigned appreciation. "I'm grateful that you've taken a moment to see me."

Rosie flashed her politician's smile. "I appreciated your family's efforts on the campaign."

Especially since everybody except Luca is a cop. It was unusual for members of SFPD to support a candidate for public defender.

Luca returned her smile. "You're family, Rosie."

"You're kind, Luca."

And generous. He contributed ten grand to Rosie's campaign.

Luca's eyes locked onto Rosie's. "We need Mike's help."

Rosie held her palms up. "He can't do it."

"It's for Johnny."

"Not even for Johnny."

"Maria and Gio would be much more comfortable if Mike handled Johnny's case."

"Mike works for the Public Defender's Office. He isn't allowed to freelance. I'm sorry, Luca. You know how we feel about your family."

"And you know how we feel about yours. That's why I need you to make an exception."

"Mike has legal and ethical obligations to his clients here."

Luca glanced at me, then he turned back to Rosie. "I have a proposition for you."

Rosie held up a hand. "Please, Luca."

"Hear me out."

She sighed. "I'm listening."

"I would propose that Mike take a temporary leave of absence from the P.D.'s Office and become 'of counsel' to my law firm. We'll sign a written agreement and put him on our malpractice policy. We'll give him an office, a secretary, a computer, and access to our associates and our library. His sole responsibility will be to handle Johnny's case. When Johnny is exonerated, we will terminate our relationship and Mike will return to his regular duties here."

Ta-da!

Rosie was no longer smiling. "That could be years from now, Luca."

"It won't take that long."

"Mike would have to resign. This office cannot function without him for more than a few weeks."

Glad to hear it.

Luca wasn't fazed. "I figured you might say that, so I would limit Mike's tenure on this case to a shorter period."

"How short?"

"Six months."

"Too long."

"Three months."

"Still too long."

"One month."

"Nothing will be resolved."

"Mike is a very good lawyer."

"Not *that* good."

That's my Rosie. I was starting to feel like I was being auctioned off like a head of cattle.

Luca finally dropped the posturing and invoked a lawyerly tone. "We would like Mike to represent Johnny for a short period to help us analyze the charges, develop a strategy, identify our options, and, if necessary, retain another attorney to whom Mike can transition the case in an orderly way. If things go well, Mike's participation will last only a few weeks."

"You don't expect him to handle the trial?"

"I would *love* for him to handle the trial, but that isn't realistic. I would not expect him to do anything beyond a preliminary hearing if we can't get the charges dropped before then. It would mean a great deal to Johnny, Gio, Maria, and me. We would, of course, compensate Mike at an hourly rate."

"That won't work, either. A city employee can't be on the payroll of another law firm."

Luca spoke to me. "If that's true, I'll need to ask you to handle this matter *pro bono*."

"Works for me."

Rosie wasn't sold. "It would set a bad precedent, and it could have political implications."

"I'm prepared to make it worth your while."

Rosie's eyes narrowed. "If you're suggesting a contribution to my re-election campaign, the answer is an emphatic no."

"I'm suggesting no such thing." He reached inside his jacket and pulled out a piece of paper. "I received this solicitation from you for a donation to the public defender's summer internship program. It says that you're trying to raise a hundred thousand dollars."

"We are."

"Coincidentally, I was going to contribute one hundred thousand dollars to underwrite this program."

Rosie paused. "We're very grateful, Luca, but there can't be any *quid pro quo*."

"There will be none. I will make an anonymous donation to this program—no strings attached. I will insist that my name and the amount of the donation *not* be revealed."

Rosie was concerned. "What if I say that Mike isn't available?"

"I'll make the donation anyway. It's a worthwhile program."

Rosie looked at me. "You're willing to do this for free for the next month?"

"Yes."

She turned back to Luca. "I think we can work something out on a very limited basis."

* * *

Rosie's eyes gleamed. "You understand that this is a bad idea, Mike."

"I do."

"Fortunately, you aren't indispensable."

I let it go.

"Do you have any active cases?" she asked.

"Not at the moment."

"Good." She lowered her voice. "I can't give you any cover if things go sideways."

I was flying solo. "Understood. Mind if I ask you something off the record?"

"Sure."

"Do you think it's a good idea to accept Luca's donation?"

"If the Bacigalupi family wants to underwrite our summer program, I have no problem accepting their generosity."

"You're turning into quite the politician."

"I'm learning. Do what you have to do, Mike. And I want you to be careful. This could get ugly."

48

Yes, it could. "Rosie?"

"Yes?"

"Thanks."

* * *

"You sure that you want me to handle Johnny's case?" I asked.

"Yes." Luca was sitting in the swivel chair opposite my desk. "My father says that the Bacigalupi family always gets what it wants."

"You sound like a character in *Game of Thrones*."

"The same concepts apply."

"The criminal justice system moves slowly. I'm going to give you a list of defense attorneys. I want you to line up somebody to bring in as co-counsel sooner rather than later."

"I will."

"And we'll need a private investigator."

"I already hired your brother."

I'm not surprised. "Excellent choice. I'll go down to the Hall and see if I can talk to the D.A. and find a judge who is willing to talk about bail."

"Great." His tone was confident. "Remember when the *State Bar Journal* said that you were the best public defender in the State of California?"

"That was a long time ago."

"Now everybody is going to remember why."

* * *

My iPhone vibrated as I was heading out the door. Pete's name appeared on the display. His tone was hushed. "Luca told me that you're going to represent Johnny."

"For now. When did you hear that?"

"About an hour ago."

That was before Luca had asked me. Luca had confidence in his powers of persuasion. "I heard that you're in, too."

"Premium rates."

"Attaboy."

"Where are you?"

"Going to the Hall to see the D.A. Then I promised Luca that I would go see if I can find a judge to talk about bail."

"A judge isn't going to talk to you about bail before the arraignment."

Probably true. "I told Luca that I would try."

"Fine. When you're finished, meet me over here in the Fillmore. They're processing the crime scene. You'll want to give it a look before they're done."

10
"ALWAYS GOOD TO SEE YOU"

The District Attorney of the City and County of San Francisco flashed a stunning and utterly phony politician's smile as she extended a supple hand. "Here we are again, Michael," she purred.

"Nice to see you, Nicole," I lied.

"*Always* good to see *you*."

As if. Nicole Ward had been San Francisco's District Attorney for almost a decade, and she wore the accouterments of her office with panache. Her creamy complexion, immaculate make-up, and designer clothing made her look like a world-class politician. We had been on opposite sides of several high-profile cases back in the days when she still appeared in court. She was a formidable adversary who won cases more on style than substance—whatever works. Her frequent appearances on CNN and MSNBC had garnered a national following.

She invited me to sit in the armchair opposite the cherrywood desk in her corner office on the third floor of the Hall. Her paneled walls were covered with photos of local power players and Washington politicos.

She took a seat in her high-backed leather chair and smiled again. "Please give Rosie my very best."

"I will." Rosie and Ward were loath to be in the same room together. I pointed at the college graduation photos of her twin daughters from her second husband. Jenna and Missy were as stunning as their mother. "Everybody okay?"

"Just fine. Jenna is in law school at Yale. Missy is applying to medical school."

"That's terrific."

She tugged at the sleeve of her St. Laurent blouse. "I'm very proud of them."

"You should be." In all the time I had known her, she had never asked about my kids.

She pointed at the middle-aged man sitting in the chair next to mine. "You've met DeSean?"

"Of course."

A native of the Bayview, DeSean Harper had arrived at the D.A.'s Office via Cal and Harvard Law School around the same time that I had started at the P.D.'s Office. Smart, meticulous, and ambitious, he had worked his way up to the head of the Felony Division upon the retirement of his mentor, the legendary Bill McNulty, who had served with distinction for almost forty years. Harper was the first African-American to hold that position.

"Good to see you again, DeSean," I said. I meant it.

"Same here."

In court, in the office, and, I suspected, in his private life, he was painstakingly concise. He was also scrupulously honest and, unlike his boss, a straight-shooter.

Ward's Botoxed forehead cracked as she continued to smile. "How can we help you?"

"I'm representing Johnny Bacigalupi."

"So we've heard." She darted a knowing glance at Harper, then she turned back to me. "You're the last person I expected to see today."

"I went to S.I. with Gio. We've known the family for decades."

"So you know that Johnny won't qualify for a public defender."

"I'm doing this on my own time."

"Rosie's okay with that?"

Sort of. "Yes."

"Really?" She arched a painted eyebrow. "We have policies

prohibiting our attorneys from handling matters outside the office. I would have thought that the P.D.'s Office did, too."

"We do. I'm taking a leave of absence."

"Do you think that's wise?"

"It's an unusual circumstance." *And it's none of your business.*

The fake smile finally disappeared. "Why did you come to see us, Mike?"

"I was hoping that you would be willing to share information on Johnny's case. For starters, have you decided on a charge?"

"First-degree murder."

"There's no malice aforethought."

"Yes, there is."

"It was self-defense."

"No, it wasn't."

"On what evidence?"

"He shot an unarmed man."

"The victim had a gun."

She corrected me. "They found a gun under the victim's body. We don't know how it got there."

"The kid was armed. Period. He was reaching for the gun when Johnny shot him."

"If you can provide sufficient evidence to prove that claim, we'll reconsider the charges, and you can return to the P.D.'s Office."

I would like nothing more. "Are you suggesting that the gun was planted?"

"I said that they found a gun under the victim's body. We don't know how it got there."

We were going in circles.

Ward shot a glance at Harper, who spoke up. "The victim's hands were up when he was shot. He wasn't holding a gun."

"How do you know?"

"I am not at liberty to discuss the evidence with you at this time."

"Video?"

"I am not at liberty to discuss the evidence with you at this time."

"You have a legal obligation to provide us with any evidence that would tend to exonerate our client."

"Which we will do in due course. The evidence that I just described does not."

"We're entitled to talk to the witnesses and see all video evidence."

"In due course."

I wasn't going to get any more from him today. "Has the arraignment been scheduled?"

"Tomorrow morning. Nine a.m. Judge Ramsey's courtroom."

An arraignment is a perfunctory legal proceeding where Johnny would enter a plea of not guilty. Our draw wasn't ideal. Judge Martellus Ramsey was a former Alameda County prosecutor. He tended to give the benefit of the doubt to the D.A.

"We're also going to ask for bail," I said.

"We'll oppose it."

"I'm going to talk to a couple of judges."

"You know as well as I do that no judge is going to grant bail before the arraignment."

Probably true. "Be reasonable, DeSean."

"We can't show preferential treatment for a cop—especially the son of an assistant chief."

"You're doing this to make an example out of my client?"

"We're following the law."

* * *

Luca's voice was strained. "What did you find out from our esteemed D.A.?"

"Not much." I held my iPhone to my ear as I walked through the lobby of the Hall. "The arraignment is tomorrow morning. They're charging Johnny with first-degree murder. They're saying he shot an unarmed man."

"He shot an armed man in self-defense."

"They claim that isn't how it went down."

"On what evidence?"

"They wouldn't say. We'll file papers to get their witnesses and video."

"What about bail?"

"It isn't likely before the arraignment."

"See if you can find a judge."

"I'll do what I can."

11
"NOT TODAY"

Judge Betsy McDaniel greeted me with a sardonic grin. "Twice in one day. I'm honored."

"So am I." I smiled back. "Rosie says hi."

"Will I see her at Pilates in the morning?"

"Unless she has to go on TV."

"Tell her that being a high-profile politico is bad for her exercise routine."

"I will."

She was sitting behind a mahogany desk in her paneled chambers on the third floor of the Hall. The workman-like office was her only remaining perk since she went on senior status. Budget cuts had decimated the court staff, so Betsy worked without a secretary.

I looked out the window at the cars on I-80. I nodded at the framed photos of her grandchildren lined up on her credenza between her laptop, multiple volumes of California Jury Instructions, and several signed first-edition Donna Leon novels. "Grandkids okay?"

"Everybody's fine. Grace and Tommy?"

"Fine. You going to keep doing this for a while?"

"Yes. If I had known how nice it is to work part-time, I would have done this years ago." Her smile disappeared. "You didn't come here to talk about my grandchildren. Does this have anything to do with Johnny Bacigalupi?"

"Yes."

"I hear you're going to handle his case."

"For now."

"Why is the P.D.'s Office representing a client whose family clearly has the wherewithal to pay a private attorney?"

"Gio was my classmate at S.I. Gio's dad was my father's commander. Johnny is my godson. I'm taking a leave of absence and working *pro bono*."

"That explains it."

Despite the substantial influx of young people who work in the tech industry, San Francisco was still a small town where old neighbors looked out for each other.

She drummed her fingers on her desk. "Rosie's okay with this?"

"She isn't crazy about it."

"Putting aside whether it's appropriate for you to take on a private client, wouldn't it make more sense for you to be talking to your client or looking for witnesses?"

"I need to talk to you about bail."

"How many other judges have you talked to?"

"You're the first."

"How many wouldn't let you inside their chambers?"

"Two."

"You figure the third time is the charm?"

"Hopefully."

"Not today, Mike."

"Hear me out, Betsy. Johnny is a good kid."

"Stuff happens."

"Something else is going on. They're rushing to judgment."

"Roosevelt doesn't arrest people on the spur of the moment."

No, he doesn't. "Maybe it wasn't his call."

"The mayor and our D.A. can't bully him."

No, they can't. "It smells."

"They're saying he shot an unarmed kid."

"Johnny says it was self-defense."

"That's why we have courts and juries."

"In the meantime, he's going to get killed if they keep him locked up."

"They'll give him his own cell."

"Not necessarily. I've made the request, but I can't get confirmation from anybody upstairs in booking."

"It will get sorted out in the next few days. Has the arraignment been set?"

"Tomorrow morning in front of Martellus Ramsey."

"It's his case. I can't help you."

"Sure you can."

"You know better, Mike. You can't forum-shop. I can't step in and interfere."

"Johnny could get beat-up tonight—or worse. Please, Betsy."

"Not today."

* * *

My iPhone vibrated as I was leaving the Hall. Luca's name appeared on the display. There were no pleasantries. "Did you find a judge?" he asked.

"I talked to Betsy McDaniel. No bail tonight."

"You need to find another judge."

"I tried Judge Stumpf, Judge Vanden Heuvel, Judge Mandel, Judge Busch, and Judge Breall. They wouldn't talk to me."

"Try again."

"It's not going to happen tonight, Luca."

There was a pause. Then I heard Luca mutter, "No bail," to somebody. It was probably Gio. Luca came back on the line. "Find another judge."

"It's not going to work tonight."

"Dammit, Mike. Johnny can't stay in jail. You need to do something."

"We'll deal with it in the morning, Luca."

"Where are you going now?"

"To the Fillmore."

12
"IT WAS AN EXECUTION"

Pete held up a hand. "Over here, Mick."

He and Roosevelt were standing in front of the post office on Geary, a half-block west of Fillmore. A cold drizzle was falling, but neither of them used an umbrella. Traffic was blocked off. The narrow street in front of the post office was bounded on the north by a chain-link fence separating upper Geary from the six-lane sub-surface Geary Boulevard built in 1961 when the Redevelopment Agency flattened a portion of the Fillmore to create a faster route between downtown and the Richmond. The sledgehammer approach to urban renewal had improved traffic flow and created an unsightly freeway through the heart of a vibrant neighborhood that survived the 1906 earthquake. More than a half-century later, people are still unhappy about it.

I walked by the old Fillmore Auditorium, a twenties-era ballroom that became the home of the Grateful Dead in the sixties. A makeshift memorial to Juwon Jones was set up outside the yellow tape on the sidewalk in front of the post office, a boxy structure flanked by the auditorium and a Korean massage studio. Three police units, an SFPD evidence van, and Roosevelt's unmarked SUV were parked in front of the gate to the parking lot. Two crime scene techs were finishing their work. Down the block, a dozen onlookers huddled under umbrellas behind a police barricade. Through a megaphone, their leader repeated the phrase, "Justice for JuJu."

I could see Roosevelt's suit and tie beneath his raincoat. He always wore dignified attire to a crime scene. "Thanks for sticking around," I said.

"I can't stay long."

I pointed at the contingent behind the police line. "Is that Reverend Tucker?"

"It is."

Reverend Isaiah Tucker was the pastor at First Union Baptist Church on Golden Gate Avenue, where he had tended his flock for three decades. The tireless community advocate wasn't afraid to stir the pot.

"Did he know the victim?" I asked.

"Yes." Roosevelt chewed on a toothpick. "And his mother. She was here earlier. She left to make funeral arrangements."

How sad.

Roosevelt eyed me. "Reverend Tucker is going to make your life complicated."

"It won't impact how I do my job."

"Yes, it will. You may be able to control what goes on inside the courtroom, but Isaiah will pull the levers outside. And you'd better be prepared for a civil suit. Jones's mother has already been approached by several plaintiff's attorneys to file a wrongful death action against the City and your client."

This was inevitable. "We'll deal with it."

He got a faraway look in his eyes as he stared at the post office. "What is it?" I asked.

"Bad memories. You remember what was here?"

"Of course."

The post office was built on the site of the notorious Peoples Temple, a cult established in Indiana by a charismatic con man named Jim Jones. In the early seventies, Jones moved his flock to Mendocino County, and later relocated to the former Albert Pike Scottish Rite Temple on this spot. The Peoples Temple preyed upon the neighboring African-American community, which was being displaced by urban renewal. The opportunistic Jones aligned himself with Mayor George Moscone, Governor Jerry Brown, Speaker of the Assembly and future Mayor Willie Brown,

Supervisor Harvey Milk, and many elected and appointed officials. Many people—including my dad—believed that illicit campaign activities by Temple members swung the 1975 mayoral election to Moscone. A few months later, D.A. Joseph Freitas ordered an inquiry on possible charges of extortion, battery, arson, kidnapping, drug use, and even homicide. Freitas's office eventually issued a report stating that there was 'no evidence of criminal wrongdoing.'

The press continued to pursue the story and hound Jones. After unflattering media reports were published and several lawsuits were filed, Jones and hundreds of his followers fled to the jungles of Guyana. The rest of the tragedy has been well documented. Jones's supporters lived in squalor until November 18, 1978, when he ordered them to drink cyanide-laced Flavor Aid. At the end of a day of unspeakable tragedy, 918 people were dead, including 270 children and Congressman Leo Ryan. It was the greatest single loss of American civilian life in a non-natural disaster until 9/11.

Roosevelt's voice was a hoarse whisper. "Never should have happened."

"It wasn't your fault. You weren't involved in the investigation."

"SFPD was. We should have seen it coming. Jones was crazy."

"A lot of people missed it."

"Not your dad." He looked at Pete. "He had Jones pegged. He said that there was something wrong with him."

"He had good instincts."

Roosevelt corrected him. "He had *great* instincts." The old warhorse shook his head. "I grew up over on Turk Street. This was *our* neighborhood. It wasn't fancy, but it was a good community until the idiots in the Redevelopment Agency decided to 'improve' our lives by tearing down our houses and putting up the projects."

I had no good answer. "It was a mistake."

"It was racism."

Yes, it was. The rain started coming down harder. I pointed at the parking lot. "Would you mind letting us take a look?"

He thought about it for a moment. "Follow me. I'll sign you in. Do exactly as I say and keep your mouths shut. And don't touch anything." He pointed down the street. "Your client and his partner pulled over Jones in the Safeway parking lot. Jones knocked your client down as he was getting out of the car and fled on foot through the plaza. He turned right on Fillmore and ran up to Geary, where he was cut off by a backup unit. He turned left and came this way. Another unit cut him off here, so he climbed over the gate into the parking lot and hid behind the postal van. Officer Bacigalupi pursued him on foot. His partner followed him a moment later."

Roosevelt lifted the yellow tape and led us into the parking lot, which was enclosed by the post office, a twenty-foot retaining wall, and the Korean spa. He signed us into the log. "Once Jones got inside, there was no way out."

We walked around the postal van parked perpendicular to the loading dock. Roosevelt nodded at the CSIs, who were picking up a dozen numbered plastic markers. "Almost done?"

The more senior of the two technicians answered him. "Yes, Inspector."

I glanced at Pete, who took my cue. It was better to let the ex-cop take the lead at a crime scene. He pointed at the markers. "Jones died here?"

Roosevelt nodded. "The shots also came from behind the van. Your client was about eight feet from Jones. Four shots. All direct hits to the chest. We found the shell casings. They match Officer Bacigalupi's service weapon. No casings from any other weapons."

Johnny had admitted it that he had fired the fatal shots.

Pete spoke to the senior technician. "Was Jones pronounced here?"

"Yes. No pulse. No vitals. Nothing. He was probably dead before he hit the ground."

"I understand that you found a weapon under his body."

"Officer Bacigalupi and Sergeant Murphy said that they found a weapon under Jones's body."

"Is there any doubt?"

"No comment."

Pete looked at Roosevelt. "Is there evidence suggesting that the weapon was planted?"

"No comment."

"What type of weapon?"

"Kel-Tec PMR-30."

It was a Saturday Night Special. "Have you identified the registered owner of the gun?"

"No. The serial number was filed off."

"Is there any record of a weapon of this type registered to Jones?"

"None."

I spoke up. "Our client told us that he ordered Jones to put his hands up. Then he instructed Jones to lie down with his arms spread."

"That's consistent with the story that he told us."

"He said that Jones reached for the gun, whereupon Johnny shot him in self-defense."

"That's his story."

"You have a different version?"

"It was an execution."

"Based on what evidence?"

"You'll find out in due course."

"Witnesses? Video?"

Roosevelt's repeated each word slowly. "In. Due. Course."

"You have a legal obligation to provide all relevant evidence."

"I have a legal obligation to provide evidence that might tend to exonerate your client. At the moment, there is none. We'll get you everything that you are legally entitled to see."

We went back a long way, but he wasn't going to budge.

Roosevelt glanced at his watch. "I need to get back to headquarters."

"But Roosevelt—,"

"We'll talk later."

He pulled up the collar on his raincoat and escorted us outside the restricted area without another word.

Pete and I put our heads down and ignored the reporters as we walked by the post office. We stopped under an overhang near the entrance to the Fillmore Auditorium. I took a moment to shake the raindrops off my overcoat and get my bearings.

"What did you make of that?" I asked Pete.

"Let's go for a walk, Mick."

13
"WE'VE MET"

Pete pointed at the rusted Honda Civic parked in the Safeway lot. It was encircled by crime-scene tape and guarded by three uniforms. "That's where Johnny and his partner pulled over Jones."

At three-thirty on Wednesday afternoon, the sky was overcast, but there was a break in the rain. The Safeway was crowded, and the plaza between the parking lot and Fillmore Street was bustling with shoppers, high school students, and homeless people.

Pete handed me an envelope. "This is Jones's rap sheet."

"You want to give me the highlights?"

"Eighteen. Single. Lived with his mother in the projects on Turk. One conviction for grand theft auto. A couple of shoplifting hits, one of which got him probation. Suspected of gang activity, but no arrests."

"He covered a lot of territory in eighteen years."

"He was a fast study. He had a baby face, but he wasn't a baby."

"I don't recall his name on the logs at the P.D.'s Office."

"He had private attorneys." My streetwise younger brother gave me a knowing look. "It's one of the perks of gang membership."

Got it. "The cops knew him?"

"Yes. Low-level delivery man. One of my sources said that he thought Jones was being groomed to be a muscle guy."

"Any chance the cops were out to get him?"

My brother stroked his mustache. "Not as far as I can tell, but nobody I talked to would have admitted it."

We walked over to the Honda, where we were stopped by an officer whose name plate read "Carter." She spoke to my brother. "How are you, Pete?"

"Fine, Christa."

"Are Donna and the baby okay?"

"Both fine. The baby just turned eight."

"Time flies."

"It does." He nodded at me. "This is my brother, Mike."

"We've met." She didn't offer a hand. She added, "In court."

I didn't remember the encounter. Then again, I'd "met" hundreds of cops under similar circumstances. I sensed that our previous meeting hadn't been a highlight-reel experience for her, so I nodded and let Pete to do the talking.

"Mike is representing Johnny," he said.

"I heard. Good cop. Nice kid."

"They've decided to charge him with murder."

"He isn't a murderer." Her tone turned pointed. "From what I hear, Johnny shot a gangbanger in self-defense after the kid pulled a gun. Instead of giving him a medal, they charge him with murder. I guess that's how the mayor, the D.A., and our new chief show us that they have our backs."

Pete nodded in agreement. "Were you working last night?"

"No."

"You hear anything about what happened this morning?"

"You need to talk to Homicide."

"Please, Christa."

"My orders are to watch this car. For anything else, you'll need to talk to Homicide."

Got it. I extended a business card. "If you change your mind, I would appreciate it if you would give us a call."

"I will."

You probably won't.

Pete tried once more. "Johnny's arraignment is tomorrow morning. Any information might be helpful. We won't mention your name."

She lowered her voice. "I heard they have something on video."

"Like what?"

"Something bad enough to charge Johnny with murder."

"Video from Johnny's body cam?"

"Could be. I don't know."

The first item on my expanding to-do list would be to prepare the paperwork to request copies of all relevant videos. In our age of digital technology, most security footage is recorded over within hours or days. Preparing subpoenas to preserve and provide video footage would be an urgent priority.

Pete pointed at the Honda. "Did they find anything in the car?"

"I thought you knew."

"Knew what?"

"They found a dozen AK-47s in the trunk."

Pete was right. Juwon Jones was no Boy Scout.

14
"SOMEBODY MUST HAVE SEEN SOMETHING"

Pete pulled up the collar of his bomber jacket, and we started walking across the plaza paved with red and black bricks in a checkerboard pattern. The rain had stopped, but the wind was picking up, and the temperature was dropping as the sun went down. People who think California has no seasons never lived through a rainy winter in San Francisco.

We stopped midway across the plaza. On the south side was an enclosed two-story mall with a Panda Express, a Verizon store, and an Indian grocery. On the north side was a Subway. Across the street, an eighties-era high-rise towered over us. Fillmore Center was built to house some of the residents who had been displaced when the Victorians were bulldozed years earlier. It turned into a financial disaster for the City. It was difficult to imagine that the nondescript shops and restaurants on Fillmore had once been the epicenter of jazz and African-American culture when the neighborhood was inhabited by transplants who had come north during World War II to escape the Jim Crow South and work in the shipyards.

The aroma of orange chicken from the Panda Express wafted across the plaza. Pete pointed at a lamp post and snapped a photo with his iPhone. "Police camera. You'll want to request the footage."

"Will do." It was helpful to have an ex-cop on your team.

"You'll also want to ask for the security videos from Subway and Panda Express right away. Subway was probably the only thing open at one a.m."

"Let's stop inside and see if anybody was here last night. If you're hungry, I'll buy you a sandwich."

"Let me look for witnesses, Mick."

"Happy to help."

"It would be better if I do it on my own."

Got it. "Fine."

Pete pointed at two street lamps. "If Jones ran by this spot, it might be tough to see anything on the security videos. They throw off some light, but it's still pretty dark."

I made notes on my iPhone.

The plaza was the dividing line between the gentrified and non-gentrified portions of the neighborhood. To the north were upscale shops and restaurants. The aroma of dim sum from the trendy State Bird Provisions restaurant melded with the aroma of coffee from Starbucks and fresh bagels at the high-end Wise Sons New York Deli. The shops south of the plaza were a hodgepodge of nail salons, hairdressers, Asian restaurants, barbeque joints, and liquor stores. Things changed from sketchy to dangerous when you crossed Turk and walked past Northern Police Station. The mini-park next to the McDonald's was populated mostly by homeless people.

The wind whipped up and the rain started falling as Pete and I walked north on Fillmore. Faded banners on the street lamps proclaimed that we were walking through San Francisco's historic Jazz District, even though the traditional jazz clubs had long-since closed, and attempts to open new venues had failed. Pete pointed out security cameras inside Starbucks and Wise Sons. He noted another police camera on a lamp post in front of a Korean Barbeque on the ground floor of the Fillmore Auditorium.

Muni buses clogged the street. A few pedestrians hurried past us, umbrellas blown by the wind. Pete and I paused at the corner of Fillmore and Geary in front of a currency exchange. I could hear the cars beneath the Fillmore Street overpass of the sunken Geary Boulevard. On the north side of Geary was the boxy white Japantown Mall, which towered over its neighbor, the Boom-Boom Room, a hip-hop and blues club.

Pete took more photos. "I'll text you a list of places with security cameras. You'll want to ask for video from Johnny's body cam and the body cams of the other cops at the scene." His eyes were moving. "If there's video showing that Jones had a gun, it will go a long way toward proving that Johnny acted in self-defense."

"Can you start looking for witnesses? Somebody must have seen something."

"Of course. Where are you off to now?"

"I'm going to talk to Johnny again."

15
"YOU GOTTA GET ME OUT OF HERE"

Johnny's voice was tense. "You gotta get me out of here."

"I need you to stay calm."

"I'm trying, Mike."

The consultation room in the jail wing of the Hall was about ninety degrees and reeked of mildew. I had removed my raincoat and was sweating through my shirt.

At six-thirty on Wednesday night, Johnny had completed the soul-crushing intake process. He had surrendered his clothing and personal items, been showered with disinfectant, received a perfunctory medical exam, and issued an orange jumpsuit. He no longer looked like a cop—he looked like an inmate.

"Did you find a judge?" he asked.

"Judge McDaniel wouldn't give us a bail hearing. Nobody else would talk to me."

"That isn't good enough, Mike."

"Your arraignment is tomorrow at nine a.m. before Judge Ramsey."

"What are the chances that they'll drop the charges?"

Almost non-existent. "Slim."

"And bail?"

About the same. "Hard to say."

He crossed his arms tightly as if he was trying to disappear. "It was self-defense. Why doesn't anybody believe me?"

"I do. I talked to the D.A. and Roosevelt Johnson. They aren't saying much."

"Did they mention the charge?"

I took a deep breath. "First-degree murder."

"You can't be serious."

"They might be overcharging to try to get you to agree to a deal for something less."

"It was self-defense," he repeated.

"I know." I let him vent for a few minutes. Then I got back to business. "Pete and I were down in the Fillmore. Inspector Johnson showed us where Jones died. You told us that your body cam fell off when you climbed over the gate. So there isn't any footage of the shooting from your cam, right?"

"Right."

"You also said that Murphy and two other officers were outside the gate when you shot Jones. Was Murph wearing his body cam?"

"I think so."

"Was it turned on?"

"I presume it was. You'll need to talk to him."

"We will. Who were the other two officers?"

"Rick Siragusa came in as backup and cut off Jones at the corner of Fillmore and Geary."

"I know him." Rick "Goose" Siragusa was a tough guy from the Excelsior. Not the brightest guy, but a solid cop.

"Charlie Connor drove over and cut off Jones in front of the post office."

"I don't know him."

"He was in the class before me at the Academy. Good cop. Nice guy."

"Were Siragusa and Connor wearing their body cams?'

"I presume. You can find them at Northern Station."

"We will."

"So you're my lawyer?"

"Yeah." I studied his face, which had aged ten years in the past twelve hours. "You want me to be your lawyer, right?"

"Right."

"Then I'm your lawyer. I need to get back to the office. I'm going to request copies of the police reports, videos, and other evidence. They're obligated to provide anything that might exonerate you. We'll track down your partner and the other officers at the scene. Pete is looking for witnesses. It would make our self-defense argument stronger if somebody can confirm that Jones had a gun. It would be even better if we can see it in a video."

"He had a gun, Mike. You'll be able to see it in the video from my body cam."

"Good." I wasn't so sure. "Did you know Jones?"

"No."

"Did Murph?"

"Not as far as I know."

"Did you know that they found a dozen AK-47s in the trunk of his car?"

His eyes opened wide. "Seriously?"

"Yeah. Jones wasn't a good guy."

"No kidding. Does it change anything?"

"Probably not."

Not the answer that he wanted. "How do you think the arraignment will play out?"

"It won't take long. I'll have your dad bring a suit and tie for you. When the judge asks for your plea, you stand up and say, 'Not guilty' in a respectful tone."

"That's it?"

"That's it."

* * *

I punched in Pete's number on my iPhone. He answered immediately. "Where are you, Mick?"

"Heading to Luca's office. Got anything we can use?"

"Working on it."

"I need you to find Kevin Murphy, Rick Siragusa, and Charlie

Connor."

"I'll track them down."

"I'll meet you in the Fillmore."

"Not a good night to come down here. There's going to be a march from City Hall to the Fillmore. They're going to have a memorial service for Jones in front of the post office. They're expecting thousands of people. The mayor is begging everybody to stay home. The chief is calling in every available cop to help with crowd control."

Or riot control.

His tone turned serious. "You remember when I told you that this could get ugly?"

"Yeah."

"It just did."

16
"THEY'RE MARCHING DOWN GEARY"

Assistant Chief Giovanni Bacigalupi III's expression was grim as he stared at the flat-screen TV in the conference room of his older brother's law firm. His raspy voice filled with a mixture of anger and frustration. "They're marching down Geary."

Luca was sitting next to him. "It'll pass, Gio."

"It's going to get worse."

It undoubtedly would.

A driving rain was beating against the windows. Gio's face was frozen into a frown. Luca had done the unthinkable and removed his suit jacket. The volume on the TV was turned off, but the closed-captioning indicated that five thousand people were marching from City Hall to the Fillmore. Many of the candles held by the marchers had been extinguished by the rain. The demonstration had been mostly peaceful, but a bus was stopped on Fillmore, and a car was overturned in front of Northern Station. Police in riot gear were stationed along the route. The media frenzy was fully engaged.

"We'll get through it, Gio," I said.

"Easy for you to say."

"We need to focus on what we can control."

"The chief won't let me come to work. He said that I have to take a leave until Johnny's case is resolved."

It was probably for the better. "I need you to focus on Johnny."

"I need you to get him out of jail."

"Working on it."

"Work harder. I heard that you couldn't get a judge to set bail."

"We'll try again at the arraignment."

"What are the chances?"

Not great. "Hard to predict. If it's first-degree murder, it's going to be an uphill battle."

"He'll wear a monitoring device. We'll agree that he'll stay with Maria and me."

"We'll make that offer in the morning."

His tone turned pointed. "We need the judge to agree."

I leveled with him. "You know how things work, Gio. I can't give you any guarantees."

"We're talking about my son, Mike."

Luca put a hand on Gio's shoulder. "Mike's doing everything that he can, Gio. It's been less than a day. Things take time."

I appreciated the vote of confidence, albeit tepid.

Gio wouldn't let it go. "My son is in jail."

"We'll fix it," I said. "It would be helpful if you, Maria, and the boys are in court in the morning. It's good to have a show of support."

"We'll be there. Anything else?"

"Try to get some sleep. Tomorrow morning is going to be stressful."

* * *

Luca stood in the doorway to my office down the hall from his. "Did Dennis get you set up on our computers?"

"Yes."

"Then why are you using your laptop?"

"It's easier to access forms on my computer. I'm working on document requests. We need to get our hands on the police reports and body cam videos as soon as we can."

"Sounds about right." He pointed down the hall. "I have my best associate standing by to help you. Her name is Nadezhda

Nikonova. She goes by Nady. UCLA undergrad and Boalt Law School. Top of her class at both. Smart as a whip. You'll like working with her."

Great. "Does she have any experience with criminal matters?"

"I'm afraid not, but you won't have to explain anything to her more than once."

"For the moment, please ask her to monitor the news, Twitter, Facebook, and YouTube. I want to know if any video is posted on our case. That will make our lives more complicated."

"Will do."

"Did you reach Tom Bearrows?" He was a solid defense lawyer who used to be a cop. "I want to engage him as co-counsel and get him up to speed."

"He's out of town. He'll be back next week."

I can make do until then. "Anything else?"

"I'm getting a lot of inquiries from the press."

I glanced at my iPhone. I had thirty-four voice messages, three dozen texts, and over a hundred e-mails. "Refer them to me."

"What are you planning to tell them?"

"That Johnny is innocent. We have no further comment."

"Should we hire a PR firm?"

"Not yet." *This isn't like trying to win over public support for a real estate deal.* "We need to make sure that all media contacts are coordinated through one person: me."

"Understood. Anything else that I can do for you?"

"Would you mind making some coffee?"

"Sure."

I wondered if he knew how to turn on the coffee pot. I glanced at my laptop, where I was streaming the live feed from Channel 4. "There is going to be a press briefing at nine o'clock tonight. We should see what they have to say."

"I'll put it up on the big screen in the conference room."

17

"THERE WERE INCONSISTENCIES"

Pete's name appeared on my iPhone. I pressed the green button and heard shouting in the background. My brother's tone was gruff. "You still at Luca's office?"

"Yeah. Where are you?"

"Geary and Fillmore."

I was streaming CNN on my laptop. "I'm watching on TV. Looks like a lot of people."

"The crowd goes all the way to Japantown. It's been pretty orderly, but they flipped over a couple of cars and broke some windows."

"Not so good."

"Reverend Tucker is coming over with Jones's mother. This could get nasty."

"Stay safe, Pete."

"My self-preservation instincts are still pretty good. I'll call you later."

* * *

"Any idea what they're going to say?" Luca asked.

"We'll see."

He was holding a can of Coke Classic. I was nursing a cup of Peet's coffee. Luca's associate, Nady, had joined us. She was a confident woman in her early thirties with intense eyes, chiseled features, and a "don't-mess-with-me" demeanor. She reminded me of Rosie.

The conference room was quiet. We were watching the feed on Channel 4. The obligatory split screen showed the anchor on one side and an aerial view of the crowd in the Fillmore on the other. The crawl noted that a press conference would begin momentarily.

The anchor invoked a melodramatic tone. "We are going to cut away from the march to carry a live press conference at police headquarters, where Rita Roberts is standing by. Rita?"

They switched over to the reporter who had covered major stories in the Bay Area for three decades. She adjusted her earpiece. "Dan? Dan? Is that you? Hello?"

They toggled between the anchor and the reporter several times before Rita finally figured out that she was, in fact, on live TV. The consummate pro pretended that nothing was amiss and started talking. "We're live at SFPD headquarters where a briefing is about to start concerning the death of a young man named Juwon Jones, who was tragically shot and killed by a police officer identified as Giovanni Bacigalupi the Fourth, the son of Assistant Chief Giovanni Bacigalupi the Third."

Luca squeezed the empty can. "Is this really necessary?"

Let it go, Luca.

Roosevelt led the mayor, the chief, and the D.A. to a podium in front of a navy background bearing the SFPD logo. Their expressions were equally grim as they tried to show solidarity while jockeying for position. As Roosevelt approached the lectern, the mayor cut him off and pulled the microphone toward himself.

"Ladies and gentlemen, Inspector Johnson will speak in a moment. A peaceful march is taking place in the Fillmore. I want to thank our citizens for remaining calm and invoking their rights of free expression and assembly in a respectful and orderly manner, thereby ensuring that neither the public nor any of our officers is injured."

It was a nice sentiment that might have been more convincing if the other side of the split screen hadn't been showing people hurtling bottles in the Fillmore. The mayor moved back, and Roosevelt stepped to the microphone.

"Inspector Roosevelt Johnson. SFPD. J-O-H-N-S-O-N. I am heading the investigation." He put on his reading glasses and read from a script. "At approximately 1:08 this morning, Officer Giovanni Bacigalupi the Fourth and Sergeant Kevin Murphy were driving east on Geary Boulevard when they made visual contact with a Honda Civic with a broken tail light. Officer Bacigalupi and Sergeant Murphy pursued the vehicle and instructed the driver to pull over. The driver pulled off Geary Boulevard at Steiner and proceeded onto the narrower portion of upper Geary for two blocks. He parked in the Safeway lot at Webster. Officer Bacigalupi and Sergeant Murphy approached the vehicle. Officer Bacigalupi acted as the contact officer. He engaged the driver, later identified as Juwon Jones, eighteen. Officer Bacigalupi requested Mr. Jones's driver's license, evidence of registration, and insurance card. Mr. Jones said that the vehicle belonged to his mother, Vanessa Jones, with whom he lived.

"Pursuant to standard procedure, Officer Bacigalupi returned to his squad car and ran the license and registration through his dashboard computer. He confirmed that the vehicle did, in fact, belong to Mr. Jones's mother. He also determined that Mr. Jones had an outstanding warrant for a probation violation. Officer Bacigalupi went back to Mr. Jones's car and requested that Mr. Jones step out of the vehicle to allow Officer Bacigalupi and Sergeant Murphy to search it, which was within their rights because of the outstanding warrant. As Mr. Jones was getting out of the car, he banged the door into Officer Bacigalupi, knocking him down. Mr. Jones fled across the nearby plaza, and proceeded north on Fillmore. Officer Bacigalupi pursued him on foot, followed by Sergeant Murphy. Officer Bacigalupi and Sergeant Murphy radioed for backup, which arrived shortly thereafter. Mr. Jones was cut off at the corner of Fillmore and Geary by a squad car driven by Officer

Richard Siragusa. Mr. Jones turned left onto Geary and proceeded westbound for a half-block, where he was intercepted by a police vehicle driven by Officer Charles Connor."

I exchanged a glance with Luca. *Nothing we didn't already know.*

Roosevelt continued reading. "When Mr. Jones saw Officer Connor's police unit, he climbed over the gate into the enclosed parking lot next to the post office at 1849 Geary. Mr. Jones hid behind a postal van. Officer Bacigalupi also climbed over the gate and cornered Mr. Jones behind the van. Officer Bacigalupi ordered Mr. Jones to put his hands up, and Mr. Jones complied."

So far, everything matched up with Johnny's version of the story.

"Officer Bacigalupi ordered Mr. Jones to lie down with arms and legs spread. Officer Bacigalupi informed Mr. Jones that if he did not comply, Officer Bacigalupi would shoot him. Officer Bacigalupi repeated the order three times. Before Mr. Jones had a chance to comply with the third order, Officer Bacigalupi shot him four times in the chest with his service weapon. Mr. Jones was pronounced dead at the scene. Nobody else was injured."

Roosevelt looked up for an instant, then he returned to the script. "We have taken statements from Officer Bacigalupi, Sergeant Murphy, Officer Siragusa, and Officer Connor. We have listened to audio recordings from police radio. We have reviewed video and audio from Officer Bacigalupi's body cam and from the body cams of other officers at the scene. We have looked at security videos from businesses in the area. We discovered inconsistencies in Officer Bacigalupi's account. After consultation with the district attorney and our chief, we determined that there was probable cause to conclude that Officer Bacigalupi committed a crime. Accordingly, we placed Officer Bacigalupi under arrest on a murder charge. He is being held at County Jail #4 at the Hall of Justice. His arraignment has been scheduled before Judge Martellus Ramsey at nine o'clock tomorrow morning." He looked up. "That's all for now. I have time for a few questions."

"Did Officer Bacigalupi admit that he shot Mr. Jones?"

"Yes."

"Do you have video of the shooting?"

"We have several videos from the scene. We will make a determination at a later time as to whether we will make any of them available."

"Was Mr. Jones armed?"

"No comment."

"We've been told that Officer Bacigalupi acted in self-defense."

"No comment."

"You mentioned that there were some inconsistencies in Officer Bacigalupi's story. Can you be more specific?"

"I can't go into details, but I will tell you that Officer Bacigalupi told us that he had not reviewed the video from his body cam before he gave his statement. We reviewed the logs and determined that Officer Bacigalupi did, in fact, look at the footage before he spoke to us, which violated department policy."

I looked at Luca. "He told me that he didn't look at the video."

"He told me the same thing."

"He lied to us."

"Maybe it was a misunderstanding. Or maybe he panicked."

"Maybe." I wonder if Johnny lied about anything else.

Roosevelt was still taking questions.

"Who is representing Officer Bacigalupi?"

"Michael Daley, who is the head of the Felony Division of the Public Defender's Office."

"Why is a public defender representing a defendant whose family can afford a private attorney?"

"You'll have to ask Mr. Daley."

* * *

My iPhone vibrated within seconds of the end of the press conference. Rosie's name appeared on the display.

"Did you see Roosevelt's presser?" she asked.

"Of course."

"He didn't mention the gun that they found under Jones's body. Why not?"

"It would help our argument that Johnny acted in self-defense."

"You sure they found a gun under the body?"

"Yes."

There was a pause. "You okay, Mike?"

"Fine."

"'Fine' as in you're okay, or 'fine' as in your life is a mess, but you're dealing with it."

"It's a mess."

"Thought so. Where are you now?"

"Luca's office. I'm going to talk to Johnny."

18
"IT WAS A MISTAKE"

Johnny owned up right away. "It was a mistake. I shouldn't have looked at my body cam footage before I gave my statement."

"Things happen," I said.

"This shouldn't have happened."

No, it shouldn't have.

At nine-forty-five on Wednesday night, we were sitting on opposite sides of a metal table in a consultation room on the seventh floor of the Hall. The blue eyes of the gifted athlete were glassy. It had been a humbling day.

I kept my voice modulated. "You must have known that they can check every login."

"I know. I panicked."

Bad move. Every San Francisco police officer is issued an Axon Body 2 HD camera. It's a popular model used by many .police departments. The officer activates the camera by pressing a button. At the end of a shift, the officer uploads the video to a secure server on the cloud. Once it's uploaded, every view is recorded.

I put my hands on the table. "You have to tell me the absolute truth about everything. It's my only non-negotiable rule. If you lie, I'm out. Understood?"

"Yes."

I wanted to believe him. "Take me through it again. When did you turn on your body cam?"

"As I was walking to Jones's car." He said that he turned it off when he went back to his unit to check on Jones's license and registration. "I turned it back on when I approached Jones's car the second time." Johnny said that the cam was recording when Jones opened the door, knocked him over, and started to run. "It was on when I pursued him across the plaza and up Fillmore. And it was still on when I turned onto Geary and saw Jones climb over the gate and into the parking lot. The camera came off when I climbed over the gate."

"So we should be able to see everything that happened up to that point?"

"Yes."

"But there isn't any footage after you got into the lot?"

"Correct."

I needed to see the video. "You told me that Jones had a gun."

"He did. It was in his hand when he got out of the car."

"Was it still in his hand when he ran up Fillmore?"

"Yes."

"And when you cornered him behind the postal van?"

He waited a half-beat. "No."

"Where was it?"

"It must have been in his pocket."

"When did he put it in his pocket?"

"I don't know for sure. Probably before he climbed over the gate."

"So we should be able to see it in the video when he got out of the car and when he was running up Fillmore."

He hesitated. "I think so. He was a half-block ahead of me and it was dark."

"You watched the video, right?"

"Right."

"Could you see a gun or not?"

"I think so. I don't know for sure."

I didn't like the equivocation. "He had a gun, right?"

"Right. We found it under his body."

We needed to see the videos as soon as possible. "They're saying that Jones's hands were up when you shot him."

"He was reaching for a gun."

"There seems to be a disagreement."

"I shot him in self-defense, Mike."

It sounded a little forced. "I need to get back to the office. I'll see you in the morning."

* * *

The rain hit my face as I was walking down the steps of the Hall at ten o'clock on Wednesday night. I pulled up my collar and trudged toward the street. Then I heard the familiar smoker's hack behind me.

"Haven't seen you in a while, Mr. Daley."

I turned around and looked at the leathery face of the *Chronicle*'s long-time crime reporter and political columnist. Jerry Edwards had been stalking the corridors of the Hall for longer than I had been a lawyer. He was a student at Cal when my older brother, Tommy, was the quarterback. Edwards went on to a long and occasionally stellar career as the *Chronicle*'s resident muckraker.

"Good to see you, Jerry," I lied.

"Same here."

Right. "I don't have time to talk."

"I would appreciate just a moment."

He was being uncharacteristically solicitous. Then again, the pit bull could appear at any time. "How'd you find me?"

"Reporter's instinct."

His were fine-tuned. "I figured you'd be over in the Fillmore."

"I was. The TV stations are getting footage of the cops and protesters yelling at each other. Lots of broken windows and overturned cars. The usual sound bites about police brutality and a broken system. You'll see it on cable tonight."

"You aren't interested in free expression?"

"I am, but I don't have anything to add, and I'd rather not stand out in the rain."

"How bad was it?"

"Pretty bad. About a dozen arrests so far. A couple of people were stabbed. Last I heard, nobody died, but that might have changed. I'm a Cal guy like you. I'm all for free speech, but I don't understand how burning cars moves us in a positive direction."

"Neither do I. It's good for business for you guys."

"I like covering big stories as much as the next guy, but I'd rather not watch people kill each other on the streets of my hometown."

"For what it's worth, neither would I."

He looked up at the Hall. "Which brings us to your client, whose actions started this series of unfortunate events. Why is the head of the Felony Division of the P.D.'s Office representing Johnny B?"

"I went to S.I. with Gio. My dad worked with Johnny's grandfather at Taraval Station."

"Do you think that's an appropriate allocation of the City's limited resources?"

"I'm taking an unpaid leave and handling the case *pro bono*."

His bushy eyebrow went up. "I didn't think you lawyers did anything for free."

"You'd be surprised."

"My three divorce lawyers never left money on the table. Your ex-wife is okay with this arrangement?"

Not exactly. "She's fine."

"I'm surprised."

"You don't know her as well as I do. If you want to take potshots at the legal profession in general or me personally, that's fine. If you promise a more civilized tone, I might be willing to give you an exclusive statement."

He reached inside his overcoat and pulled out a worn leather notebook. "I'm listening."

I gave him a knowing smile. "How long have you been doing this, Jerry?"

"Thirty-seven years."

"How many times have you interviewed attorneys like me?"

"Hundreds."

"And what have we always told you?"

He smirked. "Which version do you want me to use?"

"You tell me."

"Your client is innocent and you're looking forward to proving it in court."

"Sounds about right. You might want to add the usual stuff about a rush to judgment."

"You going to claim self-defense?"

"Probably."

"Can't you come up with something more original?"

"It's been a long day, Jerry. The arraignment is at nine o'clock tomorrow morning in Judge Ramsey's courtroom."

"I'll see you there."

* * *

My iPhone vibrated as I was about to turn on the ignition of my Corolla, which was parked in front of the P.D.'s Office on Seventh. Pete's name appeared on the display.

"Are you still in the Fillmore?" I asked.

"Just leaving."

"How bad did it get?"

"Pretty bad. Reverend Tucker got everybody worked up. A couple of people were stabbed. Some kids turned over a car. Then they turned over another one. Then they set a Dumpster on fire. The cops came in and people started breaking windows. It'll be all over the news."

"Did anybody get hurt?"

"Yeah." He didn't elaborate. "Where are you, Mick?"

"Near the Hall." I summarized my conversation with Johnny.

"How soon can you get out to the Sunset?"

"Give me twenty minutes."

"Meet me at Big John's saloon. Johnny's partner agreed to talk to us."

19
"SO THE KID SHOT HIM"

The thickset bartender's blue eyes twinkled as he placed a coaster with a Budweiser logo on the worn wooden table in a booth in the back of Dunleavy's Bar at Twenty-Third and Irving, two blocks from the house where I grew up. "What'll it be, lad?"

"Just coffee, Big John."

"Pete is on his way. You look like you could use a beer, Mikey."

"I'm working."

"I'll brew a fresh pot."

"Thanks."

The neighborhood watering hole was quiet at ten-fifteen on Wednesday night. My uncle, Big John Dunleavy, had operated the saloon bearing his name since the fifties. My father had helped him build the pine bar that ran the length of the narrow room. Now in his eighties, the one-time all-city tight-end at St. Ignatius walked a little slower and used a hearing aid. Otherwise he looked as if he could still mow down any safety who had the audacity to get in his way.

He brushed the few remaining strands of silver hair across his pale dome and invoked his Irish brogue—even though he'd never been to Ireland. "Everybody okay at home, Mikey?"

"Fine."

"You still spending a few nights a week at Rosie's house?"

"Yes."

His eyes danced. "Isn't it against City policy to sleep with your boss?"

I grinned. "Technically, it's okay for me to sleep with Rosie because she isn't my subordinate. However, it isn't okay for her to sleep with me because I report to her."

"Let me see if I have this straight. You can sleep with her, but she can't sleep with you?"

"Correct."

"How do you reconcile your natural urges with your legal obligations?"

"It's complicated, Big John. I don't think you'd like me to go into the technical details."

He let out the throaty laugh that I first heard when I was a kid. Big John wasn't just my mom's brother and my favorite uncle. He was my father's best friend. At the end of a long shift, he and Roosevelt would end the day in this very booth where they would have a beer and swap tall tales with the gregarious barkeep who helped them unwind.

His tone turned serious. "You going to be okay, Mikey?"

"Yeah."

"From everything I see on the news, Johnny B's case could get nasty."

"I just do my job. I try not to worry about things that I can't control."

"I'm worried that you won't be able to control anything this time."

"I've handled high-profile cases."

The phony brogue disappeared. "Not with riots, Mikey. Be careful, lad."

He tossed the ever-present dish towel over his shoulder and headed to the bar. I took out my iPhone and scrolled through two hundred e-mails and eighty texts.

The door opened, and Pete entered, followed by a hulking man about my age. Sergeant Kevin Murphy was wearing a blue windbreaker with the logo of his SFPD softball team imprinted on his breast. His expression was grim. His once-bright red hair was mostly silver. His jowls wiggled as he walked.

I beckoned them to join me. As they walked past the pool table, Big John exchanged stilted greetings with Murphy and handed him a Budweiser. Pete asked for coffee.

I shook Murphy's hand as he jammed his torso into the booth. Pete sat next to me. Murphy's pasty face gave him the appearance of an order of corned beef and cabbage with a boiled potato on the side. The bags under his eyes were a shade darker than the rest of his face.

"Thanks for coming in to talk to us," I said.

"Yeah."

At St. Ignatius, the sociable frat-boy-in-training always provided a keg from his father's saloon on Noriega Street for the post-football-game victory celebrations at Ocean Beach. The bawdy jokes and beer parties had stopped after an acrimonious divorce from his high school sweetheart and thirty-five years of working the streets in the Bayview, Hunters Point, and, more recently, the Fillmore. He'd moved up to the rank of sergeant, then stopped. He always professed that he liked working on the street, but Pete thought that he harbored a desire to become an inspector. Among the rank-and-file, he had a reputation as a solid cop who worked as hard as he had to and kept his nose clean. Others, including Pete, thought that Murph had evolved into a hardass who overstepped the boundaries from time to time and liked to crack a few heads.

"Your dad okay?" I asked.

"Not bad. Nothing is easy when you're north of eighty."

"And your mom?"

"Assisted living." In response to my inquiry, he informed me that his two sons—both cops—were doing fine. He changed the subject. "Gio doing okay?"

"Not bad under the circumstances."

"I'm glad you're dealing with it, Mike. The attorneys on the POA list are okay, but I'm sure Gio feels better having somebody he knows. If it were my kid, I know that I would."

"Thanks.

"I mean it." He took a draw of his beer. "Are they really going to charge the kid with first-degree murder?"

"So they say."

"That's crap. It was self-defense."

"You're prepared to testify to that effect?"

"Of course."

"Great." This represented a bit of good news. "Mind telling us what happened?"

"Sure." The first part of his story jibed with Johnny's. He and Johnny had dinner at Mel's. On their way back to the Fillmore, they saw a car with a busted tail light. Murphy told Johnny to pull him over. "Just for practice. It was a slow night. I figured it would be good to give him a little experience."

"Did you know anything about Juwon Jones?"

"Just what I found out today."

"He had a hit for grand theft auto and a couple of shoplifting charges."

"I heard."

"Some people think he had gang connections."

"I don't know anything about it."

And you might not tell us if you did. "You heard they found a dozen AK-47s in the trunk."

"Yeah. Seems he wasn't a good guy."

"Seems that way." I asked him what happened during the traffic stop.

"The kid approached the driver-side door, just like he was supposed to. He introduced himself to Jones, requested license and registration, and returned to our unit to run it through the computer."

"Where were you?"

"Right where I was supposed to be: near the rear of Jones's car on the passenger side. The kid found out that Jones had an outstanding warrant, so he did it by the book. He asked Jones to leave the vehicle so that we could search it. We had the legal right to conduct a search and, if necessary, cuff Jones."

"Why didn't Johnny cuff him?" I asked.

"He didn't have the chance. Johnny was trying not to elevate the situation. That's what he was trained to do. Other than the usual risks of stopping somebody in the middle of the night, it looked like a routine traffic stop."

"Until Jones pulled a gun."

"Correct."

"You saw it?"

"Yes."

"When?"

"When Jones got out of the car. He banged the door into Johnny and knocked him over. He ran across the plaza to Fillmore and turned right. A backup unit cut him off at Geary, so he turned left. Another unit blocked him, so he jumped the fence into the post office parking lot. Once he was inside, there was no way out. The kid was about a block behind him. I was about a half-block behind Johnny." He grinned. "I'm not as fast as I used to be."

"Johnny cornered Jones behind a postal van and ordered him to raise his hands. Jones did so on the third command. Then Johnny ordered Jones to lie down on the ground. Jones refused twice. Then he reached for a gun, so the kid shot him—in self-defense."

"You're sure he was reaching for a gun?"

"Of course. Why else would he have shot him?"

Of course.

Murphy wasn't finished. "I'm sorry that Jones died, but Johnny had no choice. He acted in self-defense. End of story."

Pete made his presence felt. "Where were you when Johnny shot him?"

"Outside the gate."

Pete pulled over a water-logged napkin and used a Bic pen to draw a rudimentary diagram. "You were here?"

"Yeah."

"If you were here and Johnny and Jones were behind the postal van, how did you see what happened?"

"I couldn't see all of it, but I heard everything. The kid ordered Jones to lie down three times. Jones disobeyed the order. The third time, he reached for a gun, so the kid shot him."

"How do you know that he was reaching for a gun?"

"I know what I saw."

Pete studied his diagram. "Are you absolutely sure that he didn't shoot him while his hands were still up?"

"Absolutely sure."

Pete glanced my way.

"Murph," I said, "were you wearing your body cam?"

A hesitation. "Yeah."

"Was it turned on when Jones was shot?"

A longer hesitation. "No. It was the end of our shift. I thought it was a routine stop."

"So you didn't turn it on even after Jones started running down Fillmore?"

"Correct."

"And even though you saw a gun in his hand?"

"Yeah." He put his massive elbows on the table. "Are you saying I did something wrong?"

Maybe. "No."

"You think we turn our cameras on every time we stop somebody for a broken tail light?'

Maybe you should. "No."

"I don't have to be here. I don't have to talk to you. In fact, if I was smart, I probably wouldn't talk to anybody other than my commander, the captain, and my union rep."

"I'm not suggesting that you did anything wrong, Murph."

"Either way, you're beating up the wrong guy. I was there. I'm prepared to testify that Jones had a gun and that the kid shot him in self-defense. I don't understand why you're crapping on me."

"We're just trying to figure out what happened."

"I just told you what happened: the kid shot him in self-defense."

"Then why is the D.A. charging him with murder?"

"Every time there's an officer-involved shooting, the mayor and the chief get nervous and try to blame the cops instead of the criminals. Helluva way to run the department."

"How many other cops were there?"

"Two: Rick Siragusa and Charlie Connor. Both work out of Northern Station."

"I presume that they talked to the chief and the D.A.?"

"No doubt."

"Were they wearing their body cams?"

"You'll need to ask them."

I lowered my voice. "Is there something else going on here, Murph?"

"I don't know." He pointed at the flat-screen above the pool table, which was tuned to the Channel 2 news. It was showing video from the march into the Fillmore. "You see that? It's already getting out of hand. You need to stop this crap."

"We will." *Well, we'll try.* "Thanks for your time, Murph."

* * *

"Can you find Siragusa and Connor?"

Pete nodded. "Will do, Mick."

We were still sitting in the booth at the back of Dunleavy's. Murphy had gone home.

Pete was staring at his iPhone. "I'm also going to look for witnesses in the Fillmore. The more time that passes, the colder the trail."

"I'm going down to the office to start putting together document requests."

"It's almost eleven o'clock."

"The day is still young."

Big John came over and refilled my coffee. "You want that beer now, Mikey?"

"Not tonight. I'm working." I pointed at the empty chair. "Got a minute?"

"For my two favorite nephews, always." He deposited his heavy frame on the wobbly wooden chair. "What is it?"

"Did you hear our conversation with Murphy?"

"I was washing the dishes."

"You were pretending."

"Maybe."

"You know Murphy better than we do. What did you think?"

"I know his father. Murph is an honest guy and a solid cop."

"You think there's any chance he's stretching the truth to protect Johnny?"

"Everybody stretches a little."

He was being more coy than I had anticipated. "What are you saying, Big John?"

"There's more to this story."

"How do you know?"

"Bartender's intuition."

His was finely tuned.

He picked up his towel. "You lads should go home and get some rest. Your jobs are going to get harder before they get easier."

He was undoubtedly right. "Thanks, Big John."

20
"THE SITUATION JUST GOT MORE COMPLICATED"

At eleven-fifteen on Wednesday night, I was sitting at my desk down the hall from Luca's office. The ceiling light buzzed as the rain pounded the window. I heard a knock on the open door. I looked up and saw Luca, his expression grim.

"Anything I can do to help?" he asked. In a moment of what passed for whimsy for him, his necktie was loosened.

"I have everything under control for now." *Well, sort of.*

"Nady is still here if you need anything."

"I'll get her started on some additional document requests as soon as I finish putting together the templates. Have you talked to Gio?"

"Briefly. Given the circumstances, he and Maria are holding up okay."

"Did he get any more information about what happened?"

"Nobody's talking to him."

Wonderful. "You reminded him to bring a suit for Johnny?"

"I did. The rest of the family will be in court for the arraignment. Did you get anything useful from Murphy?"

"He's prepared to testify that Johnny acted in self-defense."

"That's good."

"It would have been better if he had turned on his body cam."

"That's not so good."

"No, it isn't. I'm preparing documents to get access to the police videos. Pete is looking for two other officers who arrived at the scene as backup. He's also looking for witnesses in the Fillmore. We want to be sure that we have corroboration that Jones had a gun."

"Murphy can do it."

"We want at least one other witness—preferably somebody who isn't a cop."

His tone turned somber. "The situation just got more complicated." He handed me a legal document. "They've already filed a civil suit on behalf of Jones's mother."

"That was quick." *And inevitable.* "I take it that Johnny is named as a defendant?"

"Along with the City, SFPD, and the chief."

"I don't handle civil cases."

"One of my partners will represent Johnny."

"Good." While the interests of the City and Johnny converged at the moment, it was possible that the City's lawyers would throw Johnny under a bus if they could negotiate a quick and—more important—inexpensive settlement. "Will the City pay for you to defend Johnny?"

"We'll have that discussion tomorrow. In the meantime, the City Attorney's Office is representing the City for now. It's possible that they'll hire outside counsel."

"Can you extricate Johnny?"

"We'll try."

It was a more equivocal answer than I had expected. "I don't want you or the City Attorney to engage in any settlement talks without discussing it with me first."

"I can only speak for myself."

"If the City settles, it may impact the criminal case."

"I won't let that happen."

We'll see.

* * *

Pete's voice was tired. "Where are you, Mick?"

I pressed my iPhone against my ear. "Luca's office."

"It's almost midnight."

"Gonna be a long night."

"I talked to the two cops who provided backup. I know Rick Siragusa. He worked at Mission Station when I was there. He's fundamentally a good cop. Sometimes, he likes to bang heads when he can't figure out anything better. Charlie Connor just got out of the Academy. His record is clean."

"Did they tell you anything?"

"Siragusa might be willing to sit down with us. Connor needs to clear everything with his commander."

"I'm not surprised. Were either of them wearing body cams?"

"Just Connor. We need to get our hands on the video before somebody puts it up on YouTube."

* * *

Luca appeared in my doorway again at twelve-thirty on Thursday morning. "You have a visitor," he said.

Who would be here at this hour? "Pete?"

"Your ex-wife."

21

"WE THOUGHT YOU COULD USE A LITTLE HELP"

The Public Defender of the City and County of San Francisco glanced at the empty bookcases and bare walls. "Nice office," Rosie deadpanned. "Have you thought about hiring a decorator?"

"I've been busy."

At twelve-thirty on Thursday morning, she was sitting in the uncomfortable wooden chair opposite the desk. Her only minor compromise to the late hour—or, more precisely, the early hour—was the fact that she had replaced her contacts with her wire-framed glasses.

Rosie's niece, Rolanda, was sitting next to her. Rolanda was the daughter of Rosie's older brother, Tony, who ran a produce market in the Mission. Except for the longer hair and a slightly taller frame, Rolanda was a dead-ringer for her aunt in appearance, temperament, and lawyerly ability. Our long-ago babysitter and one-time law clerk was now one of the best attorneys at the P.D.'s Office.

Rolanda smiled. "You look tired, Mike."

"I am. How's Zach?"

"Fine. He's in Houston for two weeks."

Her longtime boyfriend worked for one of the big downtown firms. He spent most of his time living in hotel rooms and working on class action lawsuits that took decades to resolve. Over the seven years that they'd been together, I would guess that they'd spent about a year under the same roof. It gave Rolanda a little more elbow room in their overpriced studio apartment in the Mission.

"How are the wedding plans coming?" I asked.

"Slowly. We're still trying to work out a date."

They had been "trying" for two years. I turned back to Rosie. "All quiet at home?"

"Yes. My mother is staying with Tommy tonight."

Rosie's mother, Sylvia, was an eighty-three-year-old version of Rosie. She had been slowed a bit by knee and hip replacements, but otherwise remained spry. Her innate intelligence and occasionally sharp tongue hadn't changed since I'd met her almost a quarter of a century earlier. Sylvia continued to rebuff Rosie's suggestions that she sell the bungalow in the Mission that she and her late husband had bought in the fifties for twenty-five thousand dollars which could fetch almost two million today. She had no interest in moving into a high-end condo or independent living community. To her unending credit, she understood the demands on Rosie's time, and she spent many nights at Rosie's house. While she rarely said it aloud, she was immensely proud of her daughter.

I looked into the beautiful eyes of my ex-wife, former mentor, and current boss. "I didn't expect to see you tonight."

"Officially, we aren't here. It would violate our policies for the Public Defender and the Head of the Felony Division to meet with you."

Got it. "Why are you *not* here?"

"We thought you could use a little help."

I gave her a sideways look. "You said that the Head of the Felony Division is here. Last time I checked, that was my job."

"You're on leave." Rosie's eyes filled with pride as she looked at her niece. "Meet your replacement."

Uh-oh. "That didn't take long."

"It's an important position that I needed to fill immediately. Everybody is replaceable, Mike."

Indeed. "Congratulations," I said to Rolanda.

"Thank you."

"You feeling better? Judge McDaniel was asking about you this morning."

"I'm fine." She handed me a thumb drive. "This has everything you'll need for the next few days: document requests, subpoenas, motions, the works. You'll need to tailor them for specific witnesses and various types of evidence."

"Thanks." I smiled. "The Felony Division is in excellent hands."

"I learned from the best."

I appreciated the sentiment.

Rosie clasped her hands in front of her chin. "What have you found so far?"

"The D.A. is saying that Johnny shot an unarmed kid."

"What is Johnny telling you?"

"That Juwon Jones flashed a gun when Johnny pulled him over. Jones fled on foot. Johnny cornered him in an enclosed parking lot and shot him in self-defense when Jones reached for the gun."

"Is there video?"

"From Johnny's body cam. There may be more. I haven't seen any of it yet."

"That would be a good place to start. What's the narrative?"

I expected the question. From the day that I met Rosie in the file room of the old P.D.'s Office at the Hall, she always said that you build your case around a compelling theme. Then you tell a story with a beginning, a middle, and an ending leaving no doubt that the prosecution has not proved its case beyond a reasonable doubt. You get bonus points if you can demonstrate that your client is innocent—which rarely happens.

"Self-defense," I said. "It may change depending on what we see in the video."

"Hopefully, a gun." Rosie's eyes narrowed. "It's going to come down to a *Graham v. Connor* defense. Do you have enough evidence to make a credible argument?"

"We'll see." *Graham v. Connor* was a 1989 U.S. Supreme Court case which set forth the law in officer-involved shooting cases. Chief Justice Rehnquist's opinion held that a determination of whether an officer used appropriate force required an examination of the facts and circumstances surrounding the actions of the officer at the scene. It was intended to create an objective test where juries are supposed to consider the totality of the circumstances to decide whether an officer used reasonable force at the time (and not with the benefit of 20/20 hindsight). Among the factors are the severity of the crime, whether the suspect posed an immediate threat to the officer or others, and whether the suspect resisted arrest or attempted to flee. "Johnny said that Jones reached for a gun."

"It would be helpful if the exchange was caught on Johnny's body cam," Rosie said.

"It wasn't." I explained that Johnny's body cam fell off as he was climbing over the gate into the parking lot.

"What about his partner?"

"He didn't turn his body cam on."

"You'd better have somebody who can corroborate his story."

"His partner will."

"Another witness would be better. Preferably someone other than a cop."

"Pete's looking. In the meantime, we know that they found a gun under Jones's body."

"The D.A. will say it was planted. Are you going to be here all night?"

"Probably."

Rolanda chimed in. "I'll stick around and help you put together some of the documents."

"You don't have to do that."

"You'd do it for me."

Yes, I would. "Luca's associate is helping me. She doesn't know anything about criminal law, but she's very smart."

"That's great. For the moment, can she make us a pot of fresh coffee?"

"Of course."

Rosie pointed at the feed from Channel 4 on my laptop. "I trust you've heard that things got a little out of hand in the Fillmore."

"I did."

"They're going to do it again tomorrow."

"This is going to get ugly."

"It already is, Mike. You and Pete need to be careful. Text me when you get home."

"I will. Rosie?"

"Yes?"

"Thanks."

* * *

My head was throbbing at one-thirty on Thursday morning as Rolanda, Nady, and I were preparing requests for documents, videos, phone records, witness lists, officer statements, and other information. Pete's name appeared on my iPhone.

"You got time to come down to the Fillmore?" he asked.

"Sure." *What else would I be doing at this hour?* "What have you got?"

"A witness who was on the plaza near the Safeway. Meet me at the Subway. And bring some cash."

22
"I KNOW WHAT I DIDN'T SEE"

Fillmore Street was quiet at one-forty on Thursday morning. The protesters had gone home, and the rain had turned into a drizzle. The block between O'Farrell and Geary was lined with police cars in a display of force. Plate-glass windows were boarded up in the currency exchange, a sandwich shop, and the Starbucks.

I opened the door to the Subway next to the plaza, where I saw Pete. "Over here, Mick."

He was sitting at one of the plastic booths in the otherwise empty shop. It was the only open business in the vicinity. The kid behind the counter was staring at his cell phone. The restaurant smelled of cold cuts, vegetables, bread, and my rain-soaked jacket.

I ordered a six-inch chicken sub and a Diet Coke. I took a seat next to Pete. A homeless man of indeterminate age sat across from us. He had a scratchy gray beard and a U.S. Marines tattoo on his neck. His soiled fatigues and Salvation Army overcoat were drenched. A shopping cart holding his belongings was parked outside the door. The wrapper from a foot-long roast beef sandwich sat on the table next to an empty Doritos bag. His stench was unpleasant, but not overpowering.

"This is Dwayne," Pete said.

"Mike Daley." I shook his calloused hand. "You want another sandwich?"

"Yeah."

I went over to the counter and ordered two foot-longs, two bags of chips, and a half-dozen chocolate chip cookies. Dwayne was a cheap date. I went back to the table. "You from around here?" I asked him.

"Yeah."

"You live nearby?"

"Yeah."

This was going to take a while if he insisted on one-word answers. Then again, I wasn't going to get any sleep tonight regardless of whether I talked to Dwayne for five minutes or fifteen. "Where did you grow up?"

"The projects." His sad eyes opened a little wider. "My dad worked at the Hunters Point Shipyard. My mom waited tables."

"They still around?"

"No."

"Sorry."

"Me, too."

"Did you go to Gateway?"

"Yeah."

It was the public high school on Geary and Scott. "I went to S.I."

"A lot of cops and lawyers went there."

"Guilty." I pointed at Pete. "He used to be a cop. I'm a lawyer."

"I know. I saw you on TV."

"That's me. A TV star." I pointed at his tattoo. "Marines?"

"Yeah."

"Vietnam?"

"Iraq."

He was younger than I thought. "What did you do?"

"Artillery."

"Must have been hard keeping the equipment working in the desert."

"It was a hundred and ten in the shade every day."

"Tough duty. How many tours?"

"Three."

"Our older brother died in Vietnam."

"Sorry. Army?"

"Marines." I waited a beat. "How long have you been living on the street?"

"Couple years."

I might have guessed longer. "You have trouble finding work?"

"It was okay for a while. Then I lost my job as a mechanic. Then my wife left me. Then I got into meth. You know the drill."

"I do. I know some people who might be able to help you."

"So do I."

"At the very least, they can find you a place to stay with a roof."

"No, thanks."

"Looks like it's going to be a long rainy season."

"I'll manage."

I pulled out my wallet and dropped five twenties onto the table. "Maybe that will get you a place to stay for a night or two."

He scooped up the cash.

"I understand that you might have some information for us about what happened yesterday morning."

"I might."

"The amount of your gratuity will depend on the quality of your information."

"That's fair."

I waited.

Dwayne took a second to decide what he wanted to tell us. He pointed across the plaza. "I was in my regular spot in front of Panda Express."

"All night?"

"Until the cops showed up."

"You saw everything?"

"Maybe." He held out his hand.

I slid a twenty across the table.

"I'll need more," he said.

I palmed another twenty and held it in front of him. As he

reached for it, I pulled it back. "Did you see Juwon Jones run across the plaza?"

"Yes."

"Had you ever seen him before?"

"No."

"You saw him turn onto Fillmore and head north?"

"Yes."

"Did you see Officer Bacigalupi following him?"

"Yes." He confirmed that Murphy was a half-block behind Johnny.

"Did you see any other police officers?"

"I heard a siren and saw flashing lights near the corner of Geary and Fillmore."

That would have been Rick Siragusa. "Did a police officer get out of the car in the intersection?"

"I don't know. I couldn't see anything after Jones ran up Fillmore."

"Did Jones say anything?"

"No."

"Anything else?"

"I don't remember. It happened very fast."

I slid a twenty across the table. "Dwayne, was Officer Bacigalupi's gun drawn?"

"Yes."

"What about his partner?"

"Him, too."

"Did Jones have a gun?"

"I didn't see it."

Crap. "They found a gun under his body."

"I heard."

"You didn't see it?"

"No. He was across the plaza. It was raining."

"Maybe it was inside his pocket."

"Could have been. Or maybe it was inside your client's pocket.

Wouldn't be the first time a cop planted a piece."

"Do you have any evidence that my client planted a gun?"

"No."

"What about one of the other cops?"

"No." He's eyes narrowed. "I know what I saw. And I know what I didn't see: a gun."

This isn't helping. "Did you talk to the police?"

"Yes. I always cooperate with the cops—especially the white ones."

"You ever had any trouble?"

"Occasionally. You know the drill. White cops with guns sometimes make for an unhealthy combination for a black guy without one."

True. "You don't pack?"

"No."

"Not even a knife?"

He shrugged. "Sometimes."

"What did you tell the cops?"

"The same thing that I told you: I saw Jones run across the plaza. I didn't see a gun."

Terrific. "Who did you talk to?"

"The homicide inspector. Old black guy."

"Roosevelt Johnson?"

"Yeah."

Figures. "Was anybody else around last night?"

"I didn't see anybody."

I slid another twenty across the table along with my business card. "Would you mind asking around?"

"Sure." He picked up his extra bag of chips. "If you ask me, your client doesn't have anything to worry about."

"How do you figure?"

"When a white cop shoots a black kid, the cop always walks."

* * *

Pete took a sip of coffee from a cup bearing the Subway logo. "That didn't help, Mick."

"No, it didn't." I glanced out the window, where Dwayne was sitting next to his cart. "You think he's telling the truth?"

"Why would he lie?"

"I don't know."

"I'm going to keep an eye on him."

"You think he knows something?"

"I don't know, Mick. At the moment, I don't have any better ideas. You going home?"

"I'm going back to the office. Rolanda is helping one of Luca's associates prepare document requests."

"I thought you were supposed to be doing this outside the P.D.'s Office."

"I am. Rolanda is moonlighting out of the goodness of her heart."

"She's a nice kid."

"Yes, she is. And she isn't a kid anymore. She's a terrific lawyer."

He cocked his head to the side. "Rosie's okay with this?"

"Let's just say that she's decided to look the other way."

"I don't know how you do it, Mick. You get along better with your ex-wife than I get along with my current wife."

"I've learned to pick my arguments carefully. Everything okay with you and Donna?"

"We're fine."

Pete's first marriage didn't work out. His second marriage wasn't perfect, but it was better. "You got time to do some asking around the neighborhood here?"

"Of course, Mick."

23
"WATCH THE VIDEO"

I was driving north on the Golden Gate Bridge at two-thirty on Thursday morning when I punched in the familiar number on my iPhone.

"Homicide. Johnson."

"It's Mike, Roosevelt."

"I know." He chuckled. "You're the only defense attorney whose number is programmed into my cell."

"I'm honored."

"You should be. You're also the only defense attorney on Planet Earth whose call I would have taken at this hour."

"I'm sorry to bother you so late."

"It's early."

Yes, it is. "Are you still at the office?"

"Where else would I want to be on such a beautiful morning?"

"You going to make it home tonight?"

"Eventually. You?"

"I'm on the bridge."

"Drive carefully."

"I will."

He cleared his throat. "What can I do for you?"

"I was hoping that I could persuade you to convince our hardworking D.A. to drop the charges against my client."

"Not going to happen."

"You can save yourself a lot of time and trouble."

"I have lots of time, and I like trouble."

"In that case, I'm calling to inquire as to whether you have any new evidence that you'd like to share with me."

"No."

"I don't need to remind you that you have a legal obligation to share any evidence that might tend to exonerate my client."

"There is none."

"Come on, Roosevelt."

"This is where I'm supposed to tell you to read the police reports."

"You haven't provided them."

"In due course."

I wasn't going to get anything from him before the arraignment. "You will be receiving requests for copies of all evidence relating to Johnny's case. I would appreciate it if you would respond as quickly as possible."

"We will."

I drove into the Robin Williams tunnel between the bridge and Sausalito. When I came out on the other side, my windshield was pounded by rain. "Mind if I ask you something off the record?"

"You can ask me anything that you'd like. I'll decide whether I want to respond."

"What do you have that made you decide to arrest Johnny so quickly?"

I envisioned Roosevelt pressing the phone to his ear as he considered his answer. "Watch the video."

"You have video of the shooting?"

"Watch the video," he repeated.

It was all that he was going to say. "Thanks, Roosevelt. Give my best to Janet."

"I will. I'll see you in court."

* * *

Rosie's name appeared on my iPhone as I was driving through Mill Valley on Highway 101. "Did you make it home?" she asked.

"On my way. Why are you still up?"

"I'm catching up on e-mails.

"Are you okay?"

"I'm fine."

Rosie would never admit to anything less than 'fine.' "Everything okay at home?"

"Yeah."

Good. "Thanks for coming over with Rolanda."

"You're welcome."

"She and Luca's associate put together a stack of document requests. She said that Nady is very good."

"I know. I just talked to her."

"I appreciate it, Rosie."

"You'll make it up to Rolanda—and me."

Yes, I would.

"Why don't you stop at my house for a few minutes?" she said.

It was an offer that I couldn't refuse. "I'll see you in ten minutes."

24

"THE NEXT ELECTION IS THREE YEARS FROM NOW"

The light was on in Rosie's living room as I walked up the steps of the post-earthquake bungalow at 8 Alexander Avenue across the street from the Larkspur Little League field. Rosie and I had rented the cheery white-shingle a few months after Grace was born, and Rosie kept the house after we got divorced. One of our few affluent clients (a one-time mob lawyer) graciously purchased it for us a couple of years ago as a thank-you after we got his death penalty conviction overturned. In the Bay Area's other-worldly real estate market, it was the equivalent of winning the lottery.

Technically, Rosie "lived" in a rented one-bedroom apartment across the street from her mother's house in the Mission, but that was for show. The San Francisco Public Defender had to list an official residence in the city. In reality, she spent most of her time over here in Marin. Although I stayed at Rosie's place a couple of nights a week, I still lived at the utilitarian one-bedroom apartment behind the Larkspur fire station where I'd moved after our divorce. The rent was expensive, but it was a small price to pay for the buffer zone that we needed to maintain our sanity.

I unlocked the door and let myself in. It's nice when your ex-wife lets you keep a key. I smiled at Rosie, who was staring at her laptop on the kitchen table that doubled as her home office. I nodded at her mother, Sylvia, who was sitting in her usual spot in an armchair next to the fireplace in the living room. As always, her attention was split between her knitting and CNN.

I hung my raincoat on the rack next to the door. I was taking off my wet shoes when I received an enthusiastic greeting from an unexpected source who came barreling in from the hallway leading to the two bedrooms in the back of the house.

"Hi, Dad," he said.

"Hi, Tom."

Our twelve-year-old son gave me a hug. A recent growth spurt had made him almost as tall as I was, and he was skinny as a rail. His facial features were closer to Rosie's than mine, but his light brown hair suggested a smattering of Daley genes. With a little luck, the braces on his teeth would come off in another six months or so.

"Why are you still up?" I asked. "It's almost three o'clock in the morning."

"I heard something outside."

He was a light sleeper. And, like his mother and grandmother, he was a night owl. "It was just the rain."

"No, it wasn't."

"Then it was me."

He played with the sleeve of the Golden State Warriors T-shirt that he used as his pajamas. "Maybe."

"No kidding, Tom." He inherited his propensity for worrying from me. "You have school in less than five hours. I need you to go back to bed."

He responded with a grudging, "Okay."

"I'll come in and say good night before I leave."

He changed the subject. "I saw you on TV. They said that you're going to represent the officer who shot that guy behind the post office."

"Yeah."

"You haven't been on TV since you went back to the Public Defender's Office."

"I don't do high-profile cases anymore." *Until now.* "I'll tell you about it over the weekend."

"Are we still going to the Warriors game next week?"

"You bet."

This elicited the smile that I was hoping for. "Night, Dad."

"Night, Tom."

He bounded down the hallway into the bedroom that he used to share with his sister, and now frequently shared with his grandmother.

I walked across the living room and pecked Rosie's mom on the cheek. "You okay, Sylvia?"

"Fine, Michael."

"You're up late."

"You know that I'd be up in another hour."

True. She was always watching CNN and drinking coffee by four a.m. "Your knee working okay?"

"Good as new."

Sylvia was the proud owner of two new knees and a new hip. She liked to say that she was fully refurbished.

I pointed at the TV. "Anything new?"

"Twenty-five people were arrested in the Fillmore. Two people were stabbed. Ten marchers and four police officers were taken to the hospital."

"Not good."

"Not good at all." Her hands worked furiously on her knitting. "Why in God's name are you getting involved in this disaster?"

"Johnny is my godson. I've known his father since we were kids."

"There are other lawyers, Michael."

"Johnny's grandfather worked with my dad."

Her expression suggested that she was less than satisfied with my response.

I walked into the newly refurbished kitchen. After Rosie won the election, her first unofficial action was to replace the workman-like sixties-era appliances with workman-like new millennium appliances straight from the floor of Home Depot. Her salary didn't warrant a splurge on a Subzero refrigerator or a Wolf range.

"Did you eat?" Rosie asked.

"A couple of hours ago."

"Anything with nutritional value?"

I hate this. "I had a kale and arugula salad with free-range chicken and organic feta cheese topped with oil and vinegar dressing."

"What did you really eat?"

"A chicken sandwich with lettuce, tomato, and cucumber."

"Subway?"

"It's sort of fresh."

"Processed chicken patties aren't fresh. Did you have a bag of chips?"

"Yes."

"And a Diet Soda?"

"Just water," I lied.

"Dr. Yee says that you need to eat better and exercise more."

"I'm working on it, Rosie."

"Work harder. There's salad in the fridge."

"Thanks."

"Did you go to the gym today?"

"I walked the steps." I played baseball in high school and used to be a gym rat. Those days were long ago. Nowadays, I climbed the nearby stairway connecting Magnolia Avenue with the houses up the hill. It's a hot-spot for Marin County's fitness fanatics. "I did five up-and-downs."

"Not bad. Did you see Zvi?"

"Yes. He asked about you."

Zvi Danenberg was a ninety-two-year-old retiree who had taught physics at Mission High for forty years. The spirited nonagenarian did twenty up-and-downs every morning. He was one of the most beloved figures in Marin County.

Rosie smiled. "He's still my hero."

"Mine, too. Why are you up?"

"I was in meetings all day. I needed to catch up."

Rosie never had trouble sleeping until she became P.D. "It couldn't wait?"

"I don't get a lot of quiet time during business hours."

"Neither do I."

"You decided to represent Johnny B."

Fair enough. "Sometimes you do what you think is right."

"And, in your case, sometimes you take on everybody else's problems."

I switched topics. "Thanks for coming over tonight with Rolanda. She was a big help."

"She always is."

"Did you really appoint her as Head of the Felony Division?"

"For now."

"What happens when I come back to the office?"

"We'll talk about it then." Her expression indicated that this topic was closed. "Were you and Pete down in the Fillmore tonight?"

"We were interviewing a potential witness."

She pushed out a sigh. "A bunch of people ended up in the hospital. For my own selfish reasons, I would prefer that you and your brother don't get yourselves killed."

"We'll be careful."

Her expression indicated that she wasn't so sure. "How bad was it?"

"It was quiet when I got there. Some broken windows. The police are out in force."

"Was the witness a cop?"

"No, he was a homeless guy who was on the plaza early yesterday morning." I filled her in on the details of our conversation with Dwayne.

"Will he testify that Jones was carrying a gun?"

"He didn't see one."

"That isn't going to help your self-defense claim. Will he make a credible witness for the prosecution?"

"Not bad. He's a veteran and is reasonably articulate."

"Anything else?"

"I talked to Roosevelt. He said that we need to look at the videos."

"I don't like it." She closed her computer and looked at Sylvia. "Anything on the news?"

Rosie's mother put down her knitting. "There's video from the post office parking lot. They're trying to decide whether to release it."

Uh-oh. "What does it show?"

"They aren't saying."

We needed to see it as soon as possible—if it existed. I turned back to Rosie. "I need to go home and pick up my going-to-court suit."

"You remember how to tie a tie?"

"I'll figure it out." I reached over and touched her hand. "Are you getting any more grief about my taking Johnny's case?"

"It's part of my job."

"I hope this isn't going to cause you any political fallout."

"The next election is three years from now. People have short memories."

"You're a good sport."

"I've decided that the best part about being in your fifties is that you stop caring about what other people think." The crow's feet at the corners of her cobalt eyes became more pronounced as she displayed the glowing smile that looked as beautiful as it did when we first met. "Get some rest, Mike. You're going to have a busy day."

"Do you have time to come to the arraignment?"

"I have a meeting, but I'll try to send Rolanda."

* * *

"You up, Mick?"

I held my iPhone against my right ear as I tried to focus on the red numerals on the alarm clock on my Ikea night stand. Five twenty-two a.m. I had been asleep for a little over an hour.

"Where are you, Pete?"

"The Fillmore. I kept an eye on Dwayne. He spent the night in the basement of an apartment building on Fulton."

It seemed a bit odd for a homeless guy. "You think he knows something?"

"I'm not sure, Mick."

"I'm due in court at nine for the arraignment. I'll call you when we're done."

25
"I ALWAYS HAVE TIME FOR GOD"

The rail-thin man with the crooked white hat and the heavy knee brace smiled broadly. "Good morning, young man," he sung out.

I returned his smile. "Good morning, Zvi."

At seven a.m. on Thursday, there was a break in the rain, and the cheerful ninety-two-year-old was standing at the landing at the seventy-sixth of the one hundred thirty-nine steps between Magnolia Avenue and the top of the hill above downtown Larkspur. He showed up every morning, rain or shine. My record for my new fitness regimen was a bit spottier.

"I didn't think I would see you this morning," he said. "I saw you on CNN. You said that Officer Bacigalupi was innocent."

"He is. Johnny is a good kid."

The man in the crooked hat gave me a crooked look. "Did he kill that boy?"

"It was self-defense."

"Then I'm sure you'll be able to help him." He started walking down the steps. "Give my best to Rosie."

* * *

"Bless me father, for I have sinned."

"Didn't expect to see you this morning, Mike."

"I always have time for God, Andy."

My seminary classmate, Father Andy Shanahan, let out a hearty chuckle. "How long has it been since your last confession?"

"I was here on Monday."

"Why weren't you here Tuesday or yesterday?"

"I didn't do anything bad for a couple of days."

"Or maybe we have some catching up to do."

"Maybe."

At seven-twenty on Thursday morning, I was sitting inside the confessional at St. Patrick's Catholic Church in downtown Larkspur, a block north of the steps, and around the corner from my apartment. Long ago, Father Andy had taken advantage of his six-foot-eight-inch frame as the starting center on the S.I. varsity basketball team. A knee injury ended his college career at St. Mary's, so he turned his attention to the Church. Smart, charismatic, and politically savvy, Andy was wildly popular at St. Pat's Parish. If you believed the gossip mongers at the Archdiocese, he was on the fast track for a position with the Archbishop's office.

He scrunched his face. "You smell a bit raw, Mike. Did you do the steps?"

"Five up-and-downs."

"Zvi does twenty."

"When I'm his age, so will I."

His chiseled face transformed into a smile. "Let's go outside. The rain finally stopped."

We exchanged pleasantries as we took seats on a bench near the door. Magnolia Avenue was starting to stir. In another twenty minutes, the children would start arriving at St. Pat's School next door.

Andy's blue eyes gleamed as he took a sip of water from a paper cup. "I saw you on TV. Why is a public defender working on this case?"

"Gio."

"Thought so. How are he and Maria holding up?"

"Not great."

"And Johnny?"

"It's been a couple of rough days, Andy."

"I'll bet. And Rosie is okay with your decision to moonlight?"

"She isn't crazy about it, but we worked it out."

"You guys are doing a lot better than when you were married."

"We're older. We don't have the energy to fight."

"CNN said the D.A. is going to charge Johnny with first-degree murder."

"It was self-defense."

"Okay."

"You sound skeptical."

"Seems there's always a backstory for an officer-involved shooting."

Not you, too. "Don't jump to conclusions."

"I'm not. Either way, you've put yourself in the middle of a situation that could turn combustible."

"It already is. A dozen people ended up in the hospital last night. They're planning another march tonight."

"You sure that it's wise to do this?"

No. "I'm trying to do what's right."

"Why'd you come to see me this morning, Mike?"

"You may recall that I'm Catholic. I like to go to church." Notwithstanding the fact that I failed as a priest, that much was still true.

"It's nice of you to fit us into your busy schedule."

"I wanted a little quiet time. I figured that you'd put in a good word for me with God."

"I'll do the best that I can. Did you want to confess to something?"

"Yes. I lied to Rosie. I told her that I would be able to extricate myself from this case in just a couple of weeks. That may be unrealistic."

He pondered his options. "I'm going to go light on you and ask for just two Hail Marys."

"That's it?"

"You get mitigation points because you're helping a fellow Catholic."

"A minute ago, you were questioning Johnny's innocence."

"Fortunately, I don't have to sit in judgment of him." The corner of his mouth turned up. "I'll hit you up to do some painting in the rectory when things calm down. In the meantime, I want you and Pete to be careful. I want you to be walking up and down the steps like Zvi when you're ninety-two."

"Thanks, Andy." I glanced at my watch. "I'm due in court."

26
"MAYBE YOU AREN'T AS GOOD AS I THOUGHT"

A steady drizzle was falling as I made my way through the media horde on the steps of the Hall at eight-forty-five on Thursday morning. SFPD had blocked off Bryant Street. Reverend Tucker had assembled a contingent behind police barricades at the east end of the Hall. A pro-police group led by a dozen uniformed officers stood guard at the west end.

Media vans lined the south side of Bryant where a couple of enterprising bail bond shops had rented their driveways to CNN and Fox News for eight hundred dollars an hour. Nice coin if you can get it. I kept my eyes forward, pushed my way through the cameras, and pretended to ignore the shouted questions.

"Mr. Daley? Is your client going to plead guilty?"

"Mr. Daley? Is your client going to accept a plea bargain?"

"Mr. Daley? Is it true that there is video showing Juwon Jones was unarmed?"

"Mr. Daley? Mr. Daley? Mr. Daley?"

I turned around and faced the music. "I am pleased to have this opportunity to defend Officer Bacigalupi, who has been unjustly arrested in a rush to judgment. I am confident that this error will be corrected, and my client will be able to return to his duties."

I entered the lobby, hoping that my impassioned platitude would turn out to be true.

* * *

Luca was standing in the crowded hallway outside Judge Ramsey's courtroom on the second floor of the Hall. "Are you ready?"

"Yes." I pulled him out of earshot of the nearest reporter. "Are Gio and Maria inside?"

"First row. The boys are here, too." He lowered his voice. "Johnny had a little scrape in the lockup last night."

Crap. "How little?"

"You'll see. He's okay, but he has a nasty cut over his eye."

"They promised to put him in Ad Seg." It was the euphemism for "Administrative Segregation," meaning that Johnny would be housed in his own cell.

"They didn't."

"We'll get that fixed right away."

"I expect you to get him out of here this morning."

* * *

Judge Martellus Ramsey's courtroom was packed as Luca and I stood at the defense table on either side of Johnny at nine o'clock on Thursday morning. Nady was to my left. It was the first time she had ever been in court on official business. DeSean Harper was at the prosecution table next to Roosevelt. They were wearing matching charcoal suits. I turned and nodded to Gio and Maria, who were sitting behind us. They were flanked by their sons. The remaining three rows on the defense side were filled with uniformed cops.

The gallery behind Harper was packed. Jones's mother was sitting next to Reverend Tucker in the first row. Chief Green and four assistants were behind them. The third row was filled with members of Reverend Tucker's church. The back row was occupied by the press.

I glanced at the last row of the defense side of the gallery, where Rolanda was sitting. She gave me a subtle nod, then turned her eyes to the front of the courtroom.

I leaned over and whispered into Johnny's ear. "Stay calm and be respectful." I pointed at the TV camera next to the court reporter. "It's all theater. Everybody will be watching you. I want you to look the judge in the eye when you talk to him."

"Right."

I pointed at the bandage over his right eye. "What happened?"

"I got into a shoving match with a guy in the lockup. I'm fine."

Sure. "Did you get any sleep?"

"Not much. Can you get me out of here?"

"Yes." *Maybe not.* I needed to manage his expectations. In a first-degree murder case, the chances of bail were slim, but I didn't want to suggest that I was anything less than confident.

Luca quickly added, "Absolutely."

We'll see. I continued talking to Johnny. "They'll read the charges and ask you to enter a plea. I want you to look the judge in the eye and say, 'Not guilty,' in a respectful tone. Then we'll talk about bail."

The door to the hallway leading to the judge's chambers opened. His world-weary bailiff took off his glasses. "All rise."

The courtroom came to life as Judge Ramsey emerged from behind the bench using an electric wheelchair. He had lost the use of his legs in a skiing accident a decade earlier. The imposing jurist moved into position behind a custom-designed bench, turned on his computer, and addressed nobody in particular. "Please be seated."

We did as we were told. The courtroom was silent as the judge pretended to study his docket. He turned to his bailiff. "Would you please call our first case?"

"The People versus Giovanni Carlo Bacigalupi the Fourth."

Johnny tensed. It always sounds ominous when they recite all of your names.

There was a commotion behind the prosecution table. Jones's mother muttered, "Murderer."

Judge Ramsey spoke to her in an understated tone. "Ms. Jones,

I am very sorry for your loss. However, I want to make something clear to you and everyone in this courtroom. Except for myself, the attorneys, and the witnesses, nobody is allowed to speak." He pointed at the TV camera. "I have agreed to televise these proceedings so that our community can watch. If anyone fails to abide by my rules, I will have the bailiff escort them outside."

The courtroom was stone-cold silent.

Judge Ramsey looked at me, then he turned to Harper. "Counsel will state their names for the record."

"DeSean Harper for the People, Your Honor."

"Michael Daley, Lucantonio Bacigalupi, and Nadezhda Nikonova for the defendant."

"Which one of you will be addressing the court today?"

I nodded. "I will, Your Honor."

He pulled his microphone toward himself. "This is an arraignment. We will read the charges and the defendant will enter a plea." He looked at Johnny. "Do you understand the reason for this proceeding, Officer Bacigalupi?"

"Yes, Your Honor."

"Thank you." He spoke to Harper. "Would you please inform us of the charges?"

"First-degree murder under California Penal Code Section 187."

"Thank you." The judge went through the ceremony of reading the complaint. Then he looked at me. "Mr. Daley, do you have any questions?"

"We would like to discuss the nature of these charges."

"Denied."

"But Your Honor—,"

"You and Mr. Harper are free to discuss an amendment if you believe it is appropriate."

"These charges should be dropped," I said.

"That's up to Mr. Harper. Does your client wish to enter a plea?"

"Yes, Your Honor."

He spoke to Johnny. "On the charge of murder in the first-degree, how do you plead?"

"Not guilty, Your Honor."

"Thank you. Mr. Daley, as you are aware, by statute, I am required to schedule a preliminary hearing within ten days."

A preliminary hearing, or "prelim," is a mini-trial where the prosecution must demonstrate that there is probable cause that Johnny committed murder. It's the D.A.'s show, and all evidentiary issues are resolved in the prosecution's favor. We had the right to demand a prelim within ten days. Most defendants "waive time," which means that the prelim can be held outside that timeframe. Ordinarily, we would have had little to lose by waiving time because it would have given us more time to prepare. In this instance, I was under orders from Johnny and Luca to expedite the process.

"Your Honor, Officer Bacigalupi chooses not to waive time."

"May I ask why you believe that it is in your client's best interests?"

"He's innocent. He wishes to begin his defense as soon as possible so that we can clear his name and he can get back to work."

The veteran judge had been on the bench too long to show any appearance of surprise, but he clearly hadn't expected this. "Are you sure, Mr. Daley?"

"I am, Your Honor."

He turned to Harper. "I trust that you will be prepared to move forward within ten days?"

Harper hadn't anticipated the expedited schedule, either. "I need to check my calendar."

No you don't. "If Mr. Harper wasn't prepared to proceed on an expedited basis, he shouldn't have filed the charges." *So there.*

"Mr. Harper, in this circumstance, Mr. Daley is correct."

"We'll be ready, Your Honor."

I shot him a snarky glance. "Or you can simply drop the

charges."

"That isn't going to happen, Mr. Daley."

I didn't think it would.

The judge looked at his computer. "While this matter would ordinarily go to Department 20 for a longer hearing, it turns out that I am available to preside over the prelim on Monday, February fourteenth, at ten a.m. I trust this is acceptable to you, Mr. Daley?"

It was a quick turnaround, but we had no choice. "Yes, Your Honor."

"If there is no further business—,"

"Your Honor, we'd also like to discuss bail."

He feigned surprise. "Am I correct in assuming that bail has not been set?"

As if you didn't know. "Correct. Bail is appropriate in this case. Officer Bacigalupi has significant community ties. He is willing to wear a monitor and surrender his passport. He will also agree to other reasonable accommodations as directed by the court."

Harper wasn't buying. "The People oppose bail. The defendant is charged with first-degree murder. He is dangerous and a threat to the community. His family has significant assets making him a flight risk."

No, he isn't. "Officer Bacigalupi has no criminal record. He has lived here for his entire life. So have his father and grandfather. He isn't going anywhere, and he is entitled to bail."

Harper shot back. "It would be very unusual to grant bail in a first-degree murder case."

Yes, it would. "Not true," I lied. "Your Honor has discretion. In addition to the usual ankle bracelet, my client would agree to live with his parents until his next court appearance. I'm sure you know Officer Bacigalupi's father."

"I do."

Harper's voice went up a half-octave. "While we have great respect for Assistant Chief Bacigalupi, it would be improper to provide special treatment for his son."

"Whose record is spotless and whose integrity has never been questioned," I said.

"Until now."

Judge Ramsey listened intently as Harper and I volleyed back and forth for another five minutes. Finally, he made the call. "I am not going to grant bail at this time."

Dammit. "But Your Honor—,"

"I've ruled, Mr. Daley. Anything else?"

I sensed a cold stare from Luca, but I kept my eyes on the judge. "We have submitted requests for police reports, video, and other evidence. Given our expedited schedule, we ask you to instruct Mr. Harper and SFPD to provide all such materials by the close of business today."

Harper shook his head. "Your Honor, we have a legal obligation to provide only evidence that would tend to exonerate Mr. Daley's client. At the moment, there is none."

"Your Honor," I said, "we have the right to this information through discovery. We can do this the easy way or the hard way. The easy way means that Mr. Harper provides the information right away."

Judge Ramsey didn't hesitate. "Mr. Harper. I expect you to provide everything that you have to Mr. Daley by five p.m. today. Understood?"

"Yes."

It was a small victory. "Your Honor, we would also ask that you impose a gag order on all parties. Nobody should be playing to the press or leaking evidence which could show up on Facebook or YouTube."

"So ordered. Anything else, Mr. Daley?"

"Not at the moment."

"Then we're adjourned."

* * *

A stern-faced Luca stopped me outside the courtroom. "That

didn't go well."

"We did the best that we could, Luca."

"Gio isn't happy. Neither is Maria."

Neither am I. "The judge agreed to expedited discovery. That will help us figure out what they have and where we stand."

"You were supposed to get the charges dropped."

"That wasn't realistic."

"At the very least, you were supposed to get bail."

"The judge didn't want to be perceived as giving special treatment to the son of an assistant chief."

"That doesn't help Johnny."

My neck was burning. "I'm doing everything that I can, Luca."

"Maybe you aren't as good as I thought."

* * *

My iPhone vibrated as I was walking through the parking lot down the street from the Hall. Pete's name appeared on the display. "I heard things didn't go so well in court," he said.

"They didn't."

"You got time to come out to the old neighborhood?"

"Yeah. You got something we can use?"

"Maybe. Rick Siragusa is willing to talk to us."

27
"I'D RATHER BE JUDGED BY TWELVE THAN CARRIED BY SIX"

A look of recognition crossed the veteran cop's leathery face. Rick Siragusa's lips transformed into a half-smile. "I figured you guys would show up sooner or later."

Pete grinned. "I guess this means it's sooner, Goose."

My brother's one-time running mate at Mission Station opened the door to his bungalow at Forty-Seventh and Vicente, two blocks from the ocean in a corner of the City where the sun rarely shined. "Come on in, guys."

The lanky cop led us through the cluttered living room into a narrow kitchen. Twice divorced, Goose lived by himself in a time capsule that he had inherited from his parents. The counters and plumbing dated to the forties. The Sears appliances were seventies vintage. The Mitsubishi TV had been state-of-the-art in the mid-nineties.

We took seats in the spindle-back chairs around a butcher block table in the breakfast area overlooking an overgrown yard. The wind whipped against the windows.

Goose got up and walked over to the fridge. "Something to drink?"

Pete answered first. "Just water for me."

"Same here," I said. Even though it was only two steps to the sink, I noticed that he was limping. "You okay?"

"Yeah." He poured a glass of water for each of us, and took a seat. "I pulled something. It'll be fine."

"You working tonight?"

"Everybody is working." He pointed at the TV tuned to CNN. "I gotta be back at four. Word came down from the chief. All hands on deck until things calm down. I'm working the command center at Northern Station."

"You going to be there all night?"

"That's how we roll. When people are smashing windows and overturning cars, we look out for each other."

My dad would have said the same thing. We spent a moment catching up. He reported that his ex-wives and kids were okay. He was planning to retire in three years and seven months—everybody on the City payroll—including me—could tell you when they would start collecting their pensions. He had purchased a house in the Sierra foothills above Auburn. When he retired, he was going to sell his parents' house and pocket seven figures. It sounded pretty good.

When it was time to turn to business, I let Pete do the talking. "We heard you were at the scene on Wednesday morning."

"I was. Everything that could have gone wrong did."

We waited.

"I was sitting in my unit in front of the Boom-Boom Room. We keep an eye on things when they close."

The Boom-Boom Room was a dingy blues, funk, and hip-hop club on the northwest corner of Fillmore and Geary, a half-block from the post office parking lot where Jones died. Pete knew the owners and provided security on busy weekends. They reciprocated by letting him use the club as his unofficial office during off-hours.

"Were you by yourself?" Pete asked.

"Yeah. I was only two blocks from the Safeway, so I responded to Johnny's call for backup. I drove down Fillmore to Geary and stopped in the intersection. Jones was running toward me. I grabbed the microphone and ordered him to stop."

"Did he?"

"No. He turned left and ran west on Geary toward the post office. Johnny was about a block behind him. Murph was about a block behind him." He gave us a conspiratorial grin. "Murph isn't as light on his feet as he used to be."

Pete asked him if he got out of his car.

"First I radioed for more backup. Then I followed Murph down Geary. Charlie Connor had cut off Jones in front of the post office, so Jones climbed over the fence into the parking lot. Johnny followed him inside and cornered him behind a postal van."

"Did you go inside the lot?"

"Not until after the shooting stopped."

"What about Murphy and Connor?"

"They were outside with me."

"Did you see Johnny shoot Jones?"

"No. They were behind a postal van."

"Did you hear anything?"

"I heard everything. Johnny told Jones to lie down. He repeated the order a couple of times. Next thing I know, shots were fired."

"You're sure Johnny fired the shots?"

"I understand why you're asking, Pete, but nobody else was in the lot. The kid shot him."

My turn. "Does your unit have a dash cam?"

"Nope. SFPD is a little behind in our technology."

"Were you wearing a body cam?"

"Yes." He held his hands up. "Before you ask, I didn't turn it on. Everything happened fast. I didn't have time."

"How close was Jones to you when he ran by?"

"I'd say about thirty feet."

"And it was dark and rainy?"

"Yes, but my lights were on."

Here goes. "Did Jones have a gun?"

"Yes."

"You're sure?"

"Yeah." He added, "Murph and Johnny said they found it under his body."

"Were you with them when they found it?"

"No. I came inside the lot a few minutes later."

Pete and I exchanged a look. It was helpful that Siragusa would confirm that Jones did, in fact, have a gun. Ideally, the gun would show up in a video.

"You're prepared to testify that Jones had a gun in his hand when he ran by you?"

"Of course. You'll also want to talk to Charlie Connor. He saw more than I did, and he probably caught some of this on his body cam."

"We will. You know him?"

"Yeah. Nice kid."

I moved in another direction. "Did you know Jones?"

"I knew his name. He wasn't a good guy."

"He didn't have much of a criminal record."

His tone turned pointed. "They found a stash of AK-47s in his trunk. Those weren't going to be Valentine's presents for his girlfriend, Mike."

"Understood."

He wasn't finished. "Look, I'm sorry that Jones died. Maybe Johnny could have de-escalated the situation. Maybe not. All I know is that when you're standing there with your life on the line and you have a fraction of a second to make a decision, you do what you have to do to protect yourself. I'd rather be judged by twelve than carried by six."

It was a common sentiment among police officers.

Siragusa held up an index finger. "The reality is that Johnny saved lives last night. Some bad people were going to do bad things with those AK-47s. I'm sorry for Jones and his mother, but I feel great for the families that aren't going to lose loved ones." He glanced at his watch. "I need to take care of a few things before I go down to the station. It's going to be a long night. You know—

serve and protect."

* * *

I was pulling into the lot in Luca's building when Pete's name appeared on my iPhone. "I need you to come back to the Fillmore," he said. "Meet me at the Boom-Boom Room. I found Charlie Connor."

28

"THEY TOLD ME NOT TO TALK TO ANYONE"

Pete raised his hand. "Over here, Mick."

My lungs filled with air smelling of a combination of stale popcorn and spilled beer as I made my way to a table in the corner of the Boom-Boom Room. The music venue and dive bar wouldn't open for another six hours.

"Did you have any trouble parking?" Pete asked.

"I left my car across the street in the Japantown garage."

"Good move. It's a war zone out there."

Police cars were parked on every corner of the Fillmore. "Is there going to be another march tonight?"

"That's the plan."

"It's only going to make matters worse."

"Agreed." Pete pointed at the baby-faced cop sipping coffee. "This is Charlie Connor. He's Paulie's son."

I extended a hand. "Mike Daley. We know your dad and your uncles."

"I'm not surprised."

A dozen family members were SFPD. A few black sheep were fire fighters. "We appreciate your time."

"They told me not to talk to anyone."

"Who?"

"My commander."

Pete tried to reassure him. "It's okay, Charlie. This stays between us."

Not necessarily.

Connor wasn't so sure. "I could get in trouble."

Yes, you could. "We're trying to figure out what happened on Wednesday morning. We need your help. So does Johnny."

The well-mannered kid with the blonde hair, wide nose, and blue eyes played with his coffee cup, but didn't reply.

I had to grovel. "Please, Charlie."

He glanced at his watch. "Five minutes."

"Where were you on Wednesday morning?"

"Parked over by Kimbell Playground. We've seen an uptick in crystal meth sales."

He was a block from the post office. "Were you by yourself?"

"Yes. My partner was at the station doing paperwork."

He was killing time. I asked him what happened next.

"I heard a call from Johnny and Sergeant Murphy about a traffic stop. Sounded routine. I saw them drive up onto upper Geary. They pulled the guy over in the Safeway parking lot."

Nothing we didn't already know.

He spoke slowly. "There was a problem with the stop. Johnny called for backup. So did his partner. The suspect fled on foot. Armed and dangerous. I pulled onto Geary and stopped in front of the post office. I saw Jones running toward me. Johnny was about a half-block behind him. I turned on my lights, grabbed my microphone, and ordered Jones to stop."

"Did he?"

"He climbed over the gate into the parking lot. Johnny followed him and cornered him behind a postal van. I radioed for more backup. Then I exited my vehicle and proceeded to the area outside the parking lot, where Sergeant Murphy was standing. Officer Rick Siragusa joined us a moment later. We were outside the gate when we heard Johnny order the suspect to lie down on the ground. He repeated it at least twice."

"Did Jones respond?"

"He said, 'Don't shoot. I'm unarmed.'"

"Then what?"

He looked down. "Johnny shot him in self-defense." He added, "I called for backup and went back to my unit for the first aid kit. Sergeant Murphy climbed over the gate to assist Johnny. Officer Siragusa also called for backup and went inside the lot."

I glanced at Pete, who took the cue. "Charlie, you said that you saw Jones running toward you on Geary, right?"

"Right."

"Did he have a gun?"

He waited a half-beat. "Yes."

Pete's tone was gentle. "You sure?"

"Yes. It happened very fast. The call said that the suspect was armed and dangerous." He nodded as if to reassure himself. "He had a gun in his hand."

"And you're prepared to testify that you saw a gun in his hand when he ran toward you?"

Another hesitation. "Yes."

Good enough. "Does your car have a dash cam?"

"No."

"Were you wearing your body cam?"

"Yes. I turned it on when I was still in my unit."

"Before or after Jones came running toward you?"

"Before."

"So everything that you saw should be visible on the video?"

"Presumably."

"Including what you saw and heard when you were standing outside the parking lot?"

"Yes."

"Was it still turned on when Johnny shot Jones?"

"Yes, but we couldn't see what happened because Johnny and Jones were behind a postal van."

Pete gave me a knowing look. The video might not show everything that happened, but the audio would reveal what Johnny and Jones said.

I asked, "Did you download the video when you got back to the station?"

"Yes."

"Have you looked at it?"

"No. We aren't supposed to look at video for an officer-involved shooting until after we've given our statements."

"Did you give your statement?"

"Yes."

"Then you should be able to look at it, right?"

"My commander told me that I wasn't authorized, so I didn't."

We needed to get our hands on it right away. "You did the right thing."

"I hope so." He looked at his watch. "I need to get to the station."

"Thanks, Charlie." He was in for a long day and night. And so were we.

* * *

Pete drummed his fingers on the table in the back of the Boom-Boom Room. "We need to get our hands on the video from Charlie's body cam."

"We're on it."

He scanned his texts for a moment, then he looked at me. "Siragusa was right about one thing. Jones wasn't delivering those AK-47s to people who were going to use them for hunting."

"He didn't deserve to die, Pete."

"If he had lived, we'd probably be reading about a massacre."

"I don't know."

"Yes, you do."

Yes, I did. "My job is to represent Johnny."

"That's a cop-out."

Yes, it is. "No, it's a defense mechanism."

"That's how you keep your sanity at times like this, eh?"

"Yup."

"Pop always said that you were the smart one."

"I'm not so sure."

"You going back to the office?"

"I need to stop at City Hall."

He smirked. "You planning to talk to the mayor?"

"No. I got a text from a lawyer in the City Attorney's Office. As if I don't have enough on my plate, she wants to talk about the civil case that Jones's mother filed against the City and Johnny."

29
"I'M GETTING PRESSURE FROM MY BOSS"

The head of the civil trial division of the San Francisco City Attorney's Office leaned back in her creaky chair in her workman-like office on the second floor of City Hall. "You couldn't find somebody else to represent Johnny B?"

"His father and I were classmates at S.I. His grandfather and my dad worked together at Taraval Station."

"Uh-huh." Paula Griffith had graduated closer to the top of our class at Boalt Law School than I had. After ten years slogging away at a couple of the big firms, she moved to the City Attorney's Office, where her sharp mind, exceptional work ethic, and unapologetic tenacity were more appreciated. "Luca put the arm on you, didn't he?"

"Yeah."

"Rosie's okay with this arrangement?"

"She isn't crazy about it."

She twirled her shoulder-length red hair as she looked out the window at Civic Center Plaza, where a crowd was gathering. "Your client is in serious trouble, Mike. And his situation isn't making my life easy."

"You should see what my life is like."

"That's your problem. It would improve the quality of mine if you could get your client off—preferably quickly and with a full exoneration of any criminal charges."

"You're asking a lot."

"I can be very demanding."

Yes, you can. She had won every moot court competition in law school and became even more argumentative after she graduated. Her marriage to one of our classmates lasted less than a year. Joe didn't have the temperament to be a lawyer. And he *really* didn't have the temperament to be married to Paula. After bouncing around several firms, he moved to Mendocino and started a medical marijuana dispensary. When medicinal dope became legal a few years ago, he sold his business to a conglomerate for eight figures. Last I heard, he was enjoying a very satisfying retirement.

"You wanted to see me?" I said.

"I did. I'm working on the civil case filed by Jones's mother. I'm getting pressure from my boss to resolve it. He's under a lot of pressure from the powers-that-be."

"The mayor?"

"And the Board of Supervisors."

"Jeff won't cave under political pressure."

"You know how these cases go, Mike. They're played out in the press long before they ever get to court."

"It will set a terrible precedent if you settle without a fight."

"Depends on the terms. I'll do what's best for the City."

It was the right response. "Johnny shot Jones in self-defense."

"So he says. SFPD says that Jones was unarmed."

"Who at SFPD?"

"The chief."

"Have you seen the video?"

"Not yet. I'm told that we'll have something to look at tonight."

"Would you mind sharing if you get it before I do?"

"Sure."

I looked my classmate in the eye. "What aren't you telling me, Paula?"

"The powers-that-be think your client shot an unarmed kid."

"They found a dozen AK-47s in the trunk of Jones's car."

"He didn't have one in his possession when he was shot."

"He had a handgun. They found it under his body."

"So says your client. I've been told that Jones didn't have a gun when he was shot."

"Have you talked to Luca?"

"Briefly. Luca's firm is going to represent Johnny in the civil case. We've agreed to coordinate our defenses to the extent possible. For now, the City's and your client's interests line up, but that could change. If we get an attractive settlement offer, we might take it—even if Luca doesn't want us to do it. Johnny is a kid with minimal personal assets, which makes him judgment proof. There's a lot more at stake for the City."

"You're really thinking about settling?"

"We need to be realistic. You saw what happened last night. There's going to be another march tonight. And tomorrow. And Saturday. And Sunday. A couple of people got stabbed last night. It's only a matter of time before somebody gets killed. If we can lower the temperature by considering a settlement, we will."

It was a legitimate position. "At the very least, you should coordinate with Luca before you consider any settlements."

"I'll try, but I can't make any promises."

"It may impact the criminal case."

"That's not my problem.

"No, it's mine."

* * *

Pete's voice was tired. "Where are you, Mick?"

I pressed my iPhone to my ear as I walked through the rotunda at City Hall. "I just finished talking to Paula Griffith. She's getting pressure to settle the civil case."

"That's quick."

"Yeah. How are things down in the Fillmore?"

"Tense. The cops have blocked off the streets."

"They're worried about the march tonight?"

"They're worried about a riot."

145

30
"I DIDN'T SEE IT"

At six-thirty on Thursday evening, Pete was sipping coffee in the same booth at Subway where we'd met Dwayne a day earlier. "This is Belico," he said.

The razor-thin young man with the wisp of a mustache extended a hand. "Nice to meet you."

"Same here. You from around here?"

"Ecuador." His features were soft, but his eyes were hard. "I've been here since I was a kid. I'm a U.S. citizen."

Even in liberal San Francisco, people felt compelled to let you know that they were legal. I glanced around at the otherwise empty sandwich shop. The windows and the door were covered with plywood. "You staying open all night?"

"We're shutting down at eight. The cops told us to close early."

"Rough night last night."

"It's going to be worse tonight. Reverend Tucker is leading another march from City Hall. There's going to be trouble. We were lucky that nobody was shot last night." He glanced at his watch. "Why did you want to talk to me?"

"Did you know Juwon Jones?"

"No."

"Know anybody who did?"

"No."

"You heard that they found some AK-47s in the trunk of his car?"

"Don't know anything about it."

And he wasn't going to admit it if he did. "We heard that you were working here on Wednesday morning."

"I was."

"Our client stopped Jones in the Safeway parking lot. Did you see anything?"

"I wasn't paying attention."

"You must have seen flashing lights from the police car."

"We see lights every night. Northern Station is three blocks from here."

"Do you keep a gun behind the counter?"

"No." He eyed me. "I can't speak for anybody else who works here or any of the other businesses on the street."

"Understood. Was anybody in the restaurant when Jones was pulled over?"

"No."

"Was anybody out on the plaza?"

"Dwayne."

"We've talked to him. Anybody else?"

"I don't remember."

His involvement was going to be limited. "Do you have security cameras?"

"Two. One behind the counter. The other above the door. We gave the video to the cops."

"Did you look at it?"

"Yeah."

One-word answers were unsatisfying. "Did it show Jones running by the store?"

"Yeah."

"Could you see a gun in his hand?"

"I didn't see it."

This wasn't helping. I turned to Pete, who took the cue. "Belico, did you talk to the police?"

"I told them the same thing that I just told you. I didn't see anything. I gave them the security videos. I told them that I would be available to testify if they needed me. They said that they probably wouldn't." He stood up. "That's all I know, guys."

I handed him a card. "You'll call us if you think of anything else?"

"Yeah." He started to back away from the table, then he stopped. "Jones fell down when he turned the corner and ran up Fillmore. He got up and kept running. I don't think he was hurt."

"Did you see a gun?"

"No."

"Did you mention this to the cops?"

"Yes."

It wasn't much. I extended a hand to thank him when I heard shouting outside. Then a horn blared, and tires screeched. Pete's eyes opened wide.

The plywood-covered door exploded as a car crashed through it, sending wood and dust flying toward us. Instinctively, I covered my face as a Corolla lurched to a stop in the booth next to us.

My heart pounded as the horn blared. A young man was behind the wheel, unconscious, blood streaming from a cut above his eye. Pete walked over to the Corolla, his Glock G29 drawn. Belico followed him, a nine-millimeter handgun in his hand. I decided not to chastise him for lying to us about whether he was packing. Pete quickly put his gun back inside its holster. So did Belico. The episode had lasted less than a minute.

A moment later, Rick Siragusa arrived along with two other cops, service weapons. Siragusa saw us and lowered his gun. "What the hell are you doing here?"

"We were talking to Belico."

"Go home."

I pointed at the driver. "You know this guy?"

"Yeah. He runs errands for one of our local meth dealers."

"You think he was trying to hit us?"

"I don't think he knows who you are."

"You think this has anything to with Jones?'

"I don't know. Maybe he just lost control of his car. In addition to delivering drugs, he likes to sample the products himself. We'll take him over to San Francisco General and sort this out in the morning. In the meantime, you and Pete should get out of here. We're expecting trouble tonight."

It was good advice. "Thanks, Rick."

* * *

Pete and I stood in a cold drizzle near the corner of Geary and Fillmore at seven-fifteen on Thursday night. "You going back to the office?" he asked.

"Yes. We're supposed to get copies of the videos tonight. You want to come along? You have a good eye for this stuff."

"I'll come over later. I want to talk to a few more people down here."

I looked at the crowd assembling in front of the post office. "This might not be a good time."

"I'll be careful."

I surveyed Geary Boulevard, which was closed to traffic. Two blocks to the east, I saw thousands of people marching toward us in silence behind a police escort.

"Why don't you come back tomorrow," I said.

"I'll be careful," he repeated.

* * *

I was checking my iPhone as I was walking to my car on the lower level of the underground garage in Japantown. I pulled out my key and pressed the unlock button. As I approached the driver-side door, I heard crunching beneath my feet. The driver-side window had been smashed, and the seat was covered with glass.

Crap.

My first instinct was that the broken window had some connection to Johnny's case. Then I reminded myself that there were about seventy-five auto break-ins in San Francisco every day.

SFPD was aware of the problem. They also acknowledged that they had insufficient manpower to do anything about it.

I took a deep breath and punched in the emergency number for AAA. Stuff always happens at the most inconvenient times.

31
"CAN THEY STOP IT?"

The aroma of leftover sandwiches filled the air as Assistant Chief Gio Bacigalupi sat in silence in the conference room in his brother's law firm at nine o'clock on Thursday night. His expression was grim as he watched a live report from the Fillmore on Channel 2. "Unbelievable," he said. "Is Pete still down there?"

"He's on his way here."

"Good call."

Indeed. I stared at the flat-screen. The march had started peacefully at City Hall. The crowd had swelled as it got closer to the Fillmore. Reverend Tucker led the assembly in prayers in front of the post office. Then somebody threw a bottle. Somebody else set off a fire cracker. The police line gave way and a melee broke out between the marchers and the pro-police counter-protesters. The police responded with force. It started with shouting. Then fire hoses. Then tear gas. Then rubber bullets. The crowd went from agitated to angry.

A reporter from Channel 2 struggled to hold her microphone as she was jostled by the retreating crowd. Her hair was matted. Her voice was hoarse. "We have confirmation of at least two deaths. Dozens have been injured and taken to local hospitals. Police are trying to stabilize the scene, but protesters and counter-protesters are angry, tired, and wet. We will continue to bring you updates as we can, but the police have asked us to leave the area for our safety."

The TV cut to the studio, where the air-brushed anchor was staring into the camera in disbelief. Flustered, he blurted out, "Stay safe, Rita."

I looked over at Gio. "Can they stop it?"

"Eventually." His voice filled with frustration. "They won't let me near the area. The chief said that it would exacerbate the situation."

He was probably right. "Did they let you see Johnny tonight?"

"Briefly. They finally gave him his own cell."

That's progress—albeit minor. "How is he holding up?"

"Not great."

"We'll get him out."

"Eventually."

"These things take time."

"I know."

"I'll go see him in the morning."

"He'd like that." His tone turned pointed. "He'd like it even more if you can get him the hell out of there and get the charges dropped."

"Working on it." I filled him in on our conversations with Murphy, Siragusa, and Connor. "They're prepared to testify that they saw a gun in Jones's hand and that Johnny acted in self-defense."

"Do you have a corroborating witness who isn't a cop?"

"Pete's working on it."

"Tell him to work harder—and faster."

If my kid was sitting in a cell, I would have wanted the same thing. I turned to Luca. "I talked to Paula Griffith about the civil case."

"So did I. Is she going to fight it?"

"If it's up to her, yes."

"But?"

"Her boss is under a lot of pressure from the mayor's office to settle."

"This would be a bad time for the mayor to get squishy. It will send a signal to every plaintiff's lawyer that the City will back down when things get hot. It also sends a terrible message to SFPD."

"Politicians tend to misplace their backbones when there are rioters in the streets."

"True."

The door opened and Nady came inside. "We just got a delivery from the D.A.'s Office. Among other things, the package includes video from Johnny's body cam."

Finally. "Let's give it a look."

"I'll get my computer. And you have a couple of visitors: your brother and your ex-wife."

32
"DID ANYBODY SEE A GUN?"

The conference room was enveloped by an intense silence. Nady was loading a disk onto her laptop, which she had connected to the flat-screen. Luca sat next to Gio. I was sitting between Pete and Rosie. I was happy to see them. Pete was good at analyzing crime scenes. Rosie had an unmatched eye for detail.

I turned to my ex-wife. "For somebody who isn't involved in this case, you seem to be spending a lot of time here."

"I enjoy your company."

"Is Tommy okay?"

"Fine. My mother is at the house again tonight."

"We'll need to do something nice for her."

"*You'll* need to do something nice for her."

Fair enough. "All quiet at the office?"

"Two dozen people were arrested in the Fillmore tonight. Some will need public defenders. It's going to be busy until we get everybody processed."

"If you need help—,"

"It's under control. The Head of the Felony Division is doing an excellent job."

"Give Rolanda my thanks."

"I will." The corner of her mouth turned up slightly. "She asked me to tell you that you need to get the charges against Johnny dropped right away. We need you at work."

"I'll be back as soon as I can." I turned to Pete. "Miss being a cop?"

"I'm getting too old to dodge rocks and bottles. I have a wife and a kid."

Nady dimmed the lights and hit the Play button. The SFPD logo appeared on the TV. "This is from Johnny's body cam," she said.

I grabbed a pad of paper and a pen. Millennials took notes on their iPhones. I still did it the old-fashioned way.

All eyes turned to the TV. The technology for body cams is advanced, and the color picture and sound were clear. The cam was mounted on Johnny's chest, so we were seeing essentially what he saw, albeit from slightly below eye level. The date and time were stamped in white. There was a notation that the footage had been taken on an Axon Body 2, the most popular model among U.S. law enforcement. Johnny activated his cam as he left his car at one-eleven a.m.

As Johnny approached Jones's car, he looked at Murphy. "Quick and by the book," the veteran cop said. "And check the trunk."

"Right." Johnny pulled on the trunk. "Locked."

"Fine."

Johnny continued forward and stopped adjacent to the driver-side window. Murphy disappeared out of camera view.

Johnny pointed his flashlight at the driver's window, which reflected into the camera.

Jones lowered the window. He looked younger than eighteen. His features were soft. Full lips, a prominent nose, and facial hair that was more peach fuzz than a beard. He wore a black windbreaker. His hands were on the wheel, eyes forward. He turned slowly to face Johnny. His tone was respectful—as if somebody had coached him about how to address a cop during a traffic stop in the middle of the night. "Yes, Officer?"

"I'm Officer Bacigalupi of SFPD. Could you please put your car in Park, set the brake, and turn off the ignition?"

"Okay."

"What's your name?"

"Juwon Jones."

"Are you the owner of this vehicle?"

"It's my mother's. Her name is Vanessa Jones."

"You're out late."

"I was coming home from work."

"Where do you work?"

"The Jack-in-the-Box on Geary."

"Is the food any good?"

"Not bad."

"May I see your license and registration?"

"Is there a problem, Officer?"

"One of your tail lights is out."

Jones feigned contrition. "I meant to get it fixed."

"It's dangerous to drive at night with a broken light."

"I know. I'm sorry."

Johnny tried again. "May I see your license and registration?"

"My license is in my wallet in my pocket. The registration is in the glove compartment."

"That's fine. Please take them out slowly."

"Yes, sir." He added, "I'm not armed, Officer."

"Thank you for letting me know."

Jones pulled out his wallet, removed his license, and handed it to Johnny. Then he reached into the glove compartment, pulled out the registration certificate, and gave it to Johnny.

"Mr. Jones, I need to ask you to stay here while I check your license and registration. Standard procedure. If everything checks out, I'll write up a fix-it citation and you can go home."

"Do you have to?"

"I'm afraid so." Johnny started walking back to his unit. He told Murphy that he was going to check the license and registration. "The driver is Juwon Jones. Do you know him?"

"No."

Johnny returned to his car, took a seat behind the wheel, and turned on the dashboard computer. He turned off the body cam for a moment, then he reactivated it as he began walking toward Jones's car again.

As he reached the trunk of the Honda, he looked at Murphy, who asked, "Anything?"

"The car belongs to his mother. It isn't stolen."

"And the kid?"

"Valid driver's license."

"Rap sheet?"

"One conviction for auto theft. A couple of hits for shoplifting."

"Probation violations?"

"He missed a check-in meeting last week. There's an outstanding warrant."

Murphy glanced at his watch. "You know what to do."

"You sure?"

"Tell him that you need to search the car."

"It's late, Murph."

"Do it by the book."

Johnny walked to the driver-side window. "Mr. Jones, your driver's license and ownership records checked out."

Jones smiled. "Thank you, Officer."

"However, it seems that you missed a meeting with your probation officer last week."

The smile disappeared. "That was last week?"

"Yes. You are on probation, right?"

Jones remained silent.

"You're required to answer my question, Mr. Jones."

"Yes, I'm on probation."

"I need to ask you to step outside of your vehicle for a moment."

"Why?"

"We're required to search your car."

Jones gripped the wheel tightly. "You stopped me for a broken tail light. You said that you were going to give me a fix-it ticket."

"That's still the plan. However, since you have a probation

violation, I'm required to search your car. If you would step outside, I'll give it a look, and we can wrap this up."

Jones's eyes flashed anger. "This is harassment."

"Please, Mr. Jones. I'm just following procedure."

"This wouldn't be happening if I was white."

"This has nothing to do with race."

"Sure it does. It *always* does. You pulled me over for DWB— driving while black."

Murphy's voice was heard off-camera. "Is there a problem?"

Johnny answered him. "No. I asked Mr. Jones to get out of his vehicle."

"Is he refusing?"

"He's thinking about it."

Murphy came into camera view on the passenger side. He tapped on the window, which Jones lowered. "Mr. Jones, I need you to get out of this vehicle."

"It's raining, man."

"Let's not make this harder than it needs to be. Please get out of your vehicle."

"There's nothing here. It's my mother's car. I was just driving home from work."

"Then this will only take a minute. Please, Mr. Jones."

"I'm unarmed, man."

"I didn't suggest otherwise."

A few seconds passed. The only sound was the rain hitting the roof of Jones's car.

Out of the corner of my eye, I saw Pete, who was focused intently on the screen.

And then everything happened fast.

Jones banged the driver-side door into Johnny, who shouted an expletive. His body cam gyrated wildly for an instant, then it pointed straight up.

Pete pointed at the screen. "He landed on his back."

Jones was now off-camera, but we could hear his footsteps as he ran away. Murphy ordered him to stop. So did Johnny. Jones ignored them.

Johnny pulled himself to his feet. His body cam focused on the open door to Jones's car. Then he looked at Murphy, whose expression was a combination of anger and concern.

"You okay, kid?"

"Yeah. Which way did he go?"

Murphy pointed at the plaza. "Toward Fillmore."

"I got this. Call for backup. Jones has a gun."

"Go get him. I'll be right behind you. And be careful, kid."

Johnny's body cam vibrated as he sprinted across the plaza. It was difficult to see much because of the rain. I made out the shadow of a tall man—presumably Jones—as he ran past the Subway and turned north onto Fillmore, where he disappeared from view.

Johnny was breathing heavily as he shouted into the microphone on his shoulder. "Suspect is Juwon Jones. Eighteen. African-American. Six-six. One-eighty. Black windbreaker and jeans. Heading north on Fillmore at O'Farrell. Armed and dangerous. Repeat: armed and dangerous."

The video shook as Johnny ran by the Subway and up Fillmore. The bagel store and a jazz club flashed by. The headlights of Siragusa's police car blinded the camera as Johnny got closer to Geary. Jones was out of sight—presumably, he had already turned the corner. Johnny stopped in front of the currency exchange. Then he turned left and ran toward the post office. Jones was a half-block ahead. The headlights from Connor's police unit cast an aura around him.

Jones leapt onto the metal gate in front of the parking lot. As Johnny got closer, Jones pulled himself over and disappeared. Johnny jumped onto the gate and made it over on the second try. The video and audio came to an abrupt halt.

Nady pressed Stop. "That's it from the body cam."

"Johnny told me that it came off when he climbed over the

fence." I turned to Gio. "Did you see a gun in Jones's hand?"

He paused. "It was dark and rainy."

I asked again. "Did you see a gun?"

"I couldn't tell."

I looked around the room at my brother, my ex-wife, Johnny's uncle, and his uncle's associate. "Did anybody see a gun?"

Silence.

I pointed at Nady. "Please run it again in super slow-mo."

33
"DON'T SHOOT"

The second viewing was no more revealing than the first. Neither were the third, fourth and fifth—even in super slow-mo with enhanced video. Obstructed views, darkness, and rain made it almost impossible to see Jones.

"What else did they send over?" I asked.

Nady studied her notes. "Video from a police camera on the plaza. Footage from the security cameras at the Subway and a couple of other businesses on Fillmore. And video from Officer Connor's body cam."

"Let's roll."

Pete spoke to Nady in his most diplomatic voice. "Would you mind if I run the videos?"

"Uh, sure."

* * *

Pete pushed the Play button on Nady's laptop and narrated as we watched. "This was taken by a police security camera mounted on a street lamp in the plaza."

The video showed a wide view of the plaza with the Safeway parking lot in the background. Johnny's unit was visible, lights flashing. Jones's car was blocked by the building housing the Panda Express. I couldn't see Dwayne, who was under the overhang in front of Panda Express.

"Here comes Jones."

We watched Jones run across the empty plaza toward Fillmore.

He disappeared from camera view before he reached the Subway. Johnny appeared about fifteen seconds later. A full thirty seconds later, Murphy lumbered across the plaza.

Pete pointed at the screen. "Let me try to enhance it a bit."

He ran it again in super slow-mo. He paused as Jones ran by the light pole. "This is where Jones was closest to the camera. It's probably the best view. I don't see anything in his hands."

Neither did I.

Gio spoke up. "The gun must be inside his pocket."

Pete nodded. "Could be."

Gio's tone turned testy. "Johnny said that Jones had a gun. Why don' you believe him?"

"I *do*. His story would be easier to verify with conclusive video evidence."

"What do you mean by 'story'? It's the truth."

I invoked my priest-voice. "Pete isn't suggesting that Johnny wasn't forthcoming, Gio. He's simply noting—correctly—that it would remove all doubt if we had a photo or video showing a gun in Jones's hand."

"And if we can't?"

"We'll have testimony from Sergeant Murphy, Officer Siragusa, and Officer Connor."

"And Johnny."

"Right." *He isn't going to testify unless we're desperate.* "Let's keep going."

Pete cued the security videos from Subway, the bagel store, Starbucks, the Korean grocery, the upscale Japanese restaurant, and the downscale currency exchange. Each was just a few seconds long. We saw Jones running. Johnny was about a half-block behind him, and Murphy brought up the rear. In super slow-mo, we had reasonably good looks at Jones from multiple cameras at various angles. While some of the shots were clearer than others, no gun was visible in either of Jones's hands.

Pete started another video. "This is from Charlie Connor's body cam."

When the video began, Connor was still in his police unit in front of the post office. The footage was distorted because it was hard to see over the steering wheel and the dashboard and through the windshield. It was raining hard and the windshield wipers were swishing. Jones was running toward Connor's car, eyes glowing in the headlights. The flashing red police lights reflected off the Fillmore Auditorium, creating a disco effect.

Using his microphone, Connor ordered Jones to halt. Jones stopped for an instant, considered his options, then leapt onto the metal gate in front of the parking lot and pulled himself over. A moment later, Johnny came into view and climbed over the gate. The video was shaky as Connor got out of his car and jogged over to the front of the lot as Murphy arrived. Siragusa showed up a few seconds later.

Pete stopped the video and looked at Gio. "Did you see a gun in Jones's hand?"

Gio's voice was barely audible. "No."

"Neither did I." Pete hit Play.

The next thing we heard was Murphy's voice. "Where did they go?"

Connor answered. "Inside the parking lot." Through the metal bars, I could see a postal van. I couldn't see Johnny, but I heard his voice.

"Put your hands up and don't move."

Jones's voice filled with desperation. "Don't shoot! I'm unarmed!"

"Put your hands over your head—now."

"Don't shoot! I'm unarmed! Unarmed!"

"Do exactly as I say, or I *will* shoot you. Understood?"

"Yes. Don't shoot! I'm unarmed!"

Pete's eyes were locked onto the screen. He stopped the video and walked up to the TV. He used his index finger to draw a circle above the roof of the postal van. "You can see Jones's hands."

I moved closer to the TV. I could make out two hands above the van. Jones was tall—at least six-six. There was no gun in either hand.

Pete continued the video. We still couldn't see Johnny, but we could hear him.

"I am ordering you to lie down on your stomach with your hands above your head and your legs spread."

"Don't shoot. I'm unarmed."

"Don't lie to me."

"I'm not lying."

"Yes, you are. Do as I say."

"Don't shoot."

"If you don't do as I say, I *will* shoot."

"Please, man."

"Lie down on your stomach with your hands above your head and your legs spread."

"Okay. Okay. I'm doing it. Don't shoot. I'm unarmed."

"Now!"

"I'm doing it! Don't shoot!"

It happened in a heartbeat. Jones's hands disappeared from view just before I heard four shots in rapid succession.

There was a tense silence. Murphy uttered a string of expletives. Then he added, "The kid shot him."

34
"YOU CAN SEE IT IN THE VIDEO"

Gio stared at the dark TV screen. "It was self-defense," he insisted, desperately wanting to believe his son.

"Yes, it was." *I'm not so sure.*

"Jones was reaching for a gun. You can see it in the video."

No, you can't. You're seeing what you want to see.

After watching the final seconds of Jones's life a dozen times in super slow-mo, it was clear that Johnny had fired the first shot immediately *after* Jones's hands had disappeared from view. It was impossible to see what was happening behind the postal van, and we couldn't see facial expressions from Johnny or Jones.

Was Jones obeying Johnny's order to lie down? Was he reaching for a gun?

I kept my tone measured. "Johnny said that Jones was reaching for the gun when he shot him. That's good enough for me." *For now.*

"Will it be good enough to convince a jury?"

I don't know. "It will have to be."

* * *

Pete sipped a Coke as he sat on the windowsill in my office. "You got a big problem, Mick. The prosecution is going to play that video and say that Jones was unarmed when Johnny shot him."

"We'll argue that he was reaching for a gun."

"You can't see it in the videos."

"Johnny and three other cops said he had a gun."

"Right."

"You going home?" I asked.

"I'm heading back to the Fillmore. I want to talk to some people."

I glanced at my watch. Ten-thirty p.m. "Maybe you should take the rest of the night off. It's dangerous out there."

"The protesters went home. Nobody's going to stay out all night in the rain."

"Except you."

"I'm working." He zipped his jacket. "We need a witness to testify that Jones had a gun."

"Murphy will do it. So will Siragusa and Connor. If all else fails, Johnny will."

"We need somebody who *isn't* a cop."

He was right. "You want company?"

"No."

* * *

Luca was sitting behind his mahogany desk, jacket off, tie loosened. At eleven p.m., the only illumination came from a brass lamp. He was sipping single-malt Scotch. His melancholy mood matched the drizzle outside. "What's your take on the video, Mike?"

"Inconclusive. We'll argue that Jones was reaching for a gun."

"You can't see a gun in Jones's hands."

"It must have been inside his pocket."

"Jones said that he didn't have a gun. He repeated it several times."

"Johnny said that he did. So did Murphy. And Siragusa. And Connor."

"They'll say that they were lying. They'll say that the gun was planted."

"We have four witnesses who will say that it wasn't."

"They're all cops. They'll argue they're covering for each other."

Yes, they will. "We'll argue that they weren't. Either way, it's still an uphill climb for the D.A. to get twelve people convinced beyond reasonable doubt on a murder charge."

"Depends on the jury and the lawyers."

True. "We're just getting started, Luca."

"Johnny can't stay in jail. And he absolutely can't be convicted. It will kill him. And it will kill Gio and Maria."

"We're a long way from a conviction."

"I sure as hell hope so. You still planning to do a full prelim?"

"Yes. It will let us see the evidence and give us an idea of the D.A.'s strategy."

"Can you get the charges dropped?"

Unlikely. "Depends on what we find between now and Monday."

35
"LET ME DO MY JOB"

"Any trouble?" I asked.

"Not in the last couple of hours." Pete was less than enthusiastic to see me at twelve-thirty on Friday morning. "There's a police unit on every corner. The protesters went home."

"That's good."

"They'll be back."

His Crown Vic was parked in the Safeway lot not far from the spot where Johnny had pulled over Jones two nights earlier. The plaza was empty. The rain was pounding.

He took a sip of coffee from a canteen bearing the logo of his alma mater, San Francisco State. "I'm trying to find people who were on the street on Wednesday morning. Everybody disappears when it rains."

"It'll stop sooner or later. Heard anything from Dwayne?"

"No." His lips turned down. "Why are you here, Mick?"

"Luca is worried." *So am I.*

"Let me do my job." He finally looked at me. "Give me a little space. If Jones had a gun, somebody must have seen it. If they did, I'll find them."

He would. "I'll let you get back to work."

"Thanks. I heard about the window in your car. How you planning to get home?"

"Same way I got here: Lyft."

"Since when does a luddite like you know how to call Lyft?"

"Tommy set me up. When I need tech support, I go to my twelve-year-old."

"Keeps you young, Mick."

* * *

Roosevelt's baritone was tired. "Where are you, Mike?"

"The Golden Gate Bridge. You?"

"Home."

I was surprised. "All quiet in the Fillmore?"

"For now. Jones's funeral is tomorrow. We're expecting trouble. Why did you call?"

"Checking in." He was the only homicide inspector that I would have considered calling at this hour. "Got anything that you didn't already send over?"

"This is where I'm supposed to tell you to read my report."

"I did. Did any of your witnesses mention that Jones had a gun?"

"Just your client, Sergeant Murphy, Officer Siragusa, and Officer Connor. We couldn't verify their stories or see it in the video."

"You think they're lying?"

"I'm just summarizing information in my report. Your client and Sergeant Murphy also told us that they found a weapon under Jones's body. We have not been able to confirm how it got there."

"Are you suggesting that it was planted?"

"I'm not suggesting anything. Did you watch the videos?"

"Yes."

"Did you see a gun?"

"Hard to tell."

"Come on, Mike."

"You have an obligation to provide any evidence that may tend to exonerate my client."

"You have everything that I have."

"Does this mean that Harper is planning to argue that the gun was planted?"

"You'll have to ask him. For what it's worth, I think your client is in serious trouble."

So do I.

* * *

Rosie's name appeared on my iPhone as the Lyft was driving north on 101 through Mill Valley.

"Why are you up?" I asked.

"Tommy was working on a project. Then Mama got chatty."

"Is she okay?"

"Yes. I've been thinking about your case."

"You should let *me* think about it."

"Why don't you stop by the house for a few minutes?"

"I'm on my way."

36
"THIS ISN'T GOING TO END WELL"

Rosie took off her glasses and invoked the voice of cold, hard reality. "You saw the videos, Mike. This isn't going to end well."

"It was self-defense."

"That's not what they're saying on TV. CNN has already convicted him."

"They're wrong."

We were sitting on the sofa in her living room at one o'clock on Friday morning. The TV was tuned to CNN, the sound low. Tommy was asleep. Rosie's mother was in the bedroom. I suspected that she was probably still awake.

Rosie pointed at the TV. "They got a copy of Connor's body cam video. It's already on YouTube, Facebook, and Twitter. They're saying that Johnny shot an unarmed kid."

"People see what they want. Some will say that he acted in self-defense. The rest will call it an execution. The only person whose opinion matters is Judge Ramsey."

"No pressure, but it's your job to find the truth."

No, it's my job to get Johnny off. "They found a gun under Jones's body."

"The D.A. will say it was planted. You can't see a gun in Jones's hands in the videos."

"It must have been inside his pocket."

"Says who?"

"Me."

"Your opinion doesn't matter, and you can't testify."

CNN was showing the footage from Connor's body cam. They zoomed in on Jones's hands, visible above the postal van. Rosie picked up the remote and turned up the sound.

Anderson Cooper spoke to a retired FBI agent identified as an expert on firearms and ballistics. "What do you see here, Special Agent Fong?"

"The victim's hands are above his head. You'll note that there is no gun in either hand." He started the video and stopped it a half-second later. "Here's where he lowered his hands." He advanced it again and stopped it an instant later. "This is when the first shot was fired. It was less than a second after his hands disappeared. You will also recall that the victim stated several times that he was unarmed."

Cooper furrowed his brow. "What did you conclude?"

"There was no way that the victim could have drawn a weapon between the time he lowered his hands and the moment when the first shot was fired. Officer Bacigalupi shot an unarmed man."

"Are you saying that it was an execution?"

"I'm saying that the victim was unarmed when he was shot."

"SFPD sources told us that Officer Bacigalupi claimed that Mr. Jones was reaching for a gun."

"There is no evidence in this video."

"But you can't see what happened behind the postal van."

"That's true, Anderson. I suppose it's possible that Officer Bacigalupi *thought* that Mr. Jones was about to reach for a gun. We can't see Mr. Jones's face. We can't see a gun in his belt or his pocket. Obviously, the only person who would have known what Mr. Jones was thinking at the time was Mr. Jones."

"And he's dead."

Thanks for bringing it to our attention, Anderson.

Cooper cocked his head. "They found a gun underneath Mr. Jones's body. Wouldn't that lend credence to Officer Bacigalupi's claim that Mr. Jones was reaching for a weapon?"

"We have no idea how it got there."

"Are you suggesting that it was planted?"

"I deal only in evidence, Anderson."

Except when you're asked to speculate on cable. I grabbed the remote and turned down the sound. "We don't want this case to get to a jury."

Rosie nodded. "Then you'll need to get the charges dropped at the prelim. I presume that you're still planning to make a *Graham v. Connor* argument?"

"Yes."

"You'll say that Johnny saw a gun when he stopped Jones. He believed that Jones was still armed when he ordered him to lie down. And he thought that Jones was reaching for the gun, so he shot him."

"Correct."

"Except you can't see a gun in any of the videos."

"Doesn't matter."

"Yes, it does. Harper will claim that the gun was planted."

"He'll need to prove it beyond a reasonable doubt."

"Not at a prelim. You need video evidence that Jones had a gun. Or you need a witness."

"We have three: Murphy, Siragusa, and Connor."

"Someone *other* than a cop."

That would help. "Pete's looking." I took a sip of Diet Dr Pepper. Rosie and my doctor limited my consumption to one can a week. "If all else fails, we'll put Johnny on the stand."

"You don't want to do that."

"We may have no choice. He may be the only person who can persuade Judge Ramsey that he reasonably believed that Jones was reaching for a gun."

"It may blow up in your face—especially since CNN's expert has already decided that Johnny is guilty."

We stared at the TV, where CNN was running highlights of the march to the Fillmore and the confrontation in front of the Fillmore

Auditorium.

"How many got hurt tonight?" I asked.

"About a dozen people, including a couple of cops."

"Anybody we know?"

"No." She lowered her voice. "They're planning another march tomorrow after Jones's funeral. Somebody could get killed. Maybe you should go on TV and calm everybody down."

"I can try, but it probably won't make a difference. The only surefire way to lower the temperature would be for Johnny to plead guilty or accept a plea bargain, which isn't going to happen."

She reached over and took my hand. "Do you want to stay tonight?"

"Yes, but I'd better go over to my place. I need a fresh set of clothes and I should try to answer some e-mails."

"Are you going to do the steps in the morning?"

"I think I'll give myself the day off."

"Zvi will be disappointed."

"I'll see him over the weekend."

"Is there anything I can do to make your life a little easier?"

As if you haven't done enough already. "I could use a ride into the City in the morning. My car is in the shop to get the window fixed, and I didn't have time to arrange for a rental."

"Done."

37
"I'M SURE"

Johnny's bloodshot eyes indicated that he hadn't slept. "Can you get me out of here?"

No. "Not yet."

"When?"

"We've submitted a motion to reconsider bail. We may hear something today or tomorrow. More likely early next week."

"What are the chances?"

Non-existent. "It's up to the judge."

He slumped back into his chair.

At nine-fifteen on Friday morning, we were meeting in the musty consultation room down the hall from the intake center in the jail wing of the Hall. The air smelled of perspiration. The bags under Johnny's eyes had become more pronounced overnight.

"Your dad is planning to come see you later today. Did they give you your own cell?"

"Yes. You need to get me out of here."

"Working on it. You look tired."

"I am."

"Are you sick?"

"No." His eyes focused on mine. "I heard there was trouble in the Fillmore last night."

"There was. Who told you?"

"A couple of guys who were arrested for starting the trouble."

Figures. "Some people got hurt—including a couple of cops. Did you hear anything else?"

"No."

"A little helpful information might get you a little better treatment."

"You sound like you're thinking about negotiating a plea bargain."

I'm not ruling it out. "Not at this time."

"Not at *any* time."

"Fine."

"Why did you come to see me?"

"We got the police reports and the videos. Murph's story was consistent with yours. He said that Jones had a gun and you shot him in self-defense. Siragusa and Connor said the same thing."

"That's good, right?"

"We looked at video from your body cam. You can't see a gun in Jones's hand."

"He had a gun, Mike. He knocked me over when he got out of the car. It probably wasn't visible from my body cam."

"We also saw video from Connor's body cam and a police camera on the plaza, and security videos from stores on Fillmore. You can't see a gun in Jones's hand in any of them."

"It was dark."

Not that dark.

His eyes narrowed. "He must have put it inside his pocket."

"It would help if somebody other than police officers can testify that Jones had a gun."

"Murph found it under Jones's body."

"Okay." I cleared my throat. "Connor was standing outside the parking lot when Jones was shot. His body cam recorded video and audio of what happened inside. You can't see much because you and Jones were behind a postal van."

"What *can* you see?"

"Jones's hands above the van." I waited a beat. "You can't see a gun in either hand."

"He reached for a gun."

"His hands dropped below the roof of the postal van and out of sight less than a second before you fired the first shot. The prosecutors are going to say that there wasn't enough time for him to have reached down and pulled a gun."

"He was *going* to pull a gun."

"How do you know?"

"He looked down."

"You can't see his eyes in the video."

"You don't believe me?"

"Yes, I do."

"But you think the prosecutors are going to say that I shot him and planted the gun?"

I answered him honestly. "I think that's where we're heading. The optics are bad."

"That's crap, Mike. Murph saw the gun. So did Goose and Connor. And so did I."

"It would help if we can find somebody other than three cops to corroborate your story."

He didn't answer.

"There's something else," I said. "In the audio portion of the footage from Connor's body cam, Jones says that he's unarmed."

"He was lying."

"He said it more than once—while his hands were up."

Johnny's tone was emphatic. "He was lying. He was about to draw his weapon."

"You were the only witness."

"Fine. I'll testify."

"That's a bad idea."

"You got any better ideas?"

At the moment, no.

* * *

My iPhone vibrated as I was walking through the lobby of the Hall at ten o'clock on Friday morning. Pete's name appeared on the display.

"Where are you?" I asked.

"Down the block from First Union Baptist Church. The funeral starts at noon."

He was three blocks south of the Safeway in the Fillmore. "What's going on?"

"A big crowd marched over here from Civic Center."

"Peaceful?"

"So far. The church is full. The streets are packed. The cops blocked off the area around the church. There's a pro-cop group at Jefferson Square. There's a Black Lives Matter gathering at Kimbell Park. According to the police radio, there are some white supremacist nutcases over by Alamo Square. The cops have done a good job of keeping everybody separated—for now."

He still viewed the world through the prism of a cop. "You should get out of there."

"I want to see what happens."

"You want company?"

"There's nothing you can do down here."

38
"A GREAT AND UNNECESSARY TRAGEDY"

Luca's conference room was silent except for the rain pelting against the windows and the organ music from the TV. Luca, Nady, and I were awaiting the start of Jones's funeral.

Luca sipped coffee from a china cup. "Is Pete still down in the Fillmore?"

"Yes."

"You think that's a good idea?"

"At the moment, no."

Jones's funeral was being carried on local TV and cable. Two days earlier, he had been an unknown young man from the neighborhood. Now he was an international celebrity.

CNN was showing the obligatory split screen. On the left was the podium inside First Union Baptist Church. On the right was an aerial view of the Fillmore. Even in a heavy drizzle, the streets were filled. Many cupped their hands over candles. CNN cut back and forth between the pro-cop assembly at Jefferson Square and the Black Lives Matter gathering at Kimbell Park. They had decided not to give airtime to the white supremacists in Alamo Square.

I texted Pete to find out where he was. The reply came back immediately. "Across the street from the church. All calm so far. Lots of police."

"Get out of there," I texted.

"Soon."

The sooner the better. I closed my eyes and recalled the days when I was a kid and our family sat together in church—first at St. Peter's in the Mission, and later at St. Anne's in the Sunset. We always sat in the same order: my dad, my older brother, Tommy, me, Pete, my baby sister, Mary, who became a kindergarten teacher in L.A., and my mom. I was the only sibling who liked going to church, and I still did. It was spiritual. It had rules. And it was God's house. I decided to become a priest after we lost Tommy in Vietnam, but I didn't find any answers. I didn't get to church as often as I used to, but I liked to think that I was still a pretty good Catholic.

I opened my eyes and looked at the TV. The organist was playing a funeral dirge. Reverend Tucker and Jones's mother led a procession toward the altar. Vanessa Jones was wearing sunglasses and a black dress. It reminded me of my days as a baby priest at St. Anne's, where the low priest in the pecking order always drew funeral duty. I dreaded funerals. I always thought that I never provided much comfort to the mourners. Ironically, in my final review, an older priest told me that one of the few things at which I had excelled was conducting funerals. It seemed that our parishioners liked my graveside manner. Go figure.

Everybody stood as Reverend Tucker strode to the lectern, his white hair and trim beard matching his flowing robe. He motioned the congregation to sit down. He closed his eyes and grasped the podium, as if he was meditating. He opened his eyes and scanned his flock.

The commentator from CNN interrupted. "You are watching live coverage of the funeral of Juwon Jones, the young man who was shot to death by a San Francisco police officer early Wednesday morning."

Thanks for telling us what we could already see. For those of us who didn't trust our eyes, we could also read about it on the crawl at the bottom of the screen.

Reverend Tucker's voice was muted as he recited Psalm 23, which I still knew by heart.

The Lord is my shepherd; I shall not want.
In verdant pastures he gives me repose;
beside restful waters he leads me;
He refreshes my soul.
He guides me in right paths for His name's sake.
Even though I walk in the dark valley I fear no evil;
for you are at my side with your rod and your staff that give me
     courage.
You spread the table before me in the sight of my enemies;
you anoint my head with oil;
my cup overflows.
Only goodness and kindness follow me all the days of my life;
and I shall dwell in the house of the Lord for years to come.

Reverend Tucker led a hymn. Then he took off his glasses and spoke without notes. "My friends, we come here today to celebrate the life of Juwon Jones, who was taken from us suddenly and violently on Wednesday. He was only eighteen." He turned and spoke to Jones's mother. "It is a great and unnecessary tragedy. A beautiful life snuffed out just as it was getting started. A mother who must bear unthinkable heartbreak. We cannot change this horrible and all-too-common occurrence. But we must comfort Juwon's mother, along with her family and friends. We have heavy hearts, but we are grateful for Juwon's life, however short. He will live forever in our memories. He was a kind and gentle soul with a big smile and an enormous heart."

Luca muttered, "Except for the twelve AK-47s in the trunk of his car."

I exchanged a glance at Nady, who looked down at her laptop.

Reverend Tucker spoke about Jones's accomplishments. Overcoming the odds after his father had left home when he was a baby. A good student at Gateway High. Varsity basketball. A part-time job at McDonald's followed by a full-time job at Jack-in-the Box. He was saving for college. He wanted to go to law school.

Luca's expression was cool, but his tone turned angry. "What about the arrests? What about the probation violation? What about the AK-47s? What about the pistol that they found under his body? He's making this gangbanger sound like a saint."

I let it go. Nady didn't look up.

Tucker's voice became louder. "My friends, Juwon's fate has become too common for young black people. Too many have been gunned down in the streets of our cities—in too many cases, by police officers. We have an epidemic of violence that needs to stop."

Shouts of "Amen."

"We need to make our voices heard. We need to be loud. And clear. And united."

Somebody shouted, "We need to take revenge!"

There was a smattering of applause.

Tucker raised a hand and the church fell silent. "Violence is not the answer. I will never advocate it or condone it from this pulpit. In this church, we take our cues from our lord and savior and from Dr. King."

Another voice rang out. "Look what nonviolence has gotten us! The police are killing our kids in the streets. It isn't enough to talk. We need to take action."

"And we will," Tucker said. "But nothing is resolved by violence."

"What would you have us do?"

Tucker looked into the TV camera. "To the people in Jefferson Square who are assembled in support of the police, we want you to know that we love you, we respect you, and we want to reach out and start a dialogue. To those in Alamo Square, we want you to know that we love you, too, even though we believe that your rhetoric is hateful and counterproductive. We want to talk to you, too, because we are all God's children, and we have more in common than we do not."

There was a mixture of applause and groans.

Tucker spoke passionately for another twenty minutes, calling upon the congregation to act forcefully, but peacefully. His tone turned philosophical. "More than a hundred and fifty years ago, this country fought a great Civil War where hundreds of thousands of people died because we could not come to a common understanding about race. In some respects, I think we're still fighting that war. It's time for Christian-minded people of all races, religions, and ethnicities to celebrate our differences and everything that we have in common. That would be a positive legacy for this great tragedy. That's how we can celebrate Juwon's life, even though it ended so tragically. We cannot bring him back, but in his honor and memory, let us try to lead our lives in a more thoughtful and understanding manner."

He faced Jones's mother. "Vanessa, we are sorry for your loss. May it ease your pain knowing that Juwon is in heaven and that his spirit is an inspiration to all of us. May you find comfort in your hour of mourning, and may your son rest in eternal peace."

He led the congregation in a final hymn, and the church started to empty. Luca turned off the TV. His voice was barely audible. "He spoke nicely."

"He did."

"I feel for his mother."

"So do I."

"What do we do next?"

"Nady and I are working on additional document requests. We're starting to work on our presentation at the prelim."

My iPhone vibrated. Pete's name appeared on the display.

"Where are you?" I asked.

His voice was agitated. "Down the street from the church. Are you watching the funeral?"

"We just turned it off."

"Turn it back on. Somebody just shot two cops in front of the church."

39
"LOOKS BAD"

Pete's voice was tense. "Looks bad, Mick."

"Get out of there, Pete."

"I'm going."

I was in Luca's conference room. CNN was showing footage of the chaos in front of the church. The hearse carrying Jones's body was still parked near the front steps. People were pushing through the mob. Anderson Cooper reported that shots had been fired at police.

"Did they catch the shooter?" I asked.

Pete's voice was strained. "The cops shot him." He started talking faster. "People are throwing stuff at the cops. Now the cops are hitting people."

"Get out of there."

"They're shooting tear gas."

"Get out of there!"

He shouted, "Did you see that? Did you see that?"

"What?"

"Somebody just drove a car into the crowd! He hit about a dozen people! He's mowing people down! He's still going! Now he's stopped, and people are pounding on the windows. They just pulled him out of the car and they're beating the crap out of him. It's out of control, Mick! I'm getting out of here."

"Call me back when you're safe, Pete."

The line went dead.

Luca, Nady, and I sat in silence as we watched the bedlam on TV. Bodies were strewn on the street. Two cops were down. The air filled with a haze of tear gas. People were throwing bottles. Cars were overturned and set on fire. Police in riot gear were pelted with debris. Sirens blared. Smoke rose. People covered their faces and ran.

It was a full-blown riot.

I punched in Pete's number again. It went straight to voicemail. I left a message.

Rosie phoned in. "Are you watching what's going on in the Fillmore?" she asked.

"Yeah."

"Is Pete down there?"

"He's on his way back."

"Is he okay?"

"He was five minutes ago."

"Call me as soon as you hear from him."

It was surreal watching the riots on TV from the comfort of Luca's conference room. I texted Pete every five minutes. No response. My stomach churned.

CNN repeated unconfirmed reports that two police officers had died. Two more were wounded and taken to San Francisco General. The shooter had been killed by police. No word on his identity.

Channel 2 reported that at least a dozen people had been hit by the car that plowed into the crowd in front of the church. There were no confirmed casualties—yet. The driver had been captured and taken to the hospital. He had been badly beaten. No word on whether he was still alive. The aerial shot looked like a war zone.

A distraught Reverend Tucker was interviewed on Channel 2. Visibly shaken and trying to contain his anger, he implored everybody to stay calm, go home, and let the first responders do their jobs. "This is a House of God. This is not how we act in our community."

Forty minutes later, Pete's name appeared on my iPhone. "You okay?" I asked.

"Fine, Mick." He apologized for not calling sooner. "My battery ran out."

Relief. "Where are you?"

"St. Mary's."

The majestic Cathedral of Saint Mary of the Assumption was the mother ship of the San Francisco Archdiocese. "Why St. Mary's?"

"I figured the cops wouldn't shoot tear gas into a church." He chuckled nervously. "When you were a priest, you always used to say that when the going gets tough, you should go to church."

I was too relieved to have a glib retort. "Come down to Luca's office."

"I'll see you in an hour."

40
"YOU CAN'T GO BACK DOWN THERE"

"You smell like tear gas," I said.

Pete smirked. "How would you know?"

"I went to college in Berkeley."

"You were there *after* Vietnam."

"We had other things to protest."

"You were a third-rate protester, Mick. We had more excitement over at San Francisco State. You never even got yourself arrested."

I hadn't expected to hear my ex-cop law-and-order younger brother bragging about the time he got hauled in for breaking a window during a sit-in at State. Our dad enlisted Johnny's grandfather to pull strings to get the charges dropped.

"I always got away before the cops caught me," I explained.

"That's because you were never in the middle of the action."

Not true. "I think it had more to do with the fact that I could run fast."

We were sitting in my office at Luca's firm at three-fifteen on Friday afternoon. This was undoubtedly the first time that the aroma of tear gas had wafted through the hallowed hallways of Luca Bacigalupi and Associates, LLP.

I lowered my voice. "You okay?"

"Yeah."

"How close were you to the shooting?"

"Too close."

"Do you know either of the officers who were killed?"

"No, but I know one of the guys who was wounded. He's going to be okay."

"That's good."

"I guess."

"Did they identify the shooter?"

"Yeah. An angry kid from the neighborhood who decided to take out a couple of cops."

"Any connection to Jones?"

"I don't know. Does it matter?"

"Not really. Four people were killed by the guy in the car." I told him that twenty people had been injured, some seriously.

Pete's mustache twitched. "The driver was a white supremacist nut-job. The cops shot him dead after the people pulled him out of the car and beat the crap out of him." Pete lowered his voice. "It's probably better that he died."

It wasn't my proudest Christian thought, but I agreed. The last thing we needed was a drawn-out trial of a racist crackpot.

He wasn't finished. "You watch, Mick. Somebody is going to claim that SFPD violated the guy's constitutional right of free speech."

"Your right to express yourself stops when you start killing people."

"You would hope so."

"They called in the National Guard. The mayor announced an eight p.m. curfew. That should help."

Pete scowled. "Realistically, if somebody with an AK-47 wants to shoot a bunch of people, it'll take more than an army of cops and an early curfew to stop them. SFPD has a unit on every corner in the Fillmore. They're sitting ducks."

"You got any better ideas?"

"At the moment, no. If they keep people out of the Fillmore, they'll go down to Civic Center or the Ferry Building or Union Square. There aren't enough cops and National Guard in California to cut off every public space in San Francisco. Reverend Tucker is going to lead another march tonight. Black Lives Matter is gathering in Golden Gate Park. You can bet the white supremacists will show up somewhere. It's a mess, Mick. It isn't going to end soon."

"We can't just lock up the City."

"Might not be a bad idea for a while." He exhaled. "You still think it's a good idea to start Johnny's prelim on Monday?"

"It's the only chance that we can get the charges dropped quickly."

"Maybe you should ask for a continuance until things calm down" He stood and headed for the door. "I'll call you later. I'm going to get rid of these clothes and take a shower."

"Good plan."

"And then I'm heading back down to the Fillmore."

Bad plan. "It's too dangerous."

"There's a cop on every corner."

"You aren't going to find any witnesses. Nobody will be outside."

The corner of his mouth turned up. "I'm very resourceful."

* * *

The display on my iPhone read, "SF DA." I touched the green button. "Mike Daley."

"DeSean Harper."

What a pleasant surprise. "I'm still waiting for your witness list for the prelim."

"Working on it." He hesitated. "Can you come over to our office for a few minutes?"

Now what? "Sure. When?"

"Now."

41
"TAKE THE DEAL"

The District Attorney of the City and County of San Francisco was standing next to the window in her office, a Wedgewood tumbler in her hand. Nicole Ward looked out at the rain, exhaled heavily, and turned around to face me. As always, her wardrobe, hair, and makeup were prefect, but her tone was uncharacteristically subdued. "Thanks for coming in on short notice."

"You're welcome." Nady was sitting in the chair next to mine. We waited.

Ward took a sip of Perrier, adjusted her cashmere jacket, and took a seat in the high-back leather chair. She pointed a delicate finger at Harper, who was sitting in the side chair near the window. "It's been a challenging couple of days for DeSean and me."

And me. And Nady. And Johnny. "Did you get an ID on the guy who shot the cops?"

"Yes. He lived in the neighborhood. He had a criminal record from here to Modesto. He'd posted on social media that he wanted to take out some cops."

"Did he know Jones?"

"We don't know. At least we won't have to prosecute him for murder."

"You have other things to keep you busy. What about the guy who ran over the people in front of the church?"

"He was on the FBI's radar. He'd been spotted at rallies in other parts of the country. He'd been arrested a couple of times, but the charges never stuck."

190

"You won't have to prosecute him for murder, either."

"That's little comfort for the families of the victims." She gave me a thoughtful look. "You used to be a priest. What would you tell them?"

I hadn't anticipated the question. "Unfortunately, there are some bad people in the world. If you're unlucky and cross their path, sometimes bad things happen for no apparent reason."

"That doesn't sound very forgiving for a priest."

"Maybe that's why I'm an ex-priest. The 'Everything happens for a reason' line never worked very well for me."

"How did you comfort them?"

Her question seemed genuine. "Words are inadequate. The best that you can do is to tell them that you're sorry for their loss."

"Thank you."

"You're welcome." I waited a beat. "Why did you and DeSean want to talk to us?"

"We wanted to discuss the prelim. We've provided all of the police reports, video, and other evidence."

"We're still waiting for your witness list."

"We'll get it over to you tonight. It will be short."

Figures. "Are you planning to object to any of our motions?"

"All of them."

I wasn't surprised. "Even our motion *not* to have the prelim televised?"

"The public has a right to see what goes on in court."

"It will just inflame tensions."

"It would be worse to do it in secret. People will think we're trying to hide something."

"People play to the cameras."

Harper finally spoke up. "I won't."

"Your witnesses will. They always do. It distorts the truth."

"The truth is going to come out, Mike. It would be better if your client owns up now."

"He shot an armed man in self-defense. Jones fled the scene of a crime."

"A broken tail light isn't a crime."

"He had a probation violation. Johnny had a legitimate right to ask him to get out of the car. Jones knocked him over, flashed a gun, and fled."

"There's no gun in the video."

"There was a gun under his body."

"Your client and his partner planted it."

"You'll need to prove that beyond a reasonable doubt."

"Not at the prelim."

True. I turned to face Ward. "Why did you really want to see us, Nicole?"

"Given the circumstances, DeSean and I thought it might be a good idea to try to find a way to dial down the temperature outside."

"I'm all for it. What did you have in mind?"

"At the very least, we think it makes sense to delay the prelim for a week or two to let things calm down."

"Are you also prepared to reconsider your position on bail?"

"I'm afraid not."

"Johnny isn't a flight risk."

"It would set an unworkable precedent to agree to bail in an officer-involved shooting."

"I'm not going to let my client sit in jail for a couple of extra weeks so that you can avoid an unworkable precedent."

"Be reasonable, Mike."

"If you won't change your unreasonable view on bail, then I'm not going to change my view on timing."

"The protesters will be lined up on Bryant Street."

"The police will deal with it."

"They already have their hands full. More people are going to get hurt, Mike."

Probably. "My client has a legal right to a prelim within ten court days of his arraignment. The judge will be ready to go on

Monday. So will we."

"Fine." Ward clasped her fingers. "We'd like to discuss another possibility."

"I'm listening."

"We're going to take an enormous amount of heat for this, but DeSean and I are prepared to make you a one-time offer for a plea of voluntary manslaughter."

Things just got interesting. First-degree murder carried a minimum sentence of twenty-five years. Since Johnny used a gun, there would be an enhancement of an additional twenty-five years, resulting in a minimum sentence of fifty years. Not an attractive option. Second-degree had a minimum sentence of fifteen years, which was better, but not great. Voluntary manslaughter had a minimum sentence of three years and a maximum of eleven, and required a minimum service time of eighty-five percent of the sentence, which meant that in theory, Johnny could be out in about two and a half years. "What did you have in mind?"

"DeSean is going to kill me, but I'm prepared to recommend a sentence of three years with a chance for parole after serving eighty-five percent. Your client would, of course, have to resign from SFPD. This matter would be resolved when he's twenty-five. It's a generous deal, Mike."

Yes, it is. I kept my reaction in check, but we were now in the realm of possibility—except for the fact that Johnny would have to plead guilty to a crime, spend time in jail, and find a new career. And he would be tarred for life with a criminal record.

I decided to probe. "We might be receptive to a deal for involuntary manslaughter." On a three-year sentence, Johnny would have been eligible for parole after only eighteen months.

"That's not going to work, Mike."

"I'll talk to my client."

"We'll need your answer by five p.m. on Sunday." Her tone turned somber. "People are killing each other on the streets. We had a massacre in front of a church. This will calm everybody down."

Maybe. "I'll talk to Johnny."

"Take the deal."

She was pushing a little too hard. "We'll get back to you as soon as we can."

* * *

Nady's tone was hushed. "Does that always happen?"

"It isn't unusual to discuss a plea bargain at some point in most cases."

We were in the waiting area of the jail wing of the Hall at five-thirty on Friday evening. A deputy was bringing Johnny to the consultation room. It was quiet. The Friday night rush wouldn't start for a couple of hours.

Nady frowned. "Ward seemed intent on cutting a deal."

"People are marching in the streets. Two cops were shot. A crackpot ran down a dozen people in front of a church. This isn't normal."

"You think a plea bargain will dial things down?"

"Hard to say. If people think Johnny is getting off easy, it could make matters worse."

"You think it's a good deal, Mike?"

"Do you?"

She thought about it for a moment. "Yes, but I asked you first."

"If I thought Johnny had committed murder, it would be a great deal. It would minimize his sentence and resolve his case."

"Do you think he did?"

"No."

"Do you think he should take the deal anyway?"

I thought about it for a moment. "Probably not, but we have a legal obligation to tell him about it."

42
"I'M NOT PLEADING GUILTY"

Johnny's response was succinct. "No deal."

The fluorescent light flickered in the consultation room at five-forty on Friday evening. Johnny's expression was resolute. So was Nady's.

I kept my voice even. "You might want to think about it."

"I'm not pleading guilty. Why are you so hot to take a deal?"

"I'm just presenting options."

"You think I'm guilty."

"No, I don't."

"Then why are we talking about this?"

"I have a legal obligation to tell you about plea bargain offers presented by the D.A. My job is to help you balance the benefits and the risks. If you accept the deal, the D.A. will recommend the minimum sentence of three years. With good behavior, you'll be out after serving only eighty-five percent of the sentence, which means that you should be released in a little over two and a half years. It provides certainty."

"And if I don't?"

"If you're convicted of first-degree murder, the minimum sentence is twenty-five years. Since Jones died of a gunshot wound, that would tack on an additional twenty-five-year enhancement. And it could be longer."

"Not good."

"Not good at all. Two and a half years is a lot shorter than fifty."

"It was self-defense."

"I know, but it's easier to convince me than a jury."

"Jones had a gun. I saw it. So did Murph. And Goose and Charlie. Murph and I found it under the body."

"You can't see it in the videos. Murphy, Siragusa, and Connor will testify that they saw it, but the prosecution will try to discredit them because they're cops."

"Then I'll testify that I saw it."

"They'll say that you're lying to protect yourself. Harper will go after you. Bad things happen when defendants get on the stand."

"I can hold my own."

"It's too risky."

"It's *my* life. If I don't stick up for myself, who will?"

A very legitimate point. "We'll consider the possibility if we get to trial."

"You're going to get the charges dropped at the prelim."

"I can't make that promise."

"Then you need to make it happen."

* * *

Nady's voice was subdued as we sat in the back of the Lyft on our way to the office. "That didn't go very well, did it?"

"About what I expected. Plea bargains are never satisfying. If Johnny accepts the deal, he's still going to jail—albeit for a shorter time. And he'll lose his job and have a criminal record."

"And if he fights it?"

"We need to be realistic, Nady. Even if he's acquitted, he can't go back to SFPD, and it will be hard to find another job in law enforcement. For that matter, it won't be easy to find *any* job. He's a celebrity now. Most businesses don't want to deal with it. Do you think Luca would hire somebody who was acquitted of murder?"

"Probably not. Do you think he should take the deal?"

I watched the wipers swish as we headed north on Sixth Street.

"At the moment, no. Let's see where we are on Sunday."

"If you were in his shoes, what would you do?"

"I'd probably fight it. At the end of the day, your most valuable asset is your reputation. If he takes the deal, he'd be a convicted felon. He'd have to live with that for the rest of his life."

* * *

Gio was sitting in one of the cushy chairs in Luca's conference room at eight-thirty on Friday night. "I heard you saw Johnny," he said.

"I did. He's okay, Gio."

"They won't let me see him."

"I'll get you inside tomorrow."

"How?"

I don't know. "I'll find a way. How are you and Maria holding up?"

"Fair."

I looked into my old friend's tired eyes. "You guys solid?"

His lips formed a tight line across his face. "Yeah."

Like all couples, they'd had their ups and downs. I don't think either of them ever cheated. People who meet in high school change over the years. Sometimes, they grow apart. As far as I could tell, Gio and Maria hadn't.

"Anything I can do?"

"Get our son out of jail."

"We're doing everything that we can." This platitude was never satisfying.

"Do it faster."

"Ward and Harper offered a deal for voluntary manslaughter." I filled him in on the details.

He was unimpressed. "No."

"It's a good deal, Gio."

"It's out of the question. My son is not going to plead guilty to a crime that he didn't commit. It would destroy his future."

And that's that.

I looked at the TV. CNN was showing footage of the protests earlier in the evening. It seemed like a week had passed since Jones's funeral. They switched to the post office parking lot, where two police officers were guarding a make-shift memorial of dozens of floral arrangements wilting in the rain.

"Looks quiet," I said.

"For now." His voice filled with resignation. "Two good cops are dead. Two more are in the hospital. The shooter is dead. So are four civilians. And the asshole who drove into them. They've been marching in the streets for two days, and I can't do anything about it."

"It's better if you take a little time off, Gio."

"I have no choice. The chief told me to stay home."

It's the right call. "You have enough on your plate with Johnny."

"I feel helpless, Mike. I can't do anything for Johnny, and I can't stop the riots."

"I'll take care of Johnny. SFPD will take care of the streets."

"Is there anything that I *can* do?"

I took a moment to think. "I need you to tap your sources to help Pete find somebody who can testify that Jones pulled a gun on Johnny. Better yet, we need video footage. Pete is looking for witnesses, but he doesn't have great sources in the Fillmore, and the streets are empty because of the curfew. You know the undercover cops at Northern Station who know the people on the street. Maybe they can point you in the right direction. And if you're with Pete, the cops won't send him home for violating the curfew."

"I'm off-duty."

"You're an assistant chief. If you walk down Fillmore Street with Pete, nobody will bother you."

For the first time in a couple of days, there was light in Gio's eyes. He pulled on his jacket. "Tell Pete that I'll meet him in front of the Boom-Boom Room in twenty minutes."

* * *

An ashen-faced Luca Bacigalupi appeared in the doorway. "Where's my brother?"

"With my brother. He went to the Fillmore to help Pete look for witnesses."

"You think that's a good idea?"

"Gio knows the neighborhood. And it gives him something productive to do."

"I understand the D.A. offered a plea deal."

"She did. Voluntary manslaughter with a recommendation of a three-year sentence. With good behavior, Johnny would be out in thirty and a half months. It's a lot better than a minimum of fifty years for first-degree murder. I explained it to Johnny. He said no. So did Gio."

"We should give it a little more thought. I just got a call from Paula Griffith at the City Attorney's Office. They've agreed with Jones's mother on a settlement of the civil case."

43
"THEY'RE TRYING TO SQUEEZE US"

"How much?" I asked.

"A million," Luca said.

More than I might have thought. "Admission of liability?"

"No. Jones's mother wants her money, the mayor wants resolution, and SFPD wants the riots to end. The settlement agreement will include a full release of the City."

"It won't include a release of Johnny. Confidential?"

"No." Luca's lips turned down. "The City can't do this in secret."

You're right. "They'll need approval from the Board of Supervisors."

"Already in the works."

"It doesn't eliminate the civil case against Johnny."

"No, it doesn't."

"They're trying to squeeze us into a settlement."

"Yes, they are." He finally stepped inside my office and took a seat. "How does this impact the criminal case?"

"Legally, it doesn't. The fact that the City and Jones's mother settle the civil case is irrelevant to our case and inadmissible as evidence."

"Is there a 'but' coming?"

"Yes. Everybody will know about it. It's going to make picking a jury more difficult. Jurors are supposed to disregard this stuff, but they're human. They'll know that the City caved and paid

Jones's mother a million bucks. They'll be predisposed against Johnny."

"At a minimum, we'll want to ask for a change of venue."

"Agreed. And we will. But unless we can change the venue to Mars, it's going to be hard to find people who don't know anything about this case."

"What would you suggest?"

I had no good answers. "Let's play it out."

* * *

"Do you ever sleep?" I asked.

Nady responded with a smile. "Not much."

It was ten-thirty on Friday night. She hadn't left the office in two days.

"You're going to have to learn to pace yourself if you're going to do defense work."

"Luca says the same thing about real estate work."

Not the same. "If you aren't careful, you're going to look like me when you're fifty-seven."

"I'm going to be retired."

I liked her attitude. "Maybe I should be getting advice from you."

She grinned. "Maybe you should."

I was sitting in her modest office next door to Luca's palatial corner space. Luca had six windows. Nady had one. She had ditched her professional attire for jeans and a Cal sweatshirt. I pointed at the photo of a handsome young man taken at the top of Mt. Tam. "Husband?"

"Boyfriend. Almost seven years. He does antitrust work for Story, Short & Thompson."

Dear God. It was a mega-firm in Embarcadero Center that spun off from the now-defunct firm where I had spent five miserable years after Rosie and I had gotten divorced. "I worked at their predecessor for a while."

"I wouldn't have figured."

In hindsight, I wouldn't, either. "Let's just say that it wasn't a good fit. Is your boyfriend going to stick it out to make partner?"

"Not clear. They just extended the partnership track."

"They tend to do that."

"If he can hang in for another year, he can pay off his student loans."

This was a substantial accomplishment. Nowadays, a year at Boalt cost more than my college and law school educations combined—even for California residents.

She asked, "Are you happy that you went back to the P.D.'s Office?"

"Yes. Are you happy working for Luca?"

"For the most part."

I pointed at the photo. "You planning to get married?"

"Eventually. It's hard to organize a wedding for two lawyers."

"Don't wait too long."

"We won't."

I left it there. Given my track record, I didn't feel comfortable giving people advice on their relationships. Fortunately, Grace always came to Rosie with boyfriend issues, and Tommy wasn't interested in girls—yet.

I moved to the matters at hand. "Did anything else come in from the D.A.'s Office?"

"More police reports. Nothing new." She said that she had gone through the videos again. "You can't see a gun in Jones's hand."

Crap. "Humor me and take another look. I'll do the same. In the meantime, please put Murphy, Siragusa, and Connor on our witness list. They'll testify that Jones had a gun."

"It would help if we can find somebody to corroborate their testimony."

True. "Pete and Gio are working on it."

"What about Johnny?"

"The conventional wisdom says that you shouldn't put your

client on the stand unless you're desperate."

"This isn't a conventional situation, and we're getting desperate."

Also true. "We'll decide over the weekend. Did the D.A. send over a witness list?"

"Yes. It's short. The medical examiner will confirm that Jones died from a gunshot wound. A ballistics expert will say that the bullets that killed Jones were fired from Johnny's service weapon. Roosevelt Johnson will probably present the videos and tie everything together."

"Murphy? Siragusa? Connor?"

"No."

I wasn't surprised. They were prepared to testify that Jones had a gun. This wouldn't help Ward and Harper.

Nady took off her glasses. "Who else should I include on our witness list?"

"Depends on Pete. Maybe one of the homeless guys on the plaza." I smiled. "Be sure to include Chief Green, Reverend Tucker, and the mayor."

"Seriously?"

"Just to tweak them. And we'll want to include Johnny's name."

"Are you really planning to put him on the stand?"

"No. But I want them to have to prepare for the possibility."

* * *

It was almost midnight when Luca knocked on my open door. "You're still here," he said.

"Yup. You going home soon?"

"In a few minutes."

"Anything new on the civil case?"

"No."

"Then I guess we'll resume our respective battles in the morning."

He held up a finger. "Rosie is here to see you."

I hadn't expected it. "Thanks."

He cleared his throat. "She brought somebody with her."

"Who?"

"Johnny's mother."

44
"HE DID IT FOR HIS FATHER"

Maria Bacigalupi's modulated tone couldn't camouflage the anguish in her eyes. "I'm sorry for coming in so late."

"No problem, Maria."

She was wearing a simple beige blouse and black slacks. Her subtle makeup was perfect. She reminded me of my mother, who spent countless nights waiting for my father to come home. Mama pretended to watch TV, but she glanced out the window every few seconds, hoping to see the headlights of my dad's Buick. The stresses of being a cop are well-documented. The stresses of being a cop's spouse are sometimes forgotten. The stresses of being a cop's mother are incomprehensible.

The Law Office of Luca Bacigalupi and Associates, LLP was silent. Rosie and Maria were sitting in the chairs opposite my desk. Nady was in her office. Luca had gone home.

I offered Maria a glass of water, which she accepted. She took a sip and grasped it tightly. "Thank you for seeing me."

"I'm always available for you, Maria. How are you and Gio holding up?"

"Not so good."

"What can I do?"

She looked at Rosie for an instant. "Gio doesn't know that I'm here."

"That's okay. He's down in the Fillmore with Pete."

"I know." She waited a beat. "Do you have to tell him that I came to see you?"

"No."

She was relieved.

"Are things okay between you and Gio?"

"Same as always."

You never know what goes on inside a marriage unless you're there. "Is that good?"

"For the most part. We've been married for almost forty years."

She was being a little cryptic. "Everybody goes through rough patches."

"We've had our share."

"Nothing insurmountable, I hope."

"No. It isn't as if Gio has cheated or is mean-spirited. He has a stressful job."

"Comes with the territory, I'm afraid."

"It doesn't help that I have seven sons who are also SFPD."

"My mom dealt with the same issues. You'll get through this. So will Gio and Johnny."

"How can you be so sure?"

"Things are never as bad as they seem."

"They're pretty bad right now, Mike."

"I know. Why did you want to talk to me, Maria?"

Her eyes narrowed. "My son is in jail and accused of murder— even though he shot an armed man who had fled the scene after a legitimate traffic stop. There were a dozen AK-47s in the trunk of his car. It doesn't take a Ph.D. from Cal to understand that Jones was going to use those guns to kill people."

She was right. She also needed to vent, so I let her keep talking.

"Now two police officers are dead. Gio and I knew them. We know their families. They died because they were trying to protect the rights of the person who shot them. It doesn't make any sense. How many more?"

I had no good answer. "Things will calm down."

"Not anytime soon. They're planning another march

tomorrow."

"The City won't issue a permit."

"That won't stop them."

"Then they'll be arrested."

"And they'll be out on bail the next day. And what about the crackpot who ran over those people in front of the church? The police can't stop something like that."

"They've called in the National Guard."

"There will never be enough cops and National Guard. Your view might be different if your father was still alive or if your brother was still a cop."

True. I reached over and touched her hand. "We're doing everything that we can, Maria. For now, I want you to focus on supporting Johnny, okay? I can't imagine how hard this is for you and Gio, but you can't do anything about what's going on in the streets. Does that make sense?"

"Yes." Her façade finally broke. Tears welled in her eyes. "They won't let me see him."

"I'll make arrangements for a visit over the weekend."

"Is there any chance that the judge will grant bail?"

"Probably not in the next couple of days. We'll try again on Monday at the prelim."

She dabbed her eyes. "Gio said that the D.A. offered a plea bargain."

"They did. Voluntary manslaughter. Three years with an opportunity for early release after two and a half."

Her eyes were clear. "Take it."

"Maria—,"

"You heard me. I want you to take the deal."

"Johnny would have to plead guilty. He would have a criminal record for the rest of his life."

"It's better than fifty years or more."

"He shot Jones in self-defense."

"I know, but it doesn't matter. Juries are unpredictable. It has to stop. I can't live like this."

"I talked to Johnny about it. He doesn't want to accept the deal."

"Then I need you to talk him into it."

"I can try, but I can't make any promises."

"You're very persuasive."

I wasn't so sure. "Gio was against a plea bargain, too."

"He's stubborn."

So are you. "It's Johnny's call. If he takes the deal, he'll lose his job, and he'll never get another one in law enforcement."

"I don't care." Her eyes narrowed. "And if you can get Johnny to tell you the truth, he doesn't care, either."

"What do you mean?"

She took a deep breath. "He never wanted to be a cop. He did it for his father."

I paused to process this new information. "How long have you known?"

"Forever."

It reminded me of Pete. My mom always said that he went to the Academy just to show our father that he was as tough as he was. "It's a demanding job for somebody who doesn't really want to do it." *It's also dangerous.*

"Gio can be very demanding."

"What did Johnny want to do?"

"He wanted to design video games. He did a couple of prototypes in college. I'm no expert, but his friends told me that they were pretty good."

I hadn't anticipated this wrinkle. "Does Gio know about this?"

"Yes."

"He was still okay with Johnny becoming a cop?"

"It's the family business. Besides, Gio thinks he knows what's best for everybody."

Interesting. "Did any of your other sons want to do something other than police work?"

"A couple." She shrugged. "It doesn't really matter anymore, does it?"

"I guess not."

"Use your influence with Johnny, Mike. I don't want to lose my son."

45
"WHERE DOES THAT LEAVE YOU?"

Rosie gripped the steering wheel of her Prius as we drove across the Golden Gate Bridge at one-thirty on Saturday morning. "Didn't see that coming," she said.

"Neither did I."

The rain had stopped, and I could see the twinkling lights of San Francisco in the distance. The reassuring beacon of Alcatraz rotated in the middle of the Bay in the middle of the night.

"Thanks for coming with Maria," I said.

"I didn't want her to be alone."

"You did the right thing. Did she say anything to you about Gio?"

"They aren't talking much."

"They're both under an insane amount of stress."

"I don't think they've ever really talked things out."

"People deal with things differently."

She nodded. "My parents handled things their own way. My dad never said much. And you know that my mom isn't shy about expressing her opinions."

"Indeed." We Daleys aired our grievances every night at the dinner table until my mom would declare a truce by informing us that she had heard enough complaining for one night.

"Where does that leave you?" she asked.

"I'll talk to Johnny about the plea deal again. I don't think he'll go for it."

"Would you take it?"

I answered her honestly. "Probably not. You know me—always the idealist. I don't like the idea of somebody confessing to a crime he didn't commit."

"Might be the best deal you're going to get. You still planning to start the prelim on Monday?"

"Unless Johnny changes his mind and takes the deal. For now, that's our only chance to stop this before we go to trial."

"What are the odds?"

"Not great."

Rosie reached over and touched my hand. "Any word from Pete?"

"No."

"Anything I can do to help?"

"If you have a little time on Sunday, I might want to run a few things by you for a reality check for the prelim."

"I'll make time."

Beautiful Rosie. "Thanks, Rosita."

"You're welcome. Are you planning to go see Johnny in the morning?"

"Yes, but I'm planning to go to Tommy's basketball game first. Johnny's case will still be there."

"So will the protesters."

"Nothing I can do about that."

"Doesn't it bother you?"

"Of course, but a very wise person once told me that it's a waste of time and energy to worry about things that you can't control."

"Who was that brilliant philosopher?"

"You."

46
"IT'S HARD TO SAY NO TO MY DAD"

Johnny's eyes gleamed. "I thought I made myself clear."

"Hear me out."

"No deal."

We were sitting on uncomfortable plastic chairs in a consultation room in the visitor area of the Hall at ten-thirty on Saturday morning. Reality had returned after I had watched Tommy's basketball team win in a rout. Tommy had scored fifteen points before the coach pulled him. I still had hopes that he might become the first member of the Daley family to dunk.

"Did your dad come to see you?" I asked.

"Yes. They finally let him inside."

"He's worried, Johnny. So is your mom. I'm going to try to get her a visitor pass tomorrow."

"That would be good."

"Your dad is over in the Fillmore with Pete looking for witnesses. There's going to be another march today."

His lips turned down. "I hope they can keep things under control."

"There will be a lot of cops."

"It just takes one crackpot with a gun."

True. "Did you know either of the officers who died?"

"No, but my dad did. They were good cops." His eyes turned down. "All this crap started because of a stupid traffic stop."

"Stuff happens, Johnny."

"Right."

"We can stop this tomorrow."

"I'm not taking a plea bargain."

"You'll be out in a maximum of three years. Less with good behavior. It's a good deal."

"It doesn't change anything. My dad would never forgive me if I take the deal. That's not how we roll."

I'm not so sure. I clenched my fist. "Your mother came to see me last night."

He paused. "Let me guess: she wants me to take the deal."

"Yes, she does."

"She's okay having her son plead guilty to murder?"

"Manslaughter. It resolves this case and caps your legal exposure."

"I'd be a convicted felon. And I would plead guilty to a crime that I didn't commit. I shot Jones in self-defense."

"I believe you."

"Do you?"

"Yes."

"Then why are you pushing so hard for me to take the deal?"

"For the same reason as your mother. You'll understand it better when you have children. You always err on the side of safety and predictability. That's why Rosie and I weren't crazy about it when Grace decided to be a film major at USC. We might have been a little happier if she had studied engineering at Cal."

"I understand where my mother is coming from. My dad and my brothers are cops. She spends her life worrying about us."

"You can eliminate her need to worry about you."

"I can't do it, Mike. I'm not going to confess to a crime that I didn't commit. My dad would never get over it. Besides, I'll lose my job."

"Your mom said that you never wanted to be a cop. She said that you did it to please your dad."

"She really said that?"

"Yes." I lowered my voice. "Is it true?"

"It was always expected of my brothers and me. We got the message and stayed in our lane. We'd go to the Academy after we graduated from college. My dad always said that if any of us didn't like it, we could do something else, but he didn't mean it."

"Did any of your brothers want to do something else?"

"A couple. It's hard to say no to my dad."

I got it. My dad was less than enthusiastic about my decision to become a priest. He was really unhappy when I left the priesthood to go to law school. He barely spoke to me for a couple of years after I started working as a P.D. "Your mom said that you're interested in technology."

"I am."

"Might be an alternative career path for you someday."

"Someday."

"Do me a favor and give this a little more thought?"

"I will. Where are you off to now?"

"The Fillmore. I need to talk to my brother and your father."

47
"WORKING ON IT"

Gio took a sip of bitter coffee from a paper cup emblazoned with the Golden Arches. Wearing a navy windbreaker over a powder-blue shirt, he looked like a caged tiger, but his voice was quiet. "They let me see Johnny this morning."

"I know. I just saw him."

"Did he say anything to you about the plea bargain?"

"He doesn't want to take it. I asked him to think about it a little more. He'll be ready to go on Monday."

Gio's eyes hardened. "So will I."

Gio, Pete, and I were sitting in a booth in the McDonald's on Fillmore, across the street from Northern Station. Like the streets outside, the restaurant was quiet. The rain had stopped, but the sky was overcast—matching my mood. Pete was hunched over the table. He'd said barely a word since I arrived.

"Were you here all night?" I asked.

Gio nodded. "Yeah. It was relatively quiet." He pointed at a patrol car parked on Fillmore. "There are police units everywhere. Show of force."

Sounds like a good idea. "Are you expecting trouble again today?"

"Yes. Reverend Tucker is leading a march from City Hall to First Union. There's another pro-cop gathering at Jefferson Square. The white supremacists applied for a permit for a rally at Crissy Field, but the mayor said no."

"Good call."

"They'll show up anyway."

"They'll be arrested."

"Depends how many show up. We've been watching Twitter and Facebook. They're anticipating a crowd of ten thousand."

"There aren't that many sympathizers around here."

"You'd be amazed. They come from other cities. Even if the crowd is small, they'll probably try to provoke an overreaction from SFPD."

"Then they'll get their heads pounded—which they deserve."

The corner of his mouth turned up. "Seems pretty harsh for a bleeding-heart free-speech guy who went to college and law school over in the People's Republic of Berkeley."

"My dad and brother were cops. I draw the line at neo-Nazis." I nibbled on a French fry. "Can SFPD keep a lid on this?"

"If we can keep the groups separated. If not, things could get out of hand." He finished his coffee. "At the moment, it's out of my control. Did the judge reconsider our request for bail?"

"No."

"Dammit." He sat in silence for an interminable moment. He lowered his voice. "If Johnny was your kid, would you tell him to take the deal?"

I exchanged a glance with Pete, who quickly resumed staring at his coffee. I looked at my high school classmate and answered him honestly. "I'd probably tell him to take it. It isn't a perfect result, but it will resolve his case and provide certainty. He's only twenty-two, Gio. He'll be out before he's twenty-five. He's a smart kid who has his whole life ahead of him."

"He's a fighter."

"Sometimes you need to pick your fights."

"He'll lose his job."

"Realistically, he already has."

Gio drummed his fingers on the table. "For what it's worth, I told him to take the deal."

Huh? "You're okay with him pleading guilty to a felony?"

"He's my kid. I want him to be safe."

"He told me that you pushed him to be a cop."

"I did. And now it's time for him *not* to be a cop. Even if they drop the charges, Johnny is going to be a sitting duck. He shot a guy in self-defense, but now he's a symbol of police brutality and racism. You're a good lawyer, Mike, but sometimes, you need to cut your losses and get out of the spotlight."

It was sound advice. "Johnny was worried that you would be upset if he took the deal."

"And everybody says that I'm the stubborn one. I'll be more upset if he's convicted of murder.

"You should talk to him again."

"I will."

"We still have a couple of days. In the meantime, it would help if you guys can find somebody who can verify that Jones had a gun."

"Working on it."

"I saw Dwayne on the plaza. Any chance he might have something for us?"

Gio shot a glance at Pete. "Working on it."

* * *

A few minutes later, I was walking up Fillmore past the Subway. The rain had stopped, and the sun was peeking out from behind the clouds. The air was crisp. The usually bustling area was a ghost town. There were more cops than pedestrians. The businesses were closed. Windows were covered with plywood. Police barricades closed the street to traffic.

I pulled out my iPhone and punched in Roosevelt's number. He answered on the first ring. "Haven't heard from you since yesterday," he said. "Where are you?"

"Looking for witnesses in the Fillmore."

"You should get out of there. There's going to be trouble."

"I can handle it."

"No, you can't. Besides, you aren't going to find any more witnesses who can help you. If *I* couldn't find them, *you* won't, either."

Probably true.

He was still talking. "I understand that our D.A. has offered a plea bargain."

"We're considering it."

"Consider it harder."

"Do you have any additional evidence that you'd like to share with me?"

"We think that Jones was delivering the AK-47s to Tarik Meredith."

Meredith was one of the bigger drug dealers in town. "I didn't know that Meredith had branched out into weapons."

"Seems he's expanding his operations. The fact that Jones was a small-time runner for a big-time operator has no bearing on your client's case."

Probably not. "It demonstrates that Jones was a bad guy."

"No doubt, but your client didn't know about the AK-47s until after the fact. It's also still illegal to shoot a bad guy when his hands are up."

"It was self-defense. Johnny saw a gun."

"Nobody else did. And you can't see it on the video."

"We'll find a witness."

"Then we'll have something to discuss." He cleared his throat. "Take the deal, Mike."

* * *

I was walking by the Fillmore Auditorium when I saw a familiar face heading toward me. Jerry Edwards was wearing a soiled trench coat. If I hadn't known him, I might have mistaken him for a homeless person. He trudged with his head down, cigarette in his hand, cell phone pressed to his ear. He was probably berating somebody.

I was hoping that he wouldn't notice me, but he looked up just in time. His thin lips formed a crooked smile. He ended his call, tossed his cigarette into the street, and spoke to me in his usual guttural voice. "Didn't expect to run into you here."

"Didn't expect to see you, either, Jerry."

"I heard the City is going to settle the civil case with Jones's mother."

"Don't know anything about it," I lied. "Even if that's true, it doesn't impact our case."

"I understand that the D.A. offered you a plea bargain."

"Who told you that?"

"No comment."

It wouldn't have surprised me if Ward or Harper had leaked this news to Edwards.

He let out a violent hack. "You gonna take the deal?"

"No comment."

"Are you denying that there's a plea deal on the table?"

"No comment."

"If there is, I think that's lousy. Your client shot an unarmed kid. The legal system should take its course."

I was tempted to explain that Jones worked for one of the biggest drug kingpins in town, but there was nothing to be gained. It had no legal bearing on our case, and he might have written that I had suggested that Jones deserved to die. "I gotta get back to work, Jerry."

I was about to walk around him when I heard blaring sirens and a roar followed by a crash. Instinctively, I ducked and put a hand up in front of my face. A black SUV had barreled through the police barricade and was heading toward us. A police unit was in pursuit. Feeling a rush of adrenaline, I rammed my shoulder into the door of the Fillmore Auditorium and pulled Edwards inside. We dove into the lobby as the SUV screeched to a halt about ten feet from us. The passenger-side window rolled down and I could see a man whose face was covered.

Edwards and I ran across the lobby and dove behind the refreshment counter. An instant later, I heard popping sounds. I looked up and realized that the man in the car was firing indiscriminately across the empty lobby. Then I heard the voices of cops ordering him to halt. More shots. More shouts.

Then the shooting stopped abruptly.

Edwards and I hid for what seemed like an hour, but was only a few seconds. I peeked over the counter and saw two uniforms approaching us, flashlights and weapons drawn.

"Anybody here?" one called out. "Police."

I raised a hand. "Over here. Don't shoot. We're unarmed."

"Are you hurt?"

"No."

"Please come out slowly with your hands up."

48

"SOMEBODY HAS TO PROVIDE ADULT SUPERVISION"

"Who was he?" I asked.

Roosevelt was across the table in the interrogation room in the basement of Northern Station. "Vontae Brown. He and Jones worked for the same drug dealer."

My heart was still pounding even though more than an hour had passed since the events at the Fillmore Auditorium. "Is he dead?"

"Very. Our people took him out in the lobby of the Fillmore. You and Edwards should send them a thank-you note. You were lucky."

"Why the hell was he shooting at us?"

"Our guys had been chasing him from the Mission. Maybe he wanted to go out in a blaze of glory. He was an angry kid with a long criminal record who was a small-time enforcer for a drug boss."

"Do you think he was targeting us?"

"Doubtful. Lawyers and reporters usually aren't strategic targets."

"Is Edwards okay?"

"Fine."

"Good."

"I'll need to finish taking your statement. Then I want you to get the hell out of here. Understood?"

Sounds great. "Yes."

There was a knock on the door. A sergeant led Pete and Gio inside.

"Nice to see you," I said.

Pete answered. "We were in the neighborhood." My never-subtle younger brother pointed a finger at me. "I am going to give you a ride downtown. I want you to stick to doing lawyer stuff."

"Deal."

* * *

Rosie's name appeared on my iPhone. She didn't mince words. "Where the hell are you?"

"Luca's office."

"Are you okay?"

"Fine."

"I just saw Edwards on TV. He said that he was with you when somebody tried to run you over and started shooting at you."

"We got out of the way."

"This isn't funny, Mike."

"I know."

"Who the hell was shooting at you?"

"A kid from the neighborhood who was being chased by the cops."

"Were you targeted?"

"Roosevelt didn't think so. Neither do I."

"You think he drove by you and started shooting randomly?"

Given the current state of affairs, it wouldn't surprise me. "We were in the wrong place at the wrong time. It happens, Rosie."

"What were you doing down there?"

"Checking in with Gio and Pete."

"It's a war zone."

"I know."

She invoked the "don't-you-dare-mess with me" tone that she reserved for our kids, lying witnesses, incompetent cops, and me.

"Let me make something clear to you, Mike. I don't want you going back to the Fillmore. I need you to finish this case and get back to the office to do your job. I don't want to have to explain to the kids that you got hurt—or worse—because you decided to be a reckless idiot who walked into the middle of a neighborhood where they're having riots. Got it?"

"Yes."

"Good. I'll meet you down at Luca's office and help you get ready for Monday."

"This isn't your case, Rosie."

"*Somebody* has to provide adult supervision."

49

"WE MAY NEED YOU TO TESTIFY"

Johnny tugged at the sleeve of his orange jumpsuit at four-thirty on Sunday afternoon. "How bad is it out there?"

Not as bad as it is in here. "Could be worse. The Fillmore is quiet, but there's a police unit on every corner."

Saturday had turned into Sunday. Reverend Tucker had led peaceful marches on both days with minimal trouble. His pleas for calm and an overwhelming police presence had kept things orderly—for the most part. The neo-Nazis had gone home. Driving rainstorms also tempered the numbers and the enthusiasm of the crowds.

"Did you talk to your parents?" I asked.

"My mom was just here." Johnny's mood matched the gray walls. "She wants me to accept the plea bargain."

So do I. "She's worried. So is your dad." *Here goes.* "What do you want to do, Johnny?"

He considered his answer for a long moment. "I want to fight."

"We can end this right now and mitigate your exposure."

"You sound like a lawyer."

"I *am* a lawyer. I'm *your* lawyer. Trials are unpredictable. Lots of things can happen—most of them bad."

"You think we're going to lose?"

"Hard to predict. A lot of people are going to be predisposed against you."

"Do they understand that I acted in self-defense?"

"Doesn't matter. The perception is more important than the reality. You're a cop. The video suggests that Jones's hands were up when you shot him. He said that he was unarmed."

"He was lying."

"I know, but the only thing that matters is what twelve people in the jury box think."

"You believe they'll think that I shot Jones in cold blood?"

"A lot will depend on the composition of the jury. If it's people who have had run-ins with the police, we're in trouble. If it's law-and-order types, we're probably okay."

"It's going to be hard to find law-and-order types here in San Francisco."

"We'll ask for a change in venue."

He sat in silence for a moment. "How do you think this will go tomorrow?"

"The prosecution needs to present just enough evidence for the judge to rule that there is a reasonable basis to conclude that you committed a crime. It's a low threshold."

"And what do we do?"

"I'll go after every one of their witnesses on cross. Then we'll put Murphy, Siragusa, and Connor on the stand to testify that Jones had a gun."

"Will it be enough to get the charges dropped?"

Doubtful. "It's going to be tough, Johnny."

He folded his arms tightly. "And bail?"

"That's going to be tough."

"No deal."

"If you were my kid, I would tell you to take the deal."

"Duly noted."

"Will you give it a little more thought?"

"I'm done thinking about it. I'm not going to confess to a crime that I didn't commit."

"Okay." My stomach tightened. "There's something else that we need to discuss. We may need you to testify that Jones had a gun."

"I'm ready."

"Harper will go after you on cross."

"I'm ready."

"If we need you, I want you to follow my lead and keep your answers short."

"I will."

Game on.

50
"HE SHOULD BE TREATED LIKE A HERO"

Sergeant Kevin Murphy squeezed his ample torso into one of the rosewood chairs in Luca's conference room. He hadn't shaved since I had seen him two days earlier. "How long will this take?"

"Twenty minutes," I said. "Maybe less."

"Good. I gotta get back to work."

"You're already back on duty?"

"Every officer with a pulse is on duty."

At five o'clock on Sunday evening, we were seventeen hours from the start of Johnny's prelim, and we were no closer to getting the charges dropped. Pete and Gio were still in the Fillmore.

Murphy's voice turned sharp. "We haven't even had time to do the funerals for our guys, and now everybody is on our asses because a bunch of troublemakers came to town to raise hell. Your father never would have put up with this crap. He would have cracked some skulls."

Probably true. I shot a glance at Nady, who kept her eyes on her laptop.

Murph wasn't finished. "Everybody is afraid that San Francisco is going to turn into Ferguson. Meanwhile, we're sitting ducks. Guys like Jones are driving around town with AK-47s in their trunks, and we can't do a damn thing about it. Johnny shot a gun runner. He should be treated like a hero. Instead, he's charged with murder. How the hell are we supposed to keep the peace if we have our hands tied?"

"I wouldn't want to be a cop."

"It's reaching the point where I don't want to do this, either. I'm already eligible for early retirement and my pension. After things calm down, I may just do it."

"I wouldn't blame you."

His voice softened. "I like my job, Mike. But I'm getting sick of this stuff. Too much political correctness and not enough support for guys who put their lives on the line."

"I hear you, Murph. My dad was a cop. So was my brother."

"I saw Pete and Gio down in the Fillmore last night. I know they're working on Johnny's case, but you should tell them to get out of there before they get hurt."

"I will." I let him vent for a few more minutes. Finally, we got down to business. "I wanted to go over your testimony tomorrow."

"I'm ready."

"Did you hear from the D.A.?"

"Yeah. They said that they aren't planning to call me as a witness."

I wasn't surprised. Harper probably figured that he had enough without Murphy's testimony. More important, Murphy was prepared to testify that Jones had a gun, which was inconsistent with the prosecution's narrative.

"How do you want to play it?" he asked.

"You know the drill. Follow my lead and keep your answers short."

"I will."

"I need you to testify that Johnny acted in self-defense."

"He did."

"And that you saw a gun in Jones's hand."

"I did."

"You can't see it in the video."

"Jones knocked Johnny over. It must have been out of camera view."

"You can't see it in the videos from the plaza or in the parking lot."

"It was dark and raining. Everything happened fast. And it depends on the angles. You can't always see everything in those videos."

"But you're sure that you saw it?"

"Yes."

"You can't see a gun in his hand in the body cam video taken by Charlie Connor."

"Jones must have put it inside his pocket when he jumped the fence."

"You're sure?"

"Yeah. We found it under his body. Johnny acted in self-defense." He stood up. "Anything else?"

"Harper is going to go after you on cross."

"I've been there. I'll deal with it."

"We'll see you in court in the morning."

51
"THAT'S IT?"

"You don't need to be here," I said.

Rosie disagreed. "Yes, I do."

"You were here yesterday."

"I like it here. You have a nice office."

Right. The aroma of stale coffee wafted through the conference room at Luca's firm at eight-thirty on Sunday night. Nady was down the hall working on exhibits. I was preparing my opening.

I tried again. "Nady and I will handle it. I'll take the lead. She'll sit second chair. She's very conscientious."

"I'm sure she is. You need somebody with experience to help you with strategy."

"And who did you have in mind?"

"Me."

"Deal." I was delighted to lose this argument. "Anybody know you're here?"

"Could be. There are reporters outside."

"That won't look good."

"I'll tell them that I brought you dinner."

"I love you, Rosie."

"We don't have time for that discussion now, Mike."

The TV was tuned to CNN, the sound low. On the left side of the split screen, they were showing the mayor pleading for order. On the right was video of an overturned car on fire in front of the McDonald's in the Fillmore. Cops in riot gear were stationed on every corner.

Rosie took a sip of Diet Coke. "For once, I don't envy the

mayor."

"Neither do I. There are limits to political persuasion. At least there wasn't any trouble during the wake for the officers."

The mood had been somber, and security tight, at St. Ignatius Church on the USF campus where a wake was held for the two fallen police officers. The event was completed without incident.

"The funeral for the first police officer is on Tuesday," I said. "The second is on Wednesday. They're going to make people go through metal detectors."

"We live in a screwed-up world."

We watched the TV in silence. The mayor insisted that anybody violating curfew would be arrested. The chief tried to sound reassuring. Reverend Tucker pleaded for calm. So did Jones's mother. Ward used her moment of free air time to say that the D.A.'s Office intended to prosecute Johnny to the fullest extent of the law. A moment later, I had the surreal experience of watching myself on TV as I entered the Hall clutching a blown-out umbrella. I recited the usual defense-lawyer platitudes about my client's innocence.

Rosie couldn't contain a grin. "I'm convinced."

I hope so. I turned the TV off as Anderson Cooper began soliciting predictions from his all-star panel of eight "experts," all of whom were happy to offer their opinions, and none of whom had ever lived in San Francisco or practiced law.

"How do you think this will go tomorrow?" Rosie asked.

"Harper will keep it short. The medical examiner will testify that Jones died of gunshot wounds. His ballistics expert will confirm that the bullets were fired from Johnny's service weapon. Then they'll put Roosevelt on the stand to introduce the video from Charlie Connor's body cam showing what happened in the parking lot. He'll say that Jones was unarmed and tie their case together."

"That's probably enough for a prelim. What are you planning to do?"

"I'll pick at each of Harper's witnesses. Then we'll have

Murphy, Connor, and Siragusa testify that Jones had a gun and Johnny shot him in self-defense."

"That's it?"

"That's it."

Rosie's full lips formed a ball. She took off her reading glasses and wiped them with a cloth. Then she did what she does best—she started poking holes in our case. "How do you account for the fact that you can't see a gun in the video from Johnny's body cam?"

"Bad angles."

"You can't see a gun in the video taken by the security cameras or Connor's body cam, either."

"More bad angles. And it was dark and rainy. Jones was visible in the videos for only seconds. We'll say that the gun was in Jones's pocket. Murphy will testify that he and Johnny found it under the body."

She wasn't convinced. "And your narrative is that Johnny acted in self-defense because he thought that Jones was about to pull the gun?"

"Yes."

"At the risk of sounding just a tiny bit racist, do you think it's a good idea to have three white cops testify that their white colleague shot a seemingly unarmed black kid in self-defense?"

"You can't cherry pick the races of your witnesses."

"I take it this means that the answer is yes."

"It is. We have no other witnesses. We'll argue that based upon the circumstances at the time, Johnny believed that he was in imminent danger of being killed, and he acted in self-defense. It's a standard *Graham vs. Connor* argument."

"How are you planning to do that without having Johnny testify?"

Good question. "We'll have to rely on testimony from Murphy, Siragusa, and Connor."

"It won't be enough to get the charges dropped on Monday. You need him to testify."

"It's too risky at a prelim."

"You have no choice."

"You may be right."

"I *am* right. If you want to have any realistic chance of ending this case at the prelim, you are going to have to let Johnny testify. Frankly, I'm not sure that will be enough in front of a smart judge like Martellus Ramsey—especially at a prelim."

52
"LET HER BE HAPPY AND SAFE"

Geary Boulevard was empty as I drove my rented Ford Focus westbound through a light rain at twelve-thirty on Monday morning. The radio was tuned to KCBS. The anchor said that the mayor's curfew was holding. My hometown had been turned into a war zone—temporarily, I hoped. *How long would the chaos last?* San Francisco desperately needed to recover a sense of normalcy— whatever that might be.

I've never been particularly introspective, but my demons always come out at night. It usually happens when I'm in bed, but sometimes they appear when I'm driving alone. The visits have become more frequent as I've gotten older, and they always seem to involve my dad. He'd been gone almost twenty years. I remembered the nights when he would return home—dead tired, having done his best to keep San Francisco safe and put food on the table. After a stop at Big John's saloon, he'd show up, the ever-present Camel cigarette in his hand. I've come to appreciate the dignified fortitude of Thomas James Charles Daley, Sr. He retired at fifty-five with a full pension that he never got to enjoy. My parents' long-delayed travel plans were short-circuited when he was diagnosed with lung cancer. A year and a half later, he was gone.

My mom was never the same. The depression that overwhelmed her when my older brother died in Vietnam returned. Her pain was exacerbated by Alzheimer's, a mean-spirited disease that robbed her of her memories. After my father died, she would still sit in her chair in our living room, pretending to watch TV, hands busy with her crocheting, as if she was still waiting up for him. Her final years were filled with melancholy and, later, confusion. She always managed a smile for us, but she was overwhelmed with fear until the fateful day that she took a fall, bumped her head, and never woke up. Margaret Daley was every bit as tough as my dad. She fought her demons for eighty-two years. She never wanted anything for herself—she wanted her husband to stay safe and her kids to be happy. As with most of us, her life ended up a mixed bag—overall, more positives than negatives, I suppose.

I passed St. Mary's Cathedral and thought of my lifelong friend, Gio, and his wife, Maria. They'd raised seven kids—all of whom were solid people. I couldn't imagine their worry about their youngest son. I desperately wanted to make things right for them. Maria reminded me of my mom. Hoping the phone wouldn't ring with bad news. The endless worry. The terror of anticipation.

I thought of my client, Johnny, whose life had changed forever in a post office parking lot on a rainy night. I hoped that I could do something—anything—to help him find a way back to a promising future.

I thought of our daughter, Grace, who was just a couple of years younger than Johnny. I was immensely proud of her—even if she didn't answer my phone calls. I was also grateful that she had decided to become a film major at USC. She showed no interest in law enforcement, the military, or, heaven forbid, law school.

Let her be happy and safe.

I glanced at the Fillmore Auditorium, which was dark. Two police units were parked in the otherwise-empty intersection, lights flashing. For one night, San Francisco was quiet.

I punched in Pete's number on my iPhone.

He answered on the first ring. "What do you need, Mick?"

"Hard evidence that Johnny acted in self-defense."

"Working on it."

"You want some help?"

"No."

"Is Gio with you?"

"He went home to be with Maria." He cleared his throat. "What time does the prelim start?"

"Ten a.m."

"I'll call you."

* * *

The light from the streetlamp outside the window reflected off the cobalt eyes of the Public Defender of the City and County of San Francisco. Rosie pulled the sheet over herself and ran her fingers through my hair. She flashed the picture-perfect smile that looked the same as it did when I had first met her almost a quarter of a century earlier.

"You're getting gray, Mike," she said. "It makes you look distinguished."

"I'd rather look young."

She kissed me. "You'll always be young to me."

Beautiful Rosie. I pushed a strand of jet-black hair out of her eyes. She needed a little help from a bottle to hide the gray. "Looks nice."

"I miss having it longer."

"So do I."

"Do you think the shorter hair makes me look older?"

"No. I miss having more to play with."

This elicited another smile. We were in bed at one-fifteen on Monday morning. I was due in court in less than nine hours, but I wasn't tired, and I wanted to cherish a moment of quiet with the most beautiful woman I had ever known. Ever since our days as junior public defenders, we had always spent the night before a trial or a big prelim together. I'm not sure if it helped us in court, but it got our adrenaline flowing. Even after our divorce, we kept up our pre-game ritual out of a combination of superstition, habit, and, to be honest, enjoyment. In my prior life as a priest, I didn't have a huge sample size for comparison, but I was pretty sure that Rosie was extraordinarily good in bed.

She stroked my cheek. "Maria called about Johnny again. Can you fix this?"

"I'm not sure."

"She's worried."

"I don't blame her. Is she okay to come to court tomorrow?"

"Yes. The boys will be there, too."

"Good. A show of support."

"She said that Gio was out with Pete again tonight. You think they'll find something?"

"I'm not optimistic. Even if they find iron-clad evidence to exonerate Johnny, there will be riots."

"And if they convict him of first-degree murder, there may be riots. Somebody is going to be unhappy."

"Maria and Gio will be happy if I get their son off. That's enough for me."

"Things will never be the same for any of them."

"I know." I looked at her. "It was quiet when I was driving home."

"The cops and the National Guard are out in force."

"They can't keep a lid on this indefinitely."

"People will get tired of it sooner or later." She squeezed my hand. "Are you going to be okay, Mike? You seem more troubled than usual."

"I feel like I can't control anything."

"You can control what happens in court." I could smell her warm breath as she kissed me again. "What's bothering you?"

How much time do you have? "I'm closer to sixty than fifty. Our daughter is in college. Our son is going to start high school in a couple of years. Your mother is in her eighties. So is Big John. Everybody is counting on us. In the meantime, the cases keep getting harder. The world keeps getting nastier. And I'm getting tired."

"You've dealt with high-profile cases. You know how it goes."

"I've never had one where there are riots, and people are getting shot. There's a lot riding on this case, Rosie. I'm starting to feel like a grown-up. And I don't like it."

She chewed on her lip. It was a rare occasion where she had no answer. To her credit, she didn't try a cliché. "Maybe you should take a little time off after you finish Johnny's case."

"Maybe." I looked into her eyes. "How much longer do you want to do this?"

"One more election cycle. Can you hang in with me until then?"

"I think so."

"I'll make it worth your while."

"You always do. You like being the Public Defender, don't you?

"I do. Is that a bad thing?"

"It's a good thing. We need people like you."

"And we need people like you, Mike."

I pulled her close and kissed her. "We're going to be okay, Rosie."

"I know. Are you going to walk the steps with Zvi in the morning?"

"Yeah. The doctor says that it's good for me."

"So is sleep."

"It's overrated. I need to get up early anyway. Do you want me to go home?"

She smiled seductively. "No, I want you to stay."

53
"ALL RISE"

News vans lined Bryant at nine o'clock on Monday morning as I pushed through the reporters on the steps of the Hall. SFPD had blocked traffic. A thousand protesters stood behind police barricades. They held up signs reading "Justice for JuJu" and sang "We Shall Overcome." A battalion of cops in riot gear maintained an uneasy truce.

I was already drenched when my umbrella blew inside-out as I approached the door to the Hall. A cameraman accidentally bumped my briefcase, which banged into my knee. To his credit, he apologized. I caught myself before I fell, saving me from injury, preserving my laptop, and avoiding an embarrassing moment on YouTube.

"Mr. Daley, are you still maintaining that your client is innocent?"

"Mr. Daley, are you going to negotiate a plea bargain?"

"Mr. Daley? Mr. Daley? Mr. Daley?"

I tried to sound forceful as the rain pelted my face. "My client is innocent. I have no further comment."

I pushed my way into the lobby, where I was met by a stern-faced Luca Bacigalupi. "Gio, Maria, and the boys are upstairs," he said.

"Let's roll."

* * *

"All rise."

Judge Martellus Ramsey cut an imposing presence as he emerged from the door to the hallway leading to his chambers. His use of an electronic wheelchair did not make the one-time star linebacker at Oakland's Skyline High School appear less intimidating. The fluorescent light reflected off his shaved head as he glided to the bench between the Stars and Stripes and the California state flag. He turned on his computer, lifted a hand, and addressed his packed courtroom.

"Be seated."

An overworked fan recirculated air that smelled of mildew. A tense silence enveloped the room as Judge Ramsey pursed his lips and pulled the microphone toward himself. He scanned the faces of the fortunate souls who had seats in the five rows of the gallery. He stroked his gray beard as his gaze moved to the prosecution table, where Harper was sitting next to Roosevelt. His eyes shifted to the defense side, where Johnny was sitting between Luca and me. Nady sat to my right. Luca was at the defense table as a courtesy. Nady was here to work. As second chair, she would handle the choreography of producing evidence. I had impressed upon her that courtrooms are theaters, where stagecraft, timing, props, and presentation are essential. She had taken on her role with her customary enthusiasm and diligence. Given the opportunity and some practice, she would make a superb trial lawyer.

Johnny's mother, father, and six brothers sat behind us in the first row of the gallery. Maria's hands were in her lap, eyes locked onto the judge. Gio was wearing his dress uniform, bearing erect, expression stoic. Three assistant chiefs and a dozen cops sat behind Johnny's family. I appreciated the show of solidarity. Members of the media and a few courthouse regulars had taken the remaining seats. Rosie was in the back row.

Pete was conspicuously missing. He was still in the Fillmore. I always felt better when he was in court. He had a knack for reading judges.

The prosecution's side was also filled. Jones's mother sat

behind Harper, hands clasped. Her brother sat to her left. Reverend Tucker was on her right, clutching a Bible. Nicole Ward sat on the aisle. Members of Reverend Tucker's church took seats in the second row. Reporters sat in the last three rows. The media members who had lost the lottery had been escorted to an even dingier courtroom down the hall, where they would watch on TV.

Judge Ramsey nodded to his bailiff. "Please call our case."

"The People versus Giovanni Carlo Bacigalupi the Fourth."

"Counsel will state their names for the record."

"DeSean Harper for the People."

"Michael Daley, Lucantonio Bacigalupi, and Nadezhda Nikonova for the defense."

The judge nodded. "Mr. Bacigalupi, it's nice to see you. Ms. Nikonova, I trust that Mr. Daley has provided instructions as to how I prefer to conduct business?"

"He has, Your Honor."

"Then we'll get along fine." He pointed at Harper. "I see that Inspector Johnson is with you. I take it that he has been designated as the inspector for this case?"

"He has."

"Any objection, Mr. Daley?"

"No, Your Honor." Generally, witnesses aren't allowed in court prior to their testimony. However, the D.A. is permitted to include the lead homicide inspector at the table.

The judge nodded at Roosevelt. "Good to see you, Inspector."

"Good to see you, Your Honor."

Judge Ramsey looked into the TV camera. "Ladies and gentlemen, this matter has generated substantial media attention. Since we have limited seating and the City lacks the resources to rent a larger venue, I have ruled that these proceedings will be televised."

I stood and invoked a respectful tone. "We renew our objection."

"Noted and overruled, Mr. Daley."

I knew that was coming.

The judge gestured with his reading glasses. "In general, I don't like having cameras in my court. It changes people's behavior—usually in a bad way. First, I want to address the gallery. I am going to conduct these proceedings as if you aren't here. I expect you to remain silent. No comments, no whispers, no laughing, no outbursts, no cell phones, no texting, no tweeting, no reactions of any kind. If you disobey these instructions even once, my bailiff will escort you out the door."

I appreciated the show of control. Then again, I knew that Judge Ramsey ran his courtroom with the precision of a Swiss train.

The judge's eyes moved from the gallery to the prosecution table, and then to me. "I want to address the attorneys. My rules are simple. If you grandstand, you will spend a night in one of our fine jail cells upstairs. Understood?"

Harper and I responded in unison. "Yes, Your Honor."

"Good. I want to remind you that I have imposed a complete ban on speaking to the media or engaging in other forms of communication outside this courtroom. If I see you on TV, Twitter, Facebook, or social media of any type, I will hold you in contempt."

The judge didn't wait for a response before he continued. "Ladies and gentlemen, this is a preliminary hearing to determine whether there is sufficient evidence to bind the defendant over for trial on the charge of murder in the first degree. It is a serious matter, and I expect you to respect its gravity.

"For those who are unfamiliar with these proceedings, a preliminary hearing is different from a trial. First, there is no jury, so I am responsible for making all decisions."

True. It's all on you.

"Second, instead of proving each element beyond a reasonable doubt, the prosecution must simply show that there is sufficient evidence to justify a belief that the defendant committed a crime."

Also true. It's a relatively low standard.

"Third, by law, I am obligated to give the benefit of the doubt to the prosecution on evidentiary matters."

He'll lean over backwards to believe Harper.

The judge spoke to Johnny. "Mr. Bacigalupi, did you understand everything that I said?"

"Yes, Your Honor."

He turned to the prosecution. "Mr. Harper, while an opening statement is not customary at a prelim, I am prepared to listen if you'd like to make a few opening remarks."

"I would, Your Honor."

54
"IT WAS A COLD-BLOODED MURDER"

Harper stood at the lectern and adjusted the sleeve of his suit jacket. "It was a cold-blooded murder," he said.

Johnny gripped the armrests of his chair tightly.

Harper worked without notes. "I am here to discuss a murder committed by a San Francisco police officer. As a member of law enforcement, it is painful for me."

It's even more so for Johnny and me. It's bad form to interrupt during an opening, but I wanted to let Harper know that I would challenge him. "Objection. Alleged murder."

Harper didn't look my way. "Alleged murder," he repeated. He pointed at a poster-size photo of a smiling Jones positioned in view of the judge, the gallery, and the TV cameras. "Juwon Jones was just eighteen when he was shot and killed by the defendant. JuJu had graduated from Gateway High School. He was taking classes at City College and studying for his associate's degree. He had a job and was saving to attend State. He was a loving son."

He was also a convicted criminal and an alleged drug mule. And the cops found a dozen AK-47s in the trunk of his car. Just saying.

Harper was playing to an audience of one: Judge Ramsey. "Your Honor, like most teenagers, JuJu wasn't perfect. He was arrested a couple of times and convicted once of stealing a car. He did community service and was placed on probation. Regardless of these youthful indiscretions, he did not deserve to die, leaving a grieving mother. And he certainly didn't deserve to die in the manner that he did—unarmed and begging for his life."

Last time. "Objection. Assumes facts not in evidence."

"Please, Mr. Harper."

"Yes, Your Honor." Harper put a hand on the lectern. "JuJu was stopped for a broken tail light. When the defendant ordered him out of his vehicle, JuJu got scared and ran. The defendant gave chase and cornered him in a parking lot. In response to the defendant's command, JuJu raised his hands and surrendered. He repeatedly said that he was unarmed. He pleaded with the defendant not to shoot." He turned to face Johnny. "But that's exactly what he did."

Johnny glanced at me, panic in his eyes. I raised my hand slightly. *Stay the course.*

Harper turned back to the judge. "We will introduce police video showing exactly what happened. The defendant shot JuJu four times at point blank range. It was a horrible overreaction to a situation that should have been resolved peacefully by de-escalation. JuJu died on the spot."

Harper lowered his voice. "I wish that it hadn't happened. I wish that JuJu's mother didn't have to bury her son. I wish that I could make things right for her. But we take the facts as they are. I will provide sufficient evidence that the defendant committed first-degree murder."

Harper looked at Jones's mother, whose hands were clutched in front of her face, eyes closed, tears streaming. He turned back to Judge Ramsey. "JuJu cannot speak for himself, so it's my job to speak for him. We cannot bring him back, but we will find justice for JuJu."

Harper took his seat.

Judge Ramsey's eyes shifted to me. "Did you wish to make some brief opening remarks, Mr. Daley?"

"Yes, Your Honor."

I stood, buttoned my jacket, walked to the lectern, and placed a single notecard next to the microphone. Out of the corner of my eye, I saw Rosie, eyes focused on the judge. I could hear her voice in my head imploring me to keep it short and clear.

I invoked my confession voice. "Your Honor, Johnny Bacigalupi is a fine police officer and an exemplary young man. He feels terrible about the death of Juwon Jones, and so do I. We extend our deepest sympathies to his mother, relatives, and friends."

That was enough. There's a fine line between respectful and smarmy.

"Johnny Bacigalupi has been charged with first-degree murder in connection with a traffic stop and the ensuing foot chase, even though he acted in compliance with police procedure and, more important, in self-defense. We will not dispute the fact that Johnny shot and killed Juwon Jones. It is unfortunate that he had to do so, but he had no choice. He had to protect himself. First-degree murder requires a premeditated intent to kill. Johnny had none."

Harper got to his feet. "Objection. Mr. Daley is assuming facts not in evidence. He's also arguing the law. He should be sticking to the facts."

Yes, I should.

"Please, Mr. Daley."

"Yes, Your Honor." It was the proper call. I glanced at Harper. *Good to see that you're paying attention.*

"Your Honor, the situation began with what Officer Bacigalupi and his partner thought would be a routine traffic stop." I explained that Johnny and Murph were driving on Geary when they saw a car with a broken tail light. "Officer Bacigalupi and Sergeant Murphy decided—correctly—to pull the car over and issue a citation. They determined that the vehicle was registered under the name of Juwon Jones's mother. It was not reported as stolen or involved in criminal activity. The officers called in the traffic stop, activated their warning lights, and pursued the vehicle. Mr. Jones pulled off Geary and parked in the Safeway lot. Pursuant to standard procedure, Officer Bacigalupi approached from the driver side, and Sergeant Murphy approached on the passenger side.

Initially, the stop was uneventful.

"After Officer Bacigalupi informed the driver that his tail light was out, he returned to his police unit to check the driver's license and the car's registration. Sergeant Murphy maintained his position outside Mr. Jones's car. Officer Bacigalupi determined that Mr. Jones had a criminal record and an outstanding warrant for a probation violation. He politely asked Mr. Jones to exit the vehicle so that he and his partner could search it. This was both legally permissible and in accordance with standard SFPD practice. If Officer Bacigalupi had failed to take this step, he would have been subject to report.

"Mr. Jones became agitated and disobeyed Officer Bacigalupi's request. He flashed a handgun, banged the door into Officer Bacigalupi, knocking him down, and fled on foot. Thankfully, Mr. Jones did not shoot Officer Bacigalupi or Sergeant Murphy. Officer Bacigalupi pursued Mr. Jones with Sergeant Murphy close behind. Officer Bacigalupi and Sergeant Murphy radioed for backup and reported that Mr. Jones was armed and dangerous. Other officers were in the vicinity, so help arrived shortly thereafter.

"Officer Bacigalupi chased Mr. Jones up Fillmore to Geary, where Mr. Jones was cut off by a police car driven by Officer Richard Siragusa. Mr. Jones displayed his weapon and disobeyed Officer Siragusa's order to stop. Mr. Jones turned left and headed west. A half-block later, another police unit driven by Officer Charles Connor stopped him in front of the post office. Mr. Jones disregarded Officer Connor's commands to halt, and climbed over the gate into an enclosed parking lot. Officer Bacigalupi arrived a moment later and also climbed the fence. Sergeant Murphy and the other responding officers remained outside.

"Officer Bacigalupi found Mr. Jones hiding behind a postal van. Officer Bacigalupi ordered him to put his hands up. At first, Mr. Jones refused. Then he reconsidered and complied. Pursuant to procedure, Officer Bacigalupi announced that he was placing Mr. Jones under arrest and ordered him to lie down with arms and legs spread. Mr. Jones disobeyed the order and said that he was unarmed, which Officer Bacigalupi knew was untrue because he had seen a handgun in Mr. Jones's possession. Officer Bacigalupi repeated his order to lie down. Again Mr. Jones refused. Officer Bacigalupi repeated it a third time. Mr. Jones lowered his hands to reach for the gun. Officer Bacigalupi feared for his life and had no choice but to shoot Mr. Jones in self-defense. Officer Bacigalupi provided first aid and called an ambulance. Unfortunately, Mr. Jones died."

No discernable reaction from the judge.

"Officer Bacigalupi's life was threatened by an armed man with a criminal record who disobeyed orders and fled. A loaded handgun was found under Mr. Jones's body. Police officers subsequently found twelve AK-47 assault rifles in the trunk of his car. If Mr. Jones had cooperated, this unfortunate incident could have been avoided. If Officer Bacigalupi and Sergeant Murphy hadn't made the stop, it is likely that the AK-47s would have been used to kill innocent people."

I expected Harper to object to this statement of pure conjecture, but he did not.

I looked over at Rosie, who closed her eyes. *Time to wrap up.*

"Your Honor, the prosecution must show that Officer Bacigalupi had the requisite criminal intent to have committed murder. The evidence will demonstrate that he did not. As a matter of law, you must rule that he cannot be bound over for trial."

Judge Ramsey's chin rested in the palm of his hand. "Thank you, Mr. Daley."

I took my seat at the defense table. Johnny leaned over and whispered, "You did good."

I'm not so sure.

The judge turned to Harper. "Please call your first witness."

"The People call Dr. Joy Siu."

It was a logical starting point. Siu was the Chief Medical Examiner.

55
"A VERY RELIABLE WEAPON"

Harper stood at the lectern. "Please state your name and occupation for the record."

"Dr. Joy Siu. I am the Chief Medical Examiner of the City and County of San Francisco."

The courtroom was silent as Dr. Siu adjusted the collar of her blindingly white lab coat. From her coiffed hair to her trimmed nails, everything about her embodied understated precision. Now in her mid-forties, the Stockton native and one-time world-class figure skater had traded in her blades to attend Princeton and then Johns-Hopkins Medical School. She earned a Ph.D. at UCSF in anatomic pathology and spent twenty years doing research and consulting on autopsies all over the world. Her credentials were impeccable, and her delivery was pitch-perfect. Thankfully, her role would be brief.

Harper gave her plenty of room. "How long have you held that position?"

"Almost three years."

"What did you do before that?"

It was textbook technique. You ask simple questions that elicit soundbite responses.

"I was the Chair of the M.D./Ph.D. program in anatomic pathology at UCSF."

She was good at her job. It was also unusual for our Medical Examiner to appear at a prelim, but this was a high-profile case.

Harper wasn't taking any chances.

"Over the course of your career, how many autopsies have you performed?"

"Hundreds."

Enough. "Your Honor, we will stipulate that Dr. Siu is an expert in autopsy pathology."

"Thank you, Mr. Daley."

Johnny leaned over and whispered, "Did you need to do that?"

"The judge knows that she's qualified." *And we want to get her off the stand.*

Harper introduced Siu's autopsy report into evidence. He walked over to the witness box and presented it to her as if it was the Rosetta Stone. "Do you recognize this document?"

She pretended to study it. "Yes. It's my autopsy report for Juwon Jones."

"When did you perform the autopsy?"

"February ninth at four p.m."

"Were you able to determine the date and time of death?"

"One-twenty a.m. on February ninth."

"Can you explain how you were able to calculate the time of death with such specificity?"

"Video footage showed that the victim was shot at close range at one-twenty a.m. Based upon the location and extent of the wounds, I concluded that he died instantly."

"And the cause of death?"

"Four gunshot wounds to the chest. Two bullets struck the heart. Two more pierced his lungs. He had no chance."

"No further questions."

The first points were on the board. A murder charge requires a victim.

"Cross-exam, Mr. Daley?"

"Just a couple of questions, Your Honor. May we approach the witness?"

"You may."

I walked to the front of the box. "You mentioned that in determining time of death, you relied upon video taken at the scene."

"Correct."

"You can't see the shooter, can you?"

"No. He was standing behind a postal truck. So was the victim."

"You can't see the bullets hit the decedent, correct?"

"No."

"The decedent had a handgun in his possession when he was shot, right?"

"Objection. Mr. Daley is questioning the witness about issues that were not addressed during direct exam."

Yes, I am.

"Sustained."

I tried again. "Decedent was in possession of a gun when Officer Bacigalupi reacted and fired his weapon, correct?"

"I don't know."

"If the decedent was armed, it would have been reasonable for Officer Bacigalupi to have shot him in self-defense, right?"

"Objection. He did it again."

Yes, I did. Shame on me. "Withdrawn. No further questions, Your Honor."

"Redirect, Mr. Harper?"

"No, Your Honor."

I took my seat. Johnny leaned over and said, "Was there anything else that you could have done?"

I could have forgone cross and gotten her off the stand a little quicker. "It's early, Johnny. The prosecution always has better cards at the beginning."

* * *

The silver-haired sage exuded authority as he handled the gun encased in a clear evidence bag. "SIG Sauer P226. Forty caliber. Magazine holds twelve rounds plus one in the chamber. A very reliable weapon. Popular with law enforcement."

Harper stood in front of the witness box. "Would that include SFPD?"

"It would. It's the sidearm used by most of our officers."

And that's that.

Captain Jack Goldthorpe was a meticulous seventy-year-old who had plied his trade in an immaculate office in the basement of the Hall for forty years. From his full head of hair to his snow-white Egyptian cotton shirt to his charcoal Wilkes Bashford suit, he was a study in exactness. If you had a question about matching bullets to weapons, calculating trajectories, or analyzing distances from muzzles to bodies, "Captain Jack" was your guy. On the stand, he was a combination of expertise and geniality. Judges and juries loved him. More important, they believed him.

I stipulated to his expertise. There was no reason to let Harper lead him through his impressive resume.

"Is this an SFPD weapon?" Harper asked.

"Your Honor," I said, "we will stipulate that it is Officer Bacigalupi's service weapon."

Harper was pleased. "Will you also stipulate that the defendant was carrying this weapon on the morning of February ninth?"

"Yes."

"And that he used this weapon to shoot the victim, Juwon Jones?"

"In self-defense," I said.

"We'll discuss his state of mind later. Are you prepared to stipulate that your client used this weapon to fire the shots that killed Juwon Jones?"

"Yes."

Harper had earned another point. He had identified the weapon used to kill Jones. He took the SIG from Goldthorpe and handed him another tagged evidence bag. "Do you recognize this firearm?"

"Kel-Tec PMR-30 handgun."

"Were you able to identify the registered owner of this

weapon?"

"No. The identifying information was removed."

"Is it legal to possess this weapon in California?"

"Yes, but it is illegal to remove the identifying information."

"Where was it found?"

"Allegedly under the body of the deceased, Juwon Jones."

"Allegedly?"

"Objection," I said. "Calls for speculation."

Harper held up a hand. "We'll explain all of this momentarily."

The judge wasn't impressed. "I'm going to overrule the objection, but I want to hear the explanation now."

Harper nodded to Goldthorpe, who took the cue. "According to the defendant and his partner, they found this firearm under the deceased's body. We have no video or eyewitness evidence to corroborate this assertion."

I stood up again. "You have eyewitness testimony of the defendant and his partner."

The judge nodded. "Duly noted, Mr. Daley."

Harper pretended to ignore us and continued with Goldthorpe. "Did you find Sergeant Murphy's fingerprints on this weapon?"

"We did."

"No further questions."

"Cross-exam, Mr. Daley?"

"Yes, Your Honor." I stood, buttoned my jacket, and walked to the front of the box. "Captain Goldthorpe, did you find any prints other than Sergeant Murphy's on this weapon?"

"The victim's."

"So Mr. Jones handled this weapon?"

"Yes, although it's possible that his fingerprints could have found their way onto this weapon if somebody had put it into his hand."

True. "Other than Mr. Jones and Sergeant Murphy, did you find anybody else's fingerprints on this firearm?"

"Nothing identifiable."

"There were smudged prints, right?"

"Yes."

"So somebody else could have handled this weapon on the morning of February ninth?"

"It's possible."

Smoke and mirrors. "Would you acknowledge that Sergeant Murphy probably got his fingerprints on this weapon when he picked it up and logged it into evidence?"

"Objection. Speculation."

"Overruled."

Goldthorpe shrugged. "It's possible."

At trial, this may have been enough to get us to reasonable doubt. At a prelim, it was just another piece of evidence. "No further questions."

The judge glanced at his computer. "I need to call a recess until after lunch." He looked over at Harper. "How many more witnesses, Mr. Harper?"

"Just one, Your Honor: Inspector Roosevelt Johnson."

56
"HE MAY NOT NEED ANYBODY ELSE"

Johnny ignored his turkey sandwich. "That didn't go well."

I inhaled the stale air in the consultation room down the hall from Judge Ramsey's courtroom. "It's just two witnesses. The prosecution always gets a leg up."

"Harper said that he was going to call only one more witness: Inspector Johnson."

He may not need anybody else. "We'll see. He's going to show as little as possible. That's how prelims work."

"Maybe doing this so fast was a mistake."

"Barring new evidence, it's our only chance to get the charges dropped quickly."

He didn't respond.

Johnny, Luca, Nady, and I were squeezed around a table at one o'clock on Monday afternoon. A frustrated Gio had gone with Maria and their sons to find lunch across the street. Court wouldn't resume for another hour. I was hoping to hear from Pete. Rosie had gone back to the office. She promised to return later in the afternoon. It felt like we were attending a wake.

Johnny's eyes narrowed. "Why didn't they call Murphy?"

"His testimony runs counter to their narrative. They're saying that you guys planted the gun. Murph will testify that you didn't."

"It's the truth," Johnny said.

"I know."

"You should let me testify."

"It's too risky."

"What do we have to lose?"

Everything. "Let's see how things go this afternoon."

"You aren't going to do it."

Not until trial.

He turned to his uncle. "You're a lawyer, too. What do you think?"

Luca fiddled with his eighteen-carat-gold cufflinks. "Mike's the expert."

Not exactly a full-throated endorsement. "I'm going to check in with Pete. Then I want to go over our witness list once more."

* * *

Cigarette smoke enveloped me on the steps of the Hall as I stood in the smokers' area and pressed my iPhone to my ear. "Can you talk?"

"Briefly." Pete's voice was gravelly. "How did it go this morning?"

"About as well as expected. They're going to call Roosevelt next. Then we're up. What's going on in the Fillmore?"

"The situation is fluid. Things could change depending on what happens in court. If the judge binds Johnny over for trial, it will probably stay quiet. If you get the charges dropped or the judge grants bail, things could get out of hand."

Terrific. "You're saying that if I get a good result for my client, everybody loses?"

"Something like that, Mick."

Swell. "You got anything that we can use?"

"I'm working every angle. You aren't giving me much time."

"I don't have much time, Pete. What are the odds?"

"Not great." There was a hesitation. "When was the last time you talked to Gio?"

"About an hour ago."

"He texted me a few minutes ago. He's coming down here. Did

he say anything to you?"

"No."

"Try to slow-walk things at the prelim this afternoon until I find out what's going on."

* * *

Two familiar faces were waiting for me at the door to the courtroom. Rosie was standing next to Maria. Their muted expressions matched. I motioned to them to join me near the windows, where there were fewer prying ears.

Rosie acted as spokeswoman. "Gio went down to the Fillmore."

"I heard. He's going to meet Pete."

"I'm going to sit with Maria this afternoon."

"That's good." *And reassuring.* I turned to Maria. "Did Gio tell you anything?"

"He said that somebody may have seen something. He also said that it might be nothing."

"He's good at his job, Maria. So is Pete."

"I know." Her eyes locked onto mine. "You need to get my son out of here, Mike."

I desperately wanted to reassure her. "I will."

Her determined expression didn't change as she turned and walked into the courtroom.

Rosie waited behind. "You okay?" she asked.

"Couldn't be better." I reached over and squeezed her hand. "My lucky charm is here."

"You're going to need more than luck today."

57
"HE WAS PLEADING FOR HIS LIFE"

Harper was at the lectern. "Please state your name for the record."

"Roosevelt Johnson."

"What is your occupation?"

As if we don't know.

"I am a senior homicide inspector with the San Francisco Police Department. I have held that position for forty-seven years."

"What did you do prior to that?"

"I don't remember. It was a long time ago."

The well-rehearsed line got a chuckle from the gallery and a smile from the judge.

SFPD's most decorated homicide inspector sat in the witness box, arms folded. As always, Roosevelt was wearing a gray suit from the Men's Wearhouse, a white oxford shirt, and a striped blue and gold tie bearing the colors of his alma mater, UC-Berkeley. He had poured himself a cup of water, but he wouldn't touch it. He believed that witnesses who drank water appeared nervous.

Harper positioned himself between Roosevelt and me. It was a subtle move. I would be able to see Roosevelt's eyes, but not Harper's.

Harper introduced Roosevelt's report into evidence. "Inspector Johnson, are you the lead homicide inspector investigating the murder of Juwon Jones?"

"Objection. Move to strike the characterization of Mr. Jones's death as a murder."

"Sustained."

Harper didn't miss a beat. "Are you the lead inspector for the death of Juwon Jones?"

"Yes."

"I was under the impression that you had retired."

"I had. The mayor and the chief asked me to work on this matter. Evidently, they wanted somebody with gray hair."

More chuckles in the gallery.

I interrupted again when Harper started to walk Roosevelt through his resume. "We will stipulate to Inspector Johnson's experience."

This pleased the judge. "Thank you, Mr. Daley."

Harper pressed on. "Inspector, on the morning of February ninth, were you called to the parking lot next to the post office on Geary near Fillmore?"

"Yes. I arrived at two-thirty a.m." Roosevelt confirmed that it was about an hour after Jones had been killed. "I supervised the securing of the scene. We followed standard procedure."

I didn't expect him to suggest otherwise.

"Did you interview all of the officers at the scene?"

"Yes."

"Did that include the defendant, Officer Bacigalupi, and his partner, Sergeant Murphy?"

"Yes."

"Did either of them tell you who had shot and killed Juwon Jones?"

"Yes. Both reported that the defendant had shot Juwon."

I noted the subtle shift in Roosevelt's language. If my guess was correct, he would refer to Johnny only as "the defendant." He would call Jones by his first name.

Johnny clenched his fists as Harper led Roosevelt through a minute-by-minute chronology of the events on the morning of February ninth. The dinner at Mel's. The drive down Geary. The broken tail light. The chase. The pullover in the Safeway lot.

Roosevelt's tone was business-like. "It looked like it was going to be a routine traffic stop. The defendant and Sergeant Murphy ran a preliminary check on the vehicle, which wasn't reported as stolen. No outstanding tickets."

"Probably just a fix-it ticket?" Harper suggested.

"Yes." Roosevelt turned and spoke directly to the judge. "The defendant had just completed his probationary period. Sergeant Murphy instructed him to make the stop to give him experience handling a routine matter."

Harper introduced the video from Johnny's body cam. "Inspector, could you please walk us through what happened?"

"Of course." Roosevelt left the stand and moved in front of a flat-screen positioned where the judge and gallery could see it. He narrated as he ran the video—first at normal speed, and then in slow motion.

"The defendant handled the initial encounter with courtesy and professionalism." Roosevelt said that Johnny had approached the vehicle appropriately, introduced himself respectfully, and requested Jones's information properly. "He returned to his unit to run the license and registration through his dash computer. It took a little longer than we like."

Johnny was irritated that Roosevelt had deducted a couple of style points because his computer was slow. That was the least of our concerns.

Harper asked, "Did the defendant find anything relevant about Juwon?"

"He had an outstanding warrant for a probation violation. By law and in accordance with standard procedure, the defendant was required to search Juwon's car."

"And if he refused?"

"The defendant had the right to remove him from the vehicle and handcuff him."

"Can you show us what happened in the video from the

defendant's body cam?"

"Of course." Roosevelt ran the video again. "This is where the defendant approached the vehicle for the second time and explained to Juwon that there was an outstanding warrant. The conversation started politely, but turned heated. The defendant ordered Juwon to get out of the car. He refused. They argued. Then Juwon slammed the door into the defendant."

I had watched the next few seconds of footage dozens of times. The video was shaky as Johnny lost his balance and fell onto his back. You couldn't see Jones get out of the car because the camera was pointed up. Jones started running. Murphy ordered him to halt. It took Johnny a few seconds to pull himself to his feet. By the time that he started his pursuit, Jones was already across the plaza.

Harper asked, "Did the defendant follow procedure?"

Theoretically, I could have objected on the grounds that Roosevelt didn't qualify as an expert because he hadn't conducted a traffic stop in almost a half-century. If I had, I would have looked like an idiot.

"For the most part," Roosevelt said. "The defendant made one serious error."

Harper played the straight man. "Which was?"

"He was standing in the wrong place. We teach our trainees to position themselves slightly behind the divider between the front and the back seats to eliminate the possibility that they will be hit by the door."

I got to my feet and tried to break up their flow. "Objection. I fail to see any relevance."

"Overruled."

Harper hadn't taken his eyes off Roosevelt. "This video shows exactly what the defendant saw, right?"

"For the most part. Body cams have a more limited line of vision than the human eye. You can only see what's in-frame. In addition, the camera was mounted on the defendant's chest. As a result, the view is approximately ten inches below normal eye level."

Harper nodded as if to suggest that Roosevelt had imparted a great insight. "Did the defendant tell you that Juwon drew a weapon?"

"Yes. A Kel-Tec PMR-30 handgun."

"He knew the exact make and model?"

"Yes."

Harper ran the video once more. He stopped it an instant after Jones had opened the door. "You've studied this video in detail, right?"

"Right."

"Do you see a Kel-Tec PMR-30?"

"No."

"Did you see a handgun in Juwon's possession in any of the videos that you watched?"

"No."

"Did any witnesses corroborate the defendant's claim that Juwon had a handgun in his possession?"

"His partner, Sergeant Murphy, and two police officers: Richard Siragusa and Charles Connor."

"Was Sergeant Murphy wearing his body cam?"

"It wasn't turned on."

"What about the other officers?"

"Officer Siragusa did not activate his body cam. Officer Connor did, but it did not show a weapon in Juwon's hand."

They went through the rest of the video from Johnny's body cam again. To his credit, Roosevelt pointed out that it was difficult to see Jones because he was almost a block ahead of Johnny and it was dark and raining. He noted that the footage ended when Johnny's camera fell off as he was climbing over the gate into the parking lot.

Harper introduced the video from Connor's body cam. "Inspector, where was this taken?"

"Officer Connor activated his body cam while he was still inside his unit. The latter part of the footage was taken just outside the gate to the parking lot."

Harper ran the footage three times: first at normal speed, then in slow motion, then at normal speed again. In the video of Jones taken from Connor's car, Roosevelt noted that you could not see a gun in Jones's hand. The courtroom was silent as he ran the video taken outside the parking lot in which we could hear the fatal shots.

Harper stopped the video. "Inspector, based upon your interview with the defendant, where was he standing when this footage was taken?"

"Behind the postal van."

"And the victim?"

"Also behind the van."

"You can't see the defendant, can you?"

"No."

"But you can hear him, right?"

"Right. He had cornered Juwon behind the postal van and ordered him to lie down."

"Can you see Juwon?"

Roosevelt pointed at the screen. "If you look closely, you can see his hands above the postal truck. They were raised above his head."

"Is there anything in either of his hands?"

"No."

"The defendant and his partner told you that Juwon had a gun."

"They did."

"Yet there is no gun in either of Juwon's hands in this video, is there?"

"No."

"What did you conclude?"

"That he was not holding a gun when he was shot."

Harper re-started the video. "Inspector, while Juwon had his hands up, he was talking to the defendant, wasn't he?"

"Yes."

"What did he say?"

"'Don't shoot. I'm unarmed.'"

"How many times did he say it?"

"Three. He was pleading for his life."

"Yet the defendant shot him anyway, didn't he?"

"Yes."

"And what did you conclude from this video?"

"That the defendant had shot an unarmed man who was begging for his life."

"No further questions."

"Your witness, Mr. Daley."

As I pushed back my chair and buttoned my suit jacket, Luca whispered, "I hope you brought your A-game."

58
"THEY ALL LIED?"

I stood halfway between the prosecution table and the witness box. I wanted to start a respectful distance from Roosevelt. "Good afternoon, Inspector Johnson."

"Good afternoon, Mr. Daley."

We had faced off in court only a handful of times. San Francisco was a small town with relatively few murders and even fewer murder trials.

I spent forty-five minutes picking away at every piece of evidence that Roosevelt and Harper had introduced during direct. I challenged the collection of the evidence. I argued that the videos were at best inconclusive, and at worst, misleading. I got Roosevelt to acknowledge that Johnny had followed procedure and acted respectfully during the traffic stop. My questions were direct and probing. His answers were candid and convincing. I couldn't shake him or finesse him into an unforced error.

Finally, it was time to go toe-to-toe. "Inspector, when Mr. Jones knocked Officer Bacigalupi down with the car door, Officer Bacigalupi radioed for backup, right?"

"Right."

"And so did Sergeant Murphy?"

"Yes."

"They both clearly stated that the suspect was armed and dangerous, didn't they?"

"Yes."

"And Officer Siragusa and Officer Connor also told you that Mr. Jones had a gun, right?"

"Right."

"Just so we're clear, is it your testimony that they all lied?"

"Perhaps they were mistaken."

"You also testified that Office Bacigalupi shot an unarmed man."

"Objection," Harper said. "This mischaracterizes Inspector Johnson's prior testimony."

Well, maybe a little.

"Overruled."

Roosevelt cleared his throat. "I said that the video showed that the defendant shot Juwon while his hands were up. I was unable to determine whether the firearm allegedly found under Juwon's body was in his possession before he died, or whether it was placed there by one of the officers at the scene. Either way, he wasn't holding a gun when he was shot."

Nice parsing. "Officer Bacigalupi said that he shot Mr. Jones in self-defense."

"That's what he told me."

"Yet you seem to be suggesting that you believe he acted unilaterally."

"I can't tell you what was going on inside his head."

Let me help you. "Obviously, he was afraid because he was looking at a violent man with a gun who had just knocked him over and fled."

"Move to strike," Harper said. "Mr. Daley is testifying."

Yes, I am.

"Sustained. Please, Mr. Daley."

I glanced at Rosie, who touched her left ear. It was the signal that the judge wasn't buying what I was selling. "Inspector Johnson, a police officer with a spotless record had been accosted by a convicted felon who had a dozen AK-47s in the trunk of his car. The officer saw a gun. So did his partner. So did two other officers."

"Objection. There wasn't a question."

No, there wasn't.

"Sustained."

"Inspector, given the fact that a convicted felon disobeyed legal commands, flashed a handgun, slammed a door into Officer Bacigalupi, knocked him down, and fled, doesn't it strike you that Officer Bacigalupi acted reasonably in using lethal force to protect himself when he believed that Mr. Jones was reaching for a weapon?"

"Officer Bacigalupi could have de-escalated the situation by using lesser force."

Easy for you to say. "What would you have done if you had been in his shoes?"

"Objection. Speculation."

"Sustained."

"Inspector, we have the luxury of sitting here in court a week after the fact. Johnny had a fraction of a second to react. The law requires us to consider the circumstances at the time, not with twenty-twenty hindsight. Isn't it reasonable to conclude that Officer Bacigalupi acted in self-defense?"

"I believe that he could have de-escalated the situation."

It's your line and you're sticking to it. "Don't you think a police officer deserves the benefit of the doubt?"

"I do. But in this case, I believe that he acted improperly."

I wasn't going to shake him. "No further questions."

"Redirect, Mr. Harper?"

"No, Your Honor. The prosecution rests."

"Mr. Daley, do you wish to make a motion?"

"Yes, Your Honor. The defense moves to have the charges dropped as a matter of law. The prosecution has failed to meet its burden of proof that there is sufficient evidence to bind the defendant over for trial."

"Denied."

Big surprise.

The judge looked at the clock. "We'll take a brief recess. Please be ready to call your first witness when we resume."

59
"WE STILL HAVE CARDS TO PLAY"

Johnny's voice was flat. "That's it?"

"We haven't started our defense," I said.

"But that's all you've got with Inspector Johnson, right?"

"For now."

"Our witnesses aren't going to change anything. The judge has to give the prosecution the benefit of the doubt."

He was giving up. "We still have cards to play."

"And if they don't work?"

"We'll beat them at trial. The burden of proof will be a lot tougher."

"And I'll be sitting in jail for another year."

"We'll ask for bail again."

"Come on, Mike."

I fought back my impulse to recite a sports cliché about the fact that we were only in the first quarter. "Stay strong, Johnny. We'll get through this."

* * *

My iPhone vibrated as I was about to enter Judge Ramsey's courtroom. Pete's name appeared on the display. I told Nady that I would meet her inside. I made sure that I was out of earshot of anybody in the hall. Then I hit the green button and hoped for the best.

"Give me something that we can use," I said.

Pete cleared his throat. "Have you started your case?"

"We're about to."

"Take it slow, Mick."

"You got something?"

"Hard to say. I'll let you know."

I pressed Disconnect and headed across the hall, where Nady was waiting for me.

"Pete?" she said.

"Yes."

"Anything?"

"Maybe. He didn't give me any details."

"Is he always this coy?"

"Yes."

"Why?"

"Over the years, I've learned not to question my brother's methods."

60
"HE HAD A GUN"

"Please state your name and occupation for the record," I said.

"Kevin Murphy. Sergeant, SFPD."

"How long have you been a police officer?"

"Thirty-four years."

Judge Ramsey's courtroom was silent at four o'clock on Monday afternoon. The nervous energy in the gallery had dissipated into grim resignation. Afternoon sessions are always a slog—even without a jury.

In his pressed patrol uniform and polished badge, Murph looked the part of an old-fashioned neighborhood cop. With his wide face and engaging grin, he'd give you a friendly wave as he walked his beat. You'd never suspect that he would break your kneecaps if you crossed him. While he lacked Roosevelt's gravitas, he was, in his own way, a convincing witness.

I approached the stand. "You were Officer Bacigalupi's supervising officer?"

"Yes."

"Was he a good cop?"

"One of the best that I ever trained. Top of his class. Stellar record. Excellent marks during probation. A superb recruit and a fine officer."

He was laying it on a little thick. "You were on patrol with Officer Bacigalupi on the morning of February ninth?"

"Yes."

It took ten minutes to walk him through the events in the Fillmore. Harper didn't interrupt as Murphy followed my lead and

271

spoke in easily digestible sound bites. SFPD should have brought their recruits to watch him testify.

"Sergeant, where were you when Officer Bacigalupi approached Mr. Jones's vehicle?"

"Near the rear of Mr. Jones's car on the passenger side. I instructed Officer Bacigalupi to take the lead in the interaction. I was hoping that it would be a simple fix-it ticket."

"But the situation escalated."

"Yes, it did. Following standard police procedure, Officer Bacigalupi ran the vehicle registration and Mr. Jones's license through our computer. He determined that Mr. Jones had an outstanding warrant for a probation violation. In such circumstances, it is legally required and standard procedure to ask the perpetrator to exit the vehicle so that the officer can conduct a search. I instructed Officer Bacigalupi to proceed in this manner. I always encourage our recruits to handle every interaction by the book."

Right. "What if the individual refuses to leave the vehicle?"

"The officer is required to remove the suspect and, if necessary, subdue him."

Until this point, I had been setting the table by eliciting short answers. Now I wanted to let Murphy tell the story in his own words. "What happened next?"

He turned subtly toward the judge. "Officer Bacigalupi respectfully asked Mr. Jones to step out of the vehicle. Mr. Jones refused. Officer Bacigalupi asked again, and Mr. Jones still refused. Mr. Jones became angry. He displayed a weapon and banged the driver-side door into Officer Bacigalupi, knocking him down. Mr. Jones fled on foot."

"Did you try to stop him?"

"No. He was armed and dangerous, so I protected myself. I ordered him to halt."

"Did he?"

"He did not."

"Did you pursue him?"

"First, I radioed for backup. Second, I checked on Officer Bacigalupi, who was not seriously injured. He pursued Mr. Jones on foot. I followed him."

"Sergeant Murphy, are you certain that Mr. Jones was armed?"

"Yes." He paused for dramatic effect. "He had a gun."

Perfect. "What kind?"

"We found a Kel-Tec PMR-30 handgun under his body."

We'll get to that in a minute. I asked him to describe the chase.

"I followed Mr. Jones and Officer Bacigalupi through the plaza, north on Fillmore, and west on Geary." He confirmed that Jones jumped the gate into the parking lot. "Officer Richard Siragusa cut off the suspect in the intersection of Geary and Fillmore. Officer Charles Connor provided backup in front of the post office parking lot. Officer Siragusa, Officer Connor, and I were standing outside the parking lot when we heard shots fired."

"Could you see what happened?"

"No, but we heard Officer Bacigalupi order Mr. Jones to lie down. When Mr. Jones refused and reached for his weapon, Officer Bacigalupi had no choice but to shoot him in self-defense."

And there you have it.

Harper got to his feet. "Move to strike. Sergeant Murphy couldn't see what was happening inside the parking lot. He is therefore testifying as to matters for which he has no personal knowledge."

Yup. That's true.

Before I could respond, Murphy spoke up. "You weren't there, Mr. Harper, but I was. Mr. Jones was armed and dangerous. He repeatedly refused to follow commands or surrender. Officer Bacigalupi had no choice but to use lethal force in self-defense."

Sometimes you get help from unanticipated sources.

The judge spoke to me. "Anything else for this witness?"

"One more item." I turned back to Murphy. "After the shooting stopped, did you climb over the gate to assist Officer Bacigalupi?"

"Yes. So did Officer Connor and Officer Siragusa."

"Were you the first officer to reach Mr. Jones other than Officer Bacigalupi?"

"Yes."

"Was Officer Bacigalupi upset?"

"Yes, but he handled the situation professionally and in accordance with his training. He administered first aid and attempted to save Mr. Jones's life."

"You testified that you found a handgun under Mr. Jones's body."

"I did."

"Loaded?"

"Yes. Per procedure, I disarmed the weapon and logged it into evidence along with the unused ammunition."

"It's been suggested that the gun was planted."

"That's preposterous."

"Just to be clear, did you plant the firearm under Mr. Jones's body?"

"Absolutely not."

"Did Officer Bacigalupi?"

"No."

"Did Officer Siragusa or Officer Connor?

"Of course not."

Almost done. "Based upon your thirty-four years of experience and your proximity to the events, did Officer Bacigalupi shoot Mr. Jones in self-defense?"

"Yes, he did."

"No further questions."

"Cross-exam, Mr. Harper?"

"Yes, Your Honor." Harper strode forcefully through the well of the courtroom, where he took a position a couple of feet from Murphy.

Stay the course, Murph.

"Sergeant Murphy, you were present during the traffic stop,

right?"

"Right."

"Isn't it standard procedure to turn on your body cam when you engage a suspect?"

"Yes."

"But you didn't turn on your body cam, did you?"

"No. I thought it was going to be a routine traffic stop for a fix-it ticket."

"So you violated policy?"

"Technically, yes."

"You understand that if you had turned on your body cam, we would have more definitive evidence of what happened on the morning of February ninth, right?"

I could have objected, but I let it go. Murph could hold his own.

The veteran cop held up a hand as if to say, "That's all you've got?" "If I had to do it again, I would have turned on my camera."

Harper shook his head. "You've been a police officer for thirty-four years, right?"

"Yes."

"Ever been suspended?"

Here we go. "Objection. Relevance."

"Overruled."

Murphy held up a hand as if to tell me that he would deal with it. "Once."

"For what?"

"A convicted sex offender made wild claims that I was too rough when I arrested him."

"You cracked his skull with your baton, didn't you?"

"I acted in self-defense after he tried to kill me."

"Is that how you train the officers that you supervise?"

"Objection. Relevance."

"Sustained."

"The person that you beat up was African-American, wasn't he?"

I figured that this was coming. "Objection. Relevance."

"Overruled."

Murph didn't fluster. "Yes, the convicted felon who attacked me was African-American. He's going to be in prison for the rest of his life."

Harper moved in front of Murphy. "How long were you suspended?"

"A week."

"You didn't challenge the suspension, did you?"

"No. The process would have taken longer than serving the suspension."

"You told your superiors that you never hit the suspect, didn't you?"

"Yes."

"That wasn't true, was it?"

"No."

"Are you lying now, Officer Murphy?"

"Objection. Relevance."

"Sustained."

"You've also been put on report six times for police brutality, haven't you?"

"I've been doing this for a long time. Spurious claims are part of the job description."

"All of those claims came from African-Americans, didn't they?"

"I don't recall."

"Do I need to introduce the official complaints into the record?"

"That won't be necessary."

"So you would acknowledge that all of the claims came from African-Americans?"

"I'll take your word for it."

"You seem to have a problem with African-Americans."

"I work in a neighborhood where the population is predominantly African-American. As a result, most of the people with whom I interact happen to be African-American."

"And if you need to rough them up a bit, that's fine with you, right?"

"Objection. Relevance. Foundation."

"Sustained."

"No further questions, Your Honor."

"Please call your next witness, Mr. Daley."

"The defense calls Officer Richard Siragusa."

61
"YOU THINK I'M MAKING IT UP?"

Rick Siragusa sat in the witness box, arms at his sides. "I responded to a request for backup from Officer Bacigalupi and Sergeant Murphy at one-ten a.m. on February ninth."

"Where were you at the time?" I asked.

"Parked in front of the Boom-Boom Room."

Judge Ramsey was listening intently. The people in the gallery were getting antsy.

"Did it strike you as odd that Officer Bacigalupi and Sergeant Murphy requested backup for a traffic stop?"

"No. They requested backup after Mr. Jones attacked Officer Bacigalupi and fled."

"Did they specify whether Mr. Jones was armed?"

"They did. Listen to the audio on the police band. The perp was an African-American male dressed in black, armed and dangerous. I put on my lights and pulled into the intersection of Fillmore and Geary. A moment later, I saw Jones running toward me."

"Did you get out of your car?"

"No. The suspect was armed, so I called for more backup. I used my microphone to order him to stop, but he didn't."

Here goes. "Did you see a gun in his hand?"

"Yes."

I asked him what happened next.

"Jones turned onto Geary and headed west. Officer Bacigalupi followed him shortly thereafter. Sergeant Murphy came a moment later."

"Did you follow them down Geary?"

"Yes. I drew my sidearm, left my vehicle, and proceeded on foot to the area outside the parking lot of the post office, where I found Sergeant Murphy and Officer Charles Connor. We couldn't see Officer Bacigalupi or the perpetrator because they were behind a postal van. We heard Officer Bacigalupi order Mr. Jones to lie down. Mr. Jones disobeyed the command and reached for a weapon. Officer Bacigalupi shot him in self-defense."

"No further questions."

Harper was up quickly. "You were in your car when Mr. Jones ran by?"

"Yes."

"How far away from you was he?"

"About the length of this courtroom."

"It was dark and raining?"

"Yes, but my headlights were on."

"And your wipers?"

"I believe so."

"Did he stop in front of your unit?"

"No."

"So you saw him for about a second?"

"A little longer. Probably two or three seconds."

"And it's your testimony that Mr. Jones was holding a handgun?"

"Yes."

"What type?"

"I'm not sure."

Harper walked to the evidence cart and picked up the Kel-Tec. "Was it this handgun?"

"I presume that it was. Sergeant Murphy and Officer Bacigalupi found it under Mr. Jones's body."

"Did Mr. Jones point it at you as he ran by?"

"No."

"But you could see it in his hand?"

"Objection," I said. "Asked and answered."

"Sustained."

Harper put the Kel-Tec back on the cart, then he moved in front of Siragusa. "Did you activate your body cam?"

"No. There wasn't time."

"So, while sitting inside your police unit on a dark and rainy night with your wipers going, you were able to see a small handgun in Mr. Jones's hand as he sprinted by you?"

Siragusa didn't hesitate. "Yes."

"And you expect us to believe you?"

"Objection."

"Withdrawn. No further questions."

"Redirect, Mr. Daley?"

I had nothing to add. "No, Your Honor."

"Please call your next witness."

"The defense calls Officer Charles Connor."

* * *

Charlie Connor gulped down his second cup of water. His soft features and pale complexion made him look more like a high school student than a police officer. His starched uniform looked like he had taken it out of the box earlier that day.

I had given Siragusa some open-ended questions. I was going to lead Connor shamelessly. "You were in your unit near Kimbell Park when the call for backup came in from Officer Bacigalupi and Sergeant Murphy?"

"Yes."

"That's about a block away from the post office?"

Connor nodded a little too enthusiastically. "Yes."

"You immediately drove over to Geary?"

"Yes."

"How long did that take?"

"About fifteen seconds."

"You parked in front of the post office parking lot?"

"Yes."

"And you saw Juwon Jones running toward you?"

"Yes."

"Did you get out of your car?"

"No. I got on my speaker and ordered him to stop."

"Did he?"

"No. He climbed over the gate into the parking lot. Officer Bacigalupi followed him a few seconds later."

"Did you see a gun in Mr. Jones's hand when he ran by your car?"

"Yes."

"What did you do next?"

"I radioed for backup. Then I got out of my vehicle and walked over to the parking lot."

"Was anybody else there?"

"Sergeant Murphy. Officer Rick Siragusa joined us a moment later."

"Could you see Officer Bacigalupi inside the parking lot?"

"No. He and Mr. Jones were behind a postal van."

"Could you hear anything?"

"Yes. Officer Bacigalupi ordered Mr. Jones to put his hands up. Then he ordered Mr. Jones to lie down. Mr. Jones disobeyed Officer Bacigalupi's orders multiple times and reached for a weapon, so Officer Bacigalupi shot him in self-defense."

"How do you know it was self-defense?"

"As I said, I saw a gun in Jones's hand when he ran in front of my unit."

Good enough. "Officer Connor, did you activate your body cam?"

"Yes."

"When?"

"I was still inside my unit."

"So you took video of Mr. Jones as he was running in front of your car?"

"Yes."

"Can you see a gun in his hand?"

"No."

"Why not?"

"It happened very fast. It's hard to see anything in the video because it was dark and raining."

Good enough. "Do you have video of what happened inside the parking lot?"

"Yes. My body cam was on when I was standing outside the gate. As I mentioned, we couldn't see Officer Bacigalupi or Mr. Jones because they were behind a postal van."

"But you could hear them?"

"Yes. Officer Bacigalupi ordered Mr. Jones to lie down. He repeated the order three times."

"Are Officer Bacigalupi's commands to Mr. Jones audible on the recording from your body cam?"

"Yes."

"And when Mr. Jones did not obey Officer Bacigalupi's multiple orders to lie down, Officer Bacigalupi shot him, right?"

"In self-defense."

"In self-defense," I repeated. "No further questions."

Harper walked straight to the front of the witness box. "You testified that you saw the gun in Juwon's hand while you were still sitting in your police car, right?"

"Right."

"And you're absolutely sure that he had a gun in his hand even though it was dark and raining and he ran by you in less than a second?"

Connor hesitated. "Yes."

"And you testified that you couldn't see the gun in the video, right?"

"Objection. Asked and answered."

"Sustained."

Harper shook his head. "Officer Connor, is it your testimony that Juwon still had the gun in his hand when he climbed over the gate?"

"Yes."

"You realize that the gate is eight feet tall, right?"

"I'll take your word for it."

"So he had to leap up and pull himself over, right?"

"Right."

"But you're saying that the gun was still in his hand as he pulled himself over the fence?"

"I believe so."

Don't equivocate, Charlie.

"You recorded the events in the parking lot on your body cam, right?"

"Right. As I mentioned, we couldn't see Officer Bacigalupi or the perpetrator because they were behind a postal van."

"You heard Juwon tell the defendant that he was unarmed, right?"

"He was lying."

"He said it three times. The audio was recorded on your body cam."

Connor tried to sound more forceful. "He was lying."

"You've watched the video, right?"

"Right."

"You can see Juwon's hands above the roof of the postal van, can't you?"

"Yes."

"And you would agree that there was no gun in either of his hands, right?"

"Right."

"If there was no gun in his hands, why did Officer Bacigalupi shoot him?"

"He was reaching for a gun."

"So you say."

"You think I'm making it up?"

"As a matter of fact, I do."

"Objection," I said. "Mr. Harper is testifying."

"Sustained."

Harper returned to his seat. "No further questions, Your Honor."

"Redirect, Mr. Daley?"

"Just one question. Officer Connor, just so we're clear, did you see a gun in Mr. Jones's hand when he ran in front of your unit and then climbed over the gate into the parking lot?"

"Yes."

"No further questions."

The judge looked at his watch. "I'm going to recess until ten o'clock tomorrow morning. Do you plan to call any more witnesses, Mr. Daley?"

"Just one, Your Honor." I looked at Johnny. "We plan to call Officer Bacigalupi."

62
"JUSTICE IS ELUSIVE"

Johnny's hands were clasped, eyes red. "You said I wasn't going to testify."

"Change of plans."

Johnny, Luca, and I were sitting around a dented table in the sweltering consultation room down the hall from Judge Ramsey's courtroom. Nady had gone to the office to begin preparations for tomorrow. Rosie had returned to the P.D.'s Office.

Luca's expression was grim. "What made you change your mind?"

"We aren't going to get the charges dropped based on today's testimony. The burden of proof is low, and the judge is required to give the prosecution the benefit of the doubt. We have nothing to contradict the video showing Jones with his hands up."

"Three cops testified that he had a gun."

"It should get us to reasonable doubt at trial, but it won't stop the proceedings now."

"Why put Johnny on the stand?"

Because I don't have any better ideas. "If Johnny is convincing enough, the judge may rule in our favor. If not, maybe the prosecution will come to their senses and drop the charges—or reduce them."

"What are the chances?"

Not great. "Hard to say."

"Why didn't you ask for bail again?"

"That would have suggested that I thought the judge was going to rule in favor of the prosecution."

Luca nodded.

I turned to Johnny. "In the morning, I'm going to ask you three questions. First, did Jones have a gun when he got out of the car? Second, did he have it while he was running down the street? Third, did he still have it in the parking lot? The correct answers are yes, yes, and yes."

"Got it."

"Try to get some sleep. I'll see you in the morning."

* * *

"When was the last time you slept?" I asked.

Nady took off her glasses. "Probably around the same time that you did."

The conference room in Luca's office was quiet at eight o'clock on Monday night. The TV was tuned to CNN, the sound down. Anderson Cooper was standing under the awning in front of a currency exchange on Fillmore. Rain pelted his windbreaker as he reported that things were calm—for now.

I gulped down the remnants of my Diet Dr Pepper. "If you keep this up, you're going to burn yourself out."

She smiled. "I don't think so. I take a lot of vacations."

"Millennials."

Her grin broadened. "You Boomers blame us for everything from short attention spans to global warming. Look in the mirror. You went to college and bought your houses on the cheap. You've started a bunch of wars and destroyed the environment. Then you killed the economy when we were getting out of college. Thanks for dumping your trash on us."

Guilty. "For what it's worth, I think you have a legitimate point that our stewardship of the world has been somewhat less than exemplary."

"We're going to get the last laugh. We're going to inherit all of your money."

Yes, you will. "Not gonna happen. We're going to spend it all on ourselves."

"Like you've been doing for the past fifty years?"

"Pretty much."

She turned serious. "How is your closing argument coming along?"

"Not bad."

"What's the narrative?"

She was a quick study. "Self-defense."

"You can't see a gun in Jones's hand in the video on the street or in the parking lot. He told Johnny that he was unarmed—three times."

"Three eyewitnesses testified that he had a gun. Johnny will make four."

"They're all cops."

"The judge may be reluctant to rule that they were all lying."

"Don't be so sure. And they're all white."

"Doesn't matter."

"Yes, it does."

Yes, it does.

"Are you really going to put Johnny on the stand?" she asked.

"If I can't come up with anything else."

"You think it will help?"

"Some."

"Enough to get the charges dropped tomorrow?"

"Probably not. The prosecution's burden of proof is low."

She exhaled. "How do you deal with this stuff?"

"I've been doing it for a long time."

"I'm serious, Mike. Everybody thinks our client is guilty. There are riots in the streets. People are burning cars and throwing rocks. You're getting annihilated in the papers and on cable. Doesn't it make you a little crazy?"

Yup. "This isn't a popularity contest. I can't worry about what's going on outside. I try to focus on doing my best for Johnny."

She wasn't convinced.

I tried again. "You saw how it went in court. This isn't like a real estate contract that you edit a thousand times. Defense work is a combination of improvisational theater and making sausage. You make judgments on the fly and keep adding new ingredients. If everybody in court does their job and respects the process, there's a reasonable chance that you'll end up with a decent result."

"You really believe that, don't you?"

Most of the time. "Yes."

"What about justice?"

"Justice is elusive."

"What about O.J.?"

"We don't always get it right."

"Are you going to be able to get it right this time?"

I answered her honestly. "I don't know. If not at the prelim, we'll have another chance at the trial." I looked across the table. "For what it's worth, you'd make an excellent defense attorney. You're smart, strategic, and practical. And Lord knows, you're willing to work hard. Let me know if you'd like to give it a try. You aren't going to get rich or famous, and you'll work harder than you've ever worked, but the experience is unbelievable, and you'd be making a difference." I gave her a knowing look. "And it beats pushing paper all day."

"I'll think about it."

Pete's name appeared on my iPhone. I hit the green button and said, "This would be a good time for you to provide some information that would help our case."

"How soon can you get down to the Fillmore?"

"Twenty minutes."

"Meet me in the backroom of the Boom-Boom Room. Make sure that nobody is following you and come in through the alley."

"Is Gio with you?"

"No."

Uh-oh. "What's going on, Pete?"

"Dwayne wants to talk to us."

"The homeless guy from the plaza?"

"There's more to the story."

The line went dead.

Nady eyed me hopefully. "Your brother?"

"Who else? I need to get down to the Fillmore."

"I'll come with you."

"It could be dangerous."

"My mother and I got chased out of Uzbekistan when I was four years old with no money in our pockets and just the clothes on our backs."

And I complain when the internet goes out for ten minutes. "Get your jacket and umbrella. Let's go see if we can make some sausage."

63
"A WIN FOR EVERYBODY"

Dwayne eyed me with suspicion. "Did anybody follow you?"

"No."

He was sitting at the manager's desk in the cramped backroom of the Boom-Boom Room at eight-thirty on Monday night. Pete was guarding the door. Nady was sitting next to me. The floor vibrated from the pulsating sound of a hip-hop band.

I looked at my brother. "Why isn't Gio here?"

"He *can't* be here." He didn't elaborate.

The door opened, and Roosevelt entered. "Dwayne."

"Inspector."

Roosevelt closed the door behind him and stood guard—as if somebody else could have squeezed inside. "I understand that you have some information for us."

"I might."

Too coy for me. "Do you and Inspector Johnson know each other?"

"We've met."

I looked at Roosevelt, who held up a hand. I waited.

Dwayne pulled out a throwaway "burner" phone and placed it on the desk. "I took this video on the morning of February ninth."

Pete, Nady, and I leaned over to watch. Roosevelt looked over my shoulder.

Dwayne pressed the Play button. The video was grainy. There was no audio. I recognized the plaza. A tall African-American man sprinted across the screen. Dwayne stopped the video.

"Jones?" I asked.

"Yes." He restarted the video and stopped it a second later. He zoomed in on Jones's right hand. "You can see a handgun."

I wasn't going to disagree.

Roosevelt took off his glasses and studied the frozen shot. He didn't say anything.

"There's more," Dwayne said.

He continued the video. Just after Jones ran by the Subway, he skidded on the wet bricks, lost his balance, and fell face-first to the ground. He got up, looked around for an instant—as if he had dropped something—and then continued out of sight.

I looked at Dwayne. "He dropped the gun."

"Looks like it."

He pressed Play again. We watched Johnny sprint across the plaza, weapon drawn. He ran by the Subway, turned onto Fillmore, and disappeared. Twenty seconds later, Murphy lumbered by. He stopped beneath the Subway sign, kneeled, and reached down. He picked up an object and put it into his pocket. Then he, too, disappeared into the night.

Dwayne hit the red Stop button. We stared at each other in silence as the music pounded through the walls.

I finally spoke up. "This proves that Jones had a gun."

Dwayne nodded. "Yes, he did."

"He dropped it near the Subway. Johnny ran by it without seeing it. Murphy stopped and picked it up."

"So it seems."

Roosevelt cleared his throat. "If that's the gun that they allegedly found under Jones's body, it proves that your client shot an unarmed man."

"Johnny didn't know that Jones had dropped the gun."

"Jones told him that he was unarmed—three times."

"Johnny had a legitimate belief that Jones was lying."

"It doesn't explain how the gun got under Jones's body."

I was happy to throw somebody other than Johnny under the bus. "Murphy planted it."

"You don't know that."

"He was the last person to have the gun in his possession."

"You don't know that, either. Johnny must have known that Murphy planted it. Or maybe Murphy gave it to him and he planted it himself."

"You won't be able to prove it."

"We'll lean on Murphy. He'll roll on your client if we offer him immunity."

That's a potential problem. "The D.A. will never give immunity to a cop who planted a gun and lied about it in court."

"She might."

No, she won't. "Either way, this is a game changer. Johnny thought that Jones still had the gun when he shot him. He was acting in self-defense—or at least he thought he was. It takes the murder charge off the table."

"You'll need to have that conversation with our D.A."

Yes, I would. "Siragusa and Connor testified that Jones was holding a gun when he ran by them. We now know that Jones dropped it beforehand. It means that they were lying under oath. That's perjury and obstruction of justice."

Roosevelt's eyes narrowed. "Maybe they were mistaken. All we know is that Jones dropped a gun, and Murphy picked it up."

My mind went into overdrive. The video resolved the issue of whether Jones had a gun when he fled. But it also proved that Jones didn't have it when Johnny shot him, but Johnny didn't know it. If Johnny reasonably believed that Jones was still armed and was reaching for a gun, we had a strong case for self-defense.

We would also have to deal with the fact that the gun must have been planted. We would argue that Murphy planted it. Murphy would argue that Johnny planted it. The D.A. would argue that they conspired to plant it. Johnny was still at risk on charges of filing a false police report and obstruction of justice. Murphy was already guilty of the former and almost certainly guilty of the latter. And Siragusa and Connor were possibly guilty of perjury and obstruction, although their lawyers would argue that they were simply mistaken about seeing a gun in Jones's hand.

Bottom line: it was hard to envision a scenario where all of the cops would get through this unscathed, but I was concerned about only one: Johnny.

I turned to Dwayne. "We'll need to provide this video to the D.A."

"Fine."

"And we'll need you to authenticate it and testify."

"I can't do that."

"Why not?"

"It's complicated."

"We can subpoena you."

"You won't be able to find me."

"We're very resourceful."

"We're *more* resourceful."

What the hell? "I take it that your name isn't Dwayne?"

"No, it's not."

"And you're not really homeless?"

"Let's just say that I have another job."

"FBI?"

"Could be."

"Why are you talking to us?"

"I'm trying to make sure that the truth comes out." He pointed at Pete. "Your brother and Assistant Chief Bacigalupi figured out that I wasn't just another homeless guy. In exchange for not blowing my cover, I agreed to talk to you."

Pete's expression didn't change. I would find out how he managed this later tonight. "And Inspector Johnson?"

"My superiors determined that it would be advisable to talk to people on both sides of this case. We're trying to avoid compromising a three-year investigation of one of the biggest heroin distributors on the West Coast. If our covers are blown, our investigation will implode, and there's a good chance that some dedicated law enforcement officers will die—including me. I trust you can see why we'd like to avoid that scenario."

"I can."

"Now you understand why I can't appear in court."

"You should be talking to the D.A."

"We don't trust her."

Neither do I.

Dwayne was still talking. "We decided to talk to you first. Your brother has a reputation as a stand-up guy. So does Inspector Johnson. And so do you."

Good to hear it. "You should have been coordinating with SFPD."

"We can't." He glanced at Roosevelt. "Some cops are dirty."

"Why haven't they been arrested?"

"We're still building our case. We plan to announce arrests of major drug players and some people in law enforcement in the next few months."

"If you can't testify, this doesn't help my client."

"This video does. Take it to the D.A. and cut the best deal that you can. This should be enough to persuade her to drop the murder charge."

"She's going to need verification of the legitimacy of this video."

"That's why Inspector Johnson is here. He'll have to handle it."

I turned around and looked at Roosevelt, who nodded.

Dwayne wasn't finished. "The events of the past week have jeopardized our operation. Some of our suspects have left town. Having an army of cops, National Guard, and protesters in our territory is making our job harder. I'm willing to give you the video, but you need to keep us out of it. If you do your job, my people will stay safe, the bad guys will be arrested, the truth will come out, and your client won't go to jail for murder."

"There's no guaranty that I can persuade the D.A. or my client to accept a deal."

"I hear that you're a very good lawyer."

"What's to prevent me from revealing your identity to the D.A.?"

"Nothing, but we'll deny everything and say that you made the video yourself. Then you and your client will be in worse shape than you are now. Your client will be tried for murder, and you'll be charged with manufacturing evidence. I suspect that you'd like to avoid that scenario."

"We would. I could give the video to Jerry Edwards at the *Chronicle*."

"He won't be able to authenticate it, either. Besides, you have a reputation as a guy who wouldn't breach our confidence and get a bunch of hardworking FBI agents killed."

I wouldn't.

He handed me the burner phone. "This should be enough to persuade Ms. Ward to drop the murder charge. That's a win for you. You might even be able to convince her not to charge your client with obstruction. That would be another win for you."

True.

He pointed at Roosevelt. "You can arrest Murphy for lying under oath and obstruction of justice. You may have enough evidence to charge the other two cops for lying under oath. That's a win for you *and* the D.A."

Also true.

"We can continue our investigation, keep our covers intact, arrest a bunch of bad guys, and, hopefully, avoid getting any of our people killed. That's a win for us."

True again.

"And if we can resolve this quickly, things should calm down, the mayor can send the National Guard home, and people can get on with their lives. That's a win for everybody."

I wasn't so confident.

He held out a hand, which I shook. "For obvious reasons, you won't be seeing me again. And I will, of course, deny that this meeting ever took place."

"Understood."

"For security reasons, I'll need to know if you've been able to work this out with the D.A. by midnight. Inspector Johnson knows how to reach us."

"Thank you, Dwayne."

"Good luck, Mr. Daley."

* * *

Pete was behind the wheel and I was in the passenger seat of his Crown Vic as we drove past St. Mary's Cathedral at nine o'clock on Monday night. Rain reflected off his headlights.

Nady spoke up from the back seat. "Didn't see that coming."

Neither did I. "I told you that it's like making sausage."

"Can you cut a deal with Ward and Harper?"

"We're going to find out."

She spoke to Pete. "How did you know that Dwayne worked undercover?"

"I used to be in law enforcement. I notice things."

"Like what?"

"He didn't pass the smell test."

"He smelled terrible."

"Not terrible enough for a homeless guy. You haven't spent as much time on the street as I have." The corner of his mouth turned up. "And I played a hunch."

"Did Gio have anything to do with it?"

"Might have."

Nady wasn't satisfied. "You didn't just walk up to him and say, 'You smell too good to be a real homeless guy, so you must be an undercover cop.'"

"I tailed him. He was sleeping in an SRO on Fulton. It isn't the Ritz, but it's better than the street. I told him that I wouldn't blow his cover if he was straight with me. He agreed to trust me after I told him that I used to be a cop. He said that he was working on something big. I told him that if he could help us, I could get

Johnny's case resolved and get the National Guard out of the neighborhood. If you want something, you gotta give something."

"How did you plan to resolve Johnny's case?"

"I called my big brother." He turned to me. "Speaking of which, did you hear back from the D.A.?"

"Yeah. She's agreed to meet with us tonight."

64
"WE CAN END THIS RIGHT NOW"

"You're absolutely sure this is legitimate?" Ward asked. She and Harper had just viewed Dwayne's video for the third time.

Roosevelt didn't waver. "Yes."

The District Attorney of the City and County of San Francisco was sitting ramrod straight in her ergonomic leather chair. For the first time since I'd met her, her makeup wasn't perfect, and the bags under her eyes were visible. She stared daggers at me. "You're playing games."

I darted a glance at Nady, who was sitting in the chair next to mine. Then I turned back to Ward. "I'm trying to save lives and stop the chaos on the streets. We can end this right now."

"Based upon a video that you could have made on your iPad?"

"Inspector Johnson just confirmed that the individual who shot the video is working undercover on busting a major heroin ring. I'm going to leave it up to Inspector Johnson to decide whether he wants to give you more information about that person. I can assure you that if we reveal his identity, it will put his life and the lives of a dozen law enforcement officers at risk. If we work together, we can avoid a disaster."

"And if I refuse?"

"I will send this video to Jerry Edwards at the *Chronicle*."

"You're prepared to put the undercover officers at risk?"

No, I'm not. "If I have to. My loyalty is to my client. Obviously, I would prefer to work something out with you."

"You're bluffing."

"No, I'm not." *Yes, I am.* "I'm trying to work with you."

"I would appreciate it if you and Ms. Nikonova would wait outside for a few minutes."

* * *

At some point in every case, it always seems to come down to an interminable wait. As Nady and I sat in the darkened reception area outside Ward's office, five minutes turned into ten, ten turned into fifteen, and fifteen turned into a half-hour. Unlike Ward's opulent office, the waiting area hadn't been remodeled. It looked the same as it did when I was a baby public defender almost a quarter of a century earlier.

My mind wandered as I checked my e-mails and texts. Pete asked for an update. So did Luca. Gio was standing by, hoping for a shred of positive news. Rosie reported that she was working late. I smiled when Tommy texted me a reminder about his next basketball game.

I leaned back in the plastic seat, closed my eyes, and replayed the prelim in my head. I thought about Johnny, whose life would never be the same. I reminded myself of his mother's words that he never really wanted to be a cop. I understood the endless fears and worries that she had endured as the wife of an assistant chief and the mother of seven police officers. I thought of my old friend, Gio, who was a standup guy and a hardworking cop.

Then my thoughts turned to my dad. He never said much, and we didn't always see eye to eye. As I've gotten older, I've started to understand him better. He did his job, played by the rules, paid his taxes, was faithful to his wife, and wanted his kids to have a better life. In his own way, he was an excellent role model. I would have given anything to have spent a little more time with him.

The door to Ward's office opened. Harper appeared, expression serious. "We need to talk."

* * *

Ward sat in her chair, features contorted into an extreme frown. Harper sat to my left, demeanor subdued. Nady was to my right. Roosevelt sat in an armchair in front of the flat-screen TV, the ever-present cup of coffee in his hand.

Ward's tone was grave. "You've put us in an impossible situation."

"We can fix this, Nicole."

"I'm not so sure, Mike."

Let's not get melodramatic. "The video changes everything."

"No, it doesn't."

"Yes, it does. Jones had a gun. It proves that Johnny acted in self-defense."

"Jones dropped the gun."

"Johnny didn't know it. He *thought* that he was acting in self-defense. We're back to *Graham vs. Connor.* Johnny had a legitimate belief that Jones still had the gun. When Jones lowered his hands, Johnny believed that he was reaching for it, so he shot him in self-defense."

"Jones repeatedly said that he was unarmed."

"Johnny had a reasonable basis to believe that he was lying."

"Come on, Mike."

"You come on, Nicole. Judge Ramsey isn't going to move this case to trial on a murder-one charge. Even if he does, you'll never get to guilt beyond a reasonable doubt."

Her full lips turned down. "I might be willing to go down to murder-two."

Progress. "You won't get a conviction. We'll get to reasonable doubt on self-defense."

Her eyes betrayed her poker face. She knew that I was right. "You expect us to drop the charges?"

"Yes."

"I can't do that, Mike."

"Yes, you can. And it isn't as if you'll come up empty. Based on the video, you have a slam-dunk case against Murphy for filing a false police report, obstruction of justice, and perjury. You can get Siragusa and Connor for lying about seeing the gun in Jones's hand."

"You expect me to let your client walk away scot-free?"

"He didn't do anything illegal."

"He lied."

"No, he didn't. He didn't know that Jones had dropped the gun. He didn't know that Murphy had picked it up and planted it under Jones's body."

"He colluded with Murphy, Siragusa, and Connor to obstruct justice."

Maybe. "You don't know that. And you certainly can't prove it."

"You expect me to just let him out?"

Ideally. "Yes."

She exchanged frustrated looks with Harper and Roosevelt, then she looked straight into my eyes. "I can't do it, Mike. I can't just let him go."

It was time to put our cards on the table. "What *can* you do?"

There was an interminable hesitation. "First, I'm prepared to drop the murder charge."

Don't react—hear her out. "That's a good start."

"Second, your client will agree to be a fully cooperating witness in the cases that we will be bringing against Murphy, Siragusa, and Connor. If he lies about anything, all bets are off."

"Fine."

"Third, your client will submit his resignation from SFPD."

As a practical matter, Johnny couldn't continue as a member of SFPD if he testified against three other cops. "I'll talk to him."

"Finally, your client will plead guilty to obstruction of justice."

Crap. "He didn't obstruct justice."

"He colluded with three other officers to lie about planting the gun."

"No, he didn't."

"Yes, he did."

"You can't make that case beyond a reasonable doubt."

"We'll get Murphy, Siragusa, and Connor to testify against him in exchange for lighter sentences."

Yes, you will. "You're asking me to convince my client to plead guilty to a crime that he didn't commit?"

"He shot an unarmed kid."

"In self-defense."

"He and his partner lied. So did Siragusa and Connor. This is absolutely the best deal that I'm going to offer, and it's a lot better than I *should* offer."

I believed her. "He can't do time."

"He has to do time."

"Probation."

"The maximum sentence is just one year. That's the best that I can do."

"Too long."

"I'm being generous."

"Probation," I repeated.

"One year."

"Three months."

"One year. With good behavior, he'll only have to serve six months."

"Credit for time served."

"Yes. That's the absolute best that I can do."

That's as good as I'm going to get. "I'll take it back to my client."

She looked at her watch. "This offer will remain open for the next hour. If you breathe a word of this to anybody else, it's revoked, and I will deny that I ever made it."

* * *

Nady and I walked down the empty corridor outside Ward's office. "Can I join you when you talk to Johnny?" she asked.

"Ordinarily, I'd say yes, but I think it's probably better if I talk to him alone."

"Understood. I'll meet you back at the office."

"Thanks." I pulled out my iPhone and punched in a now-familiar number.

Gio answered on the first ring. "You got something, Mike?"

"I need you to come over to the Hall right away. We need to talk to Johnny."

"Did you get the charges dropped?"

"Not yet, but I might have something that could be workable."

"I'll be right there. You want me to bring Luca?"

"I think it would be better if just you and I talked to Johnny."

65
"IT'S BETTER THIS WAY"

Johnny's face was flushed as he sat on the opposite side of the table from his father and me. He spoke in a hoarse whisper. "They want me to confess to a crime that I didn't commit?"

Yes. "Plea bargain deals are never perfect, Johnny."

"You want me to lie?"

Yes. "In my judgment, it's the best deal that we're going to get. It takes the murder charge off the table. It caps your exposure."

"You sound like a lawyer."

I am a lawyer. "You can put all of this behind you in a year—six months with good behavior. A trial won't even start for another year—maybe longer. I can't guarantee that I'll be able to persuade the judge to grant bail."

"I'd have to quit my job."

"I'm afraid so." *Your mother says you never wanted to be a cop.* "Either way, it wouldn't be safe for you to remain with SFPD."

"I would have to live with the fact that I'm a convicted criminal."

There's no way around it. "Yes."

"And I'd have to testify against Murph, Goose, and Charlie?"

"You'd have to cooperate."

"You want me to rat them out?"

"I want you to tell the truth."

"So, you want me to tell the truth about them, but not me?"

Ironically, it would work to your advantage. "That's part of the deal."

"You're okay with that?"

"I'm not crazy about it, but I think it's the best alternative for you."

"So you think morality has a sliding scale?"

"This is about expedience."

"Is that what you used to tell people when you were a priest?"

Occasionally. "I wasn't the world's greatest priest."

"Maybe you aren't the world's greatest lawyer, either."

I let it go. He was under an ungodly amount of stress.

Johnny considered his options for an interminable moment. "You're the hotshot lawyer. What would you do if you were me?"

I'd probably fight it, but I don't always do the rational thing. "I'd take the deal. It minimizes your exposure and ends this today."

He turned to his father. "And you?"

Assistant Chief Giovanni Bacigalupi III looked straight into the eyes of his youngest child. "Take the deal, son. It's better this way."

"You're okay with me admitting that I'm a criminal?"

"It minimizes the risk of greater damage."

"It will ruin my reputation."

"People have short memories."

"It will ruin our family's reputation."

"We'll be fine."

"I'll lose my job."

"There are other jobs."

"It won't be the family business."

"We've been doing this for four generations. Maybe it's time for us to try something new."

"I always wanted to be a cop."

Gio's tone was empathetic. "No, you didn't. *I* always wanted you to be a cop."

"You'd be okay with it?"

"Absolutely. And your mother would have one less cop to worry about when she goes to bed every night." He added, "So will I."

Johnny swallowed hard.

My old classmate stood up and hugged his youngest son. "You're the seventh son of the seventh son, Giovanni. That makes you special. I know that I've never said this enough, but I am immensely proud of you."

The room was silent as my friend and my godson hugged. When they finally separated, Johnny choked back tears and whispered, "Please tell the D.A. that I accept the deal."

"I will."

There were tears in Gio's eyes when he whispered to his son, "I'll go call your mother."

66
"I WORK HERE"

The light was on in Rosie's office when I walked in at eleven o'clock on Monday night. The plaintive sound of Bonnie Raitt singing John Prine's "Angel from Montgomery" came from the speaker next to her computer.

"You're here late," I observed.

She looked up. "I needed to get caught up on paperwork."

"Kids okay?"

"Fine."

"Your mom?"

"Status quo. What brings you here?"

"I work here."

She took off her reading glasses. "Do you?"

"I used to."

"Do you still *want* to work here?"

"Yes."

"Good." She took a sip of water. She pointed at the chair opposite her desk. "Sit."

I did as she said.

"Diet Dr Pepper?"

"No, thanks."

"Bourbon?"

"That sounds better."

"Thought so." She pulled a bottle of Bulleit Bourbon and two glasses from her bottom drawer and poured a finger for each of us. "Enough?"

"I think so."

"There's more at home."

"That might be a good thing."

"Did you get your car fixed?"

"It'll be ready tomorrow."

She took a sip of her drink. "I heard you cut a deal for Johnny."

Word travels fast. "Where did you hear that?"

"Maria. She didn't have details."

"Is she holding up okay?"

"Relieved. And she expressed her gratitude for all of your efforts."

"Glad to hear it."

"What's the deal?"

"Ward will drop the murder charge. Johnny will plead guilty to obstruction with a recommendation of a one-year sentence. With good behavior, he'll be out in six months. He'll resign from SFPD and be a cooperating witness in obstruction and perjury cases against Murphy, Siragusa, and Connor."

"Good result for Johnny. Ward gets to claim victory, too. Not bad at all. I take it that you found some new evidence?"

"Pete did."

"I should have known. What was it?"

"Video of Jones running across the plaza with a gun in his hand." I filled her in on the details. "Murphy planted the gun— maybe with Johnny's knowledge. Maybe not. Either way, Murphy lied in his police report and probably obstructed justice. Siragusa and Connor lied about seeing a gun in Jones's hand, or they were mistaken. Either way, they were wrong."

"They lied."

"Murphy did for sure. I'm not so sure about Siragusa and Connor."

"They testified that they saw a gun in Jones's hand. How is that *not* lying?"

"They responded to a call saying that Jones was armed and dangerous. It was dark and rainy. Maybe we should give them the benefit of the doubt and say that they were mistaken."

"You really believe that?"

"I don't know. It doesn't matter for Johnny's case. My dad used to say that you shouldn't cast aspersions on the cops until you've spent some time in the line of fire."

"You're sure that Murphy planted the gun?"

"Yes."

"Do you think Johnny knew?"

"I don't know, and I didn't ask him."

"And you're okay with cops lying for each other?"

"I didn't say that."

"What *are* you saying?"

"I don't condone it, but I think I understand why they might have done it."

"When all is said and done, you're still the son of a cop."

"Yup."

She smiled. "Whatever happened to 'Mr. Morality'?"

"Now you know why I'm no longer a priest."

"You have more tolerance for lying than I do."

"Seems I've become more practical in my old age. I just persuaded a client to plead guilty to a crime that—arguably—he didn't commit—because it was expedient and minimized his risks. You could say that I encouraged him to lie to cut a better deal for himself."

"He's a grown-up."

"To me, he'll always be a kid. Roosevelt was also instrumental in persuading Ward to put together the deal."

"I'm not surprised."

I took another sip of bourbon. "I may have found us a promising young attorney: Nady Nikonova."

"She's a real estate lawyer."

"She's just pretending until she can find something better to do. She's a fighter. And she's really smart."

"Invite her in for an interview."

"I already did."

She downed the rest of her drink. "All quiet outside?"

"For now."

"How do you think this will play down in the Fillmore?"

"Hard to say. Some people are going to say that Johnny got away with murder."

"Legally, it was self-defense. The new video proves it."

"People aren't always impressed by legal arguments."

"It's a fact."

"Nowadays, people aren't impressed by facts, either."

Her tone turned thoughtful. "What happened to the wisecracking head of the felony division?"

"I'm tired, Rosie. I'm not as young as I was a week ago."

"You aren't as funny as you used to be, either."

"Did you like me better when I was funnier?"

"I like you just the way you are." She reached over and squeezed my hand. "Did Gio and Maria thank you?"

"Profusely."

"What about Luca?"

"He was more subdued. He may be a little ticked off if we swipe his associate."

"What happens to the civil case?"

"Nothing changes. The City agreed to pay Jones's mother a million dollars. If she wants to continue her case against Johnny, Luca will have to deal with it."

"Are you okay with the plea bargain?"

"It isn't perfect, but it seems like a good result for our client."

"Let it go, Mike. You can't control everything."

"You've told me the same thing for the past twenty-five years."

"Maybe you'll finally start listening to me." She flashed her non-politician's smile. "Don't beat yourself up this time. You found the truth and got a good result. Justice is never perfect, but it sounds like it was served pretty well today."

"Maybe so. Nobody on either side is especially happy. It usually means that we came up with a reasonable compromise."

"You don't seem satisfied."

"Jones is still dead. So are the cops who were killed in the Fillmore. And the people who were run down in front of the church. And the kid who tried to run us over on Fillmore."

"There's nothing you could have done. Give yourself a break, Mike."

"I'll try." I looked up into her eyes. *Beautiful Rosie.* "So?"

"So what?"

"Do I still have a job?"

"Of course."

Excellent. "You weren't happy when I decided to represent Johnny."

"I fire people when they screw up, not when they do what they think is right—even if I happen to disagree with them."

"You sure?"

"I'm not going to change who you are. I don't want to. Frankly, it would be futile, and I happen to like you this way."

"So we'll just go back and pick up where we left off?"

"For the most part."

Uh-oh.

"In your absence, I appointed Rolanda as the permanent co-head of the Felony Division. She's more conscientious about administrative matters than you are."

True.

"It will also give you a chance to spend more time in court and train some of our younger attorneys."

"I'd like that."

"It will be good experience for Rolanda."

"Agreed."

"I wasn't asking for your permission."

You never do. "I know."

She glanced at her watch. "You got plans tonight?"

"I thought I might go home, have another sip of bourbon, and go to sleep for the first time in a week. You?"

"I'm taking the rest of the night off."

"You want some company?"

"Absolutely." She logged off her computer. "Do you know what today is?"

I glanced at my iPhone. *Oh, crap.* "I didn't get you anything for Valentine's Day."

"Are you trying to tell me something?"

"I'm an idiot."

"For what it's worth, so am I. I didn't have time to get you anything, either."

"That's not very romantic—even for two people who've been divorced a lot longer than they were married."

"We have other redeeming qualities. Mind if I ask you something?"

"Ask away."

"Do you remember the last time we had sex?"

"Does last night count?"

"No."

"I think it was a couple of weeks ago."

She picked up her iPhone and looked at the display. "It was two weeks, three days, eighteen hours and forty-four minutes."

"You keep track?"

She smiled. "I have an App on my iPhone."

"You're kidding."

Her grin broadened. "Yes, I am."

"I'm exhausted, Rosita."

"Not too tired for to celebrate Valentine's Day, I hope."

"I think I can summon a little extra energy."

"Then we can go home and I'll give you your present." She walked around her desk and took my hand. As we were leaving her office, she turned out the light and leaned over and kissed me. "Happy Valentine's Day, Mike."

"Happy Valentine's Day, Rosie."

A NOTE TO THE READER

Dear Reader,

Thanks very much for reading this story. I hope you liked it. If you did, I hope you will check out my other books. In addition, I would appreciate it if you would let others know. In particular, I would be very grateful if you would tell your friends and help us spread the word by e-mail, Amazon, Facebook, Goodreads, Twitter, LinkedIn, etc. In addition, if you are inclined (and I hope you are), I hope you will consider posting an honest review on Amazon.

If you have a chance and would like to chat, please feel free to e-mail me a sheldon@sheldonsiegel.com. We lawyers don't get a lot of fan mail, so it's always nice to hear from my readers. Please bear with me if I don't respond immediately. I answer all of my e-mail myself, so sometimes it takes a little extra time.

Regards,

Sheldon

Connect with Sheldon Siegel

Email: sheldon@sheldonsiegel.com

Website: www.sheldonsiegel.com

Amazon: amazon.com/author/sheldonsiegel

Facebook: SheldonSiegelAuthor

Twitter: @SheldonSiegel

Goodreads: Author Profile

Sheldon Siegel

ACKNOWLEDGMENTS

Writing stories is a collaborative process. I would like to thank the many kind people who have been very generous with their time.

Thanks to my beautiful wife, Linda, who still reads my manuscripts and keeps me going when I'm stuck. You are a kind and wonderful soul and I am very grateful.

Thanks to our twin sons, Alan and Stephen, for your support and encouragement for so many years. I am more proud of you than you can imagine.

Thanks to my teachers, Katherine Forrest and Michael Nava, who encouraged me to finish my first book. Thanks to the Every Other Thursday Night Writers Group: Bonnie DeClark, Meg Stiefvater, Anne Maczulak, Liz Hartka, Janet Wallace and Priscilla Royal. Thanks to Bill and Elaine Petrocelli, Kathryn Petrocelli, and Karen West at Book Passage.

Thanks to my friends and colleagues at Sheppard, Mullin, Richter & Hampton (and your spouses and significant others). I can't mention everybody, but I'd like to note those of you with whom I've worked the longest and those who read drafts of this manuscript: Randy and Mary Short, Cheryl Holmes, Chris and Debbie Neils, Bob Thompson, Joan Story and Robert Kidd, Donna Andrews, Phil and Wendy Atkins-Pattenson, Julie and Jim Ebert, Geri Freeman and David Nickerson, Ed and Valerie Lozowicki, Bill and Barbara Manierre, Betsy McDaniel, Ron and Rita Ryland, Bob Stumpf, Mike Wilmar, Mathilda Kapuano, Guy Halgren, Aline Pearl, Ed Graziani, Julie Penney, Mike Lewis, Christa Carter, Doug Bacon, Lorna Tanner, Larry Braun, Nady Niknonova, Joy Siu, and Yolanda Hogan.

A huge thanks to Jane Gorsi for her incomparable editing skills.

Another huge thanks to Vilsaka Nguyen of the San Francisco Public Defender's Office for your thoughtful comments and terrific support.

A big thanks to Officer David Dito of the San Francisco Police Department for assistance on police procedural matters.

Another big thanks to Bob Puts for his help on the inner workings of SFPD.

Thanks to Jerry and Dena Wald, Gary and Marla Goldstein, Ron and Betsy Rooth, Debbie and Seth Tanenbaum, Joan Lubamersky, Jill Hutchinson and Chuck Odenthal, Tom Bearrows and Holly Hirst, Julie Hart, Burt Rosenberg, Ted George, Phil Dito, Sister Karen Marie Franks, Brother Stan Sobczyk, Jim Schock, Chuck and Nora Koslosky, Jack Goldthorpe, Scott Pratt, Bob Dugoni, and John Lescroart. Thanks to Lauren, Gary and Debbie Fields.

Thanks to Tim and Kandi Durst, Bob and Cheryl Easter, and Larry DeBrock at the University of Illinois. Thanks to Kathleen Vanden Heuvel, Bob and Leslie Berring, and Jesse Choper at Boalt Law School.

Thanks to the incomparable Zvi Danenberg, who motivates me to walk the Larkspur steps and inspires everybody who knows him.

Thanks as always to Ben, Michelle, Margie and Andy Siegel, Joe, Jan, and Julia Garber, Roger and Sharon Fineberg, Jan Harris, Scott, Michelle, Kim and Sophie Harris, Stephanie and Stanley Coventry, Cathy, Richard, and Matthew Falco, and Julie Harris and Matthew, Aiden and Ari Stewart.

ABOUT THE AUTHOR

Sheldon Siegel is the New York Times, Amazon, and USA Today bestselling author of the Mike Daley/Rosie Fernandez series of critically acclaimed courtroom dramas featuring San Francisco criminal defense attorneys Mike Daley and Rosie Fernandez. He is also the author of the thriller novel The Terrorist Next Door featuring Chicago homicide detectives David Gold and A.C. Battle. His books have sold millions of copies worldwide and been translated into  a dozen languages. A native of Chicago, Sheldon earned his undergraduate degree from the University of Illinois in Champaign in 1980 and his law degree from Boalt Hall School of Law at UC-Berkeley in 1983. He has been an attorney for more than thirty years, and he specializes in corporate and securities law with the San Francisco office of the international law firm of Sheppard, Mullin, Richter & Hampton LLP.

Sheldon began writing his first novel, SPECIAL CIRCUMSTANCES, on a laptop computer during his daily commute on the ferry from Marin County to San Francisco. Sheldon is a San Francisco Library Laureate, a former president of the Northern

California chapter and a member of the national board of directors of the Mystery Writers of America, and an active member of the International Thriller Writers and Sisters in Crime. His work has been displayed at the Bancroft Library at UC-Berkeley and he has been recognized as a distinguished alumnus of the University of Illinois and a Northern California Super Lawyer.

Sheldon lives in Marin County with his wife, Linda, and their twin sons, Alan and Stephen. He is currently working on his next novel.

ACCLAIM FOR SHELDON SIEGEL'S NOVELS

Featuring Mike Daley and Rosie Fernandez

<u>SPECIAL CIRCUMSTANCES</u>

"An A+ first novel." *Philadelphia Inquirer.*

"A poignant, feisty tale. Characters so finely drawn you can almost smell their fear and desperation." *USA Today.*

"By the time the whole circus ends up in the courtroom, the hurtling plot threatens to rip paper cuts into the readers' hands." *San Francisco Chronicle.*

<u>INCRIMINATING EVIDENCE</u>

"Charm and strength. Mike Daley is an original and very appealing character in the overcrowded legal arena—a gentle soul who can fight hard when he has to, and a moral man who is repelled by the greed of many of his colleagues." *Publishers Weekly.*

"The story culminates with an outstanding courtroom sequence. Daley narrates with a kind of genial irony, the pace never slows, and every description of the city is as brightly burnished as the San Francisco sky when the fog lifts." *Newark Star-Ledger.*

"For those who love San Francisco, this is a dream of a novel that capitalizes on the city's festive and festering neighborhoods of old-line money and struggling immigrants. Siegel is an astute observer of the city and takes wry and witty jabs at lawyers and politicians." *USA Today.*

CRIMINAL INTENT

"Ingenious. A surprise ending that will keep readers yearning for more." *Booklist.*

"Siegel writes with style and humor. The people who populate his books are interesting. He's a guy who needs to keep that laptop popping." *Houston Chronicle.*

"Siegel does a nice job of blending humor and human interest. Daley and Fernandez are competent lawyers, not superhuman crime fighters featured in more commonplace legal thrillers. With great characters and realistic dialogue, this book provides enough intrigue and courtroom drama to please any fan of the genre." *Library Journal.*

FINAL VERDICT

"Daley's careful deliberations and ethical considerations are a refreshing contrast to the slapdash morality and breakneck speed of most legal thrillers. The detailed courtroom scenes are instructive and authentic, the resolution fair, dramatic and satisfying. Michael, Rosie, Grace and friends are characters worth rooting for. The verdict is clear: another win for Siegel." *Publishers Weekly.*

"An outstanding entry in an always reliable series. An ending that's full of surprises—both professional and personal—provides the perfect finale to a supremely entertaining legal thriller." *Booklist.*

"San Francisco law partners Mike Daley and Rosie Fernandez spar like Tracy and Hepburn. Final Verdict maintains a brisk pace, and there's genuine satisfaction when the bad guy gets his comeuppance." *San Francisco Chronicle.*

THE CONFESSION

"As Daley moves from the drug and prostitute-ridden

underbelly of San Francisco, where auto parts and offers of legal aid are exchanged for cooperation, to the tension-filled courtroom and the hushed offices of the church, it gradually becomes apparent that Father Ramon isn't the only character with a lot at stake in this intelligent, timely thriller." *Publishers Weekly.*

"This enthralling novel keeps reader attention with one surprise after another. The relationship between Mike and Rosie adds an exotic dimension to this exciting courtroom drama in which the defense and the prosecutor interrogation of witnesses make for an authentic, terrific tale." *The Best Reviews.*

"Sheldon Siegel is to legal thrillers as Robin Cook is to medical thrillers." *Midwest Book Review.*

JUDGMENT DAY

"Drug dealers, wily lawyers, crooked businessmen, and conflicted cops populate the pages of this latest in a best-selling series from Sheldon Siegel. A compelling cast and plenty of suspense put this one right up there with the best of Lescroart and Turow." *Booklist Starred Review.*

"An exciting and suspenseful read—a thriller that succeeds both as a provocative courtroom drama and as a personal tale of courage and justice. With spine-tingling thrills and a mind-blowing finish, this novel is a must, must read." *New Mystery Reader.*

"It's a good year when Sheldon Siegel produces a novel. Siegel has written an adrenaline rush of a book. The usual fine mix from a top-notch author." *Shelf Awareness.*

PERFECT ALIBI

"Siegel, an attorney-author who deserves to be much more well-known than he is, has produced another tightly plotted, fluidly written legal thriller. Daley and Fernandez are as engaging as when we first met them in Special Circumstances, and the story is typically intricate and suspenseful. Siegel is a very talented writer, stylistically closer to Turow than Grisham, and this novel should be eagerly snapped up by fans of those giants (and also by readers of San Francisco-set legal thrillers of John Lescroart)." *Booklist*.

"Sheldon Siegel is a practicing attorney and the married father of twin sons. He knows the law and he knows the inner workings of a family. This knowledge has given him a great insight in the writing of Perfect Alibi, which for Siegel fans is his almost perfect book." *Huffington Post*.

FELONY MURDER RULE

"Outstanding! Siegel's talent shines in characters who are sharp, witty, and satirical, and in the intimate details of a San Francisco insider. Nobody writes dialogue better. The lightning quick pace is reminiscent of Elmore Leonard—Siegel only writes the good parts." *Robert Dugoni, New York Times and Amazon best-selling author of MY SISTER'S GRAVE.*

Featuring Detective Gold and Detective A.C. Battle

THE TERRORIST NEXT DOOR

"Chicago Detectives David Gold and A.C. Battle are strong entries in the police-thriller sweepstakes, with Sheldon Siegel's THE TERRORIST NEXT DOOR, a smart, surprising and bloody take on the world of Islamic terror. As a crazed bomber threatens to shut down American's third-largest city, the Chicago cops, the FBI, Homeland Security and even the military sift through every available clue to the bomber's identity, reaching for a climax that is both shocking and credible." *New York Times* best-selling author Sheldon Siegel tells a story that is fast and furious and authentic." *John Sandford. New York Times Best Selling author of the Lucas Davenport Prey series.*

"Sheldon Siegel blows the doors off with his excellent new thriller, THE TERRORIST NEXT DOOR. Bombs, car chases, the shutdown of Chicago, plus Siegel's winning touch with character makes this one not to be missed!" *John Lescroart. New York Times Best Selling Author of the Dismas Hardy novels.*

"Sheldon Siegel knows how to make us root for the good guys in this heart-stopping terrorist thriller, and David Gold and A.C. Battle are a pair of very good guys." *Thomas Perry. New York Times Best Selling Author of POISON FLOWER.*

Sheldon Siegel

BOOKS BY SHELDON SIEGEL

Mike Daley/Rosie Fernandez Novels
Special Circumstances
Incriminating Evidence
Criminal Intent
Final Verdict
The Confession
Judgment Day
Perfect Alibi
Felony Murder Rule
Serve and Protect

David Gold/A.C. Battle Novel
The Terrorist Next Door

Connect with Sheldon Siegel
Email: sheldon@sheldonsiegel.com
Website: www.sheldonsiegel.com
Amazon: amazon.com/author/sheldonsiegel
Facebook: www.facebook.com/SheldonSiegelAuthor
Twitter: @SheldonSiegel